Big Puck Energy

Rush Hockey #1

Elise Faber

BIG PUCK ENERGY
BY ELISE FABER
Newsletter sign-up

BIG PUCK ENERGY
Copyright © 2022 Elise Faber
Hardcover Print ISBN: 978-1-63749-075-4
Print ISBN-13: 978-1-63749-074-7
Ebook ISBN-13:978-1-63749-073-0
Cover Art by Jena Brignola

Rush Hockey

Big Puck Energy
Filthy Puckboy
So Pucking Over It

PROLOGUE

BILLIE ROSE

B illie Rose waded through a graveyard of beer bottles.

Chairs were overturned, glasses were broken, pool cues had been reduced to splinters. Even the door to the bathroom had been torn off one hinge, the cheap wood hanging lazily from the bottom one, swaying gently in the breeze that came courtesy of the shattered window just to the right of the bar's entrance.

Suffice to say, the bar was trashed.

Absolutely trashed.

As was Axel Finnegan, the captain of the Rush and ringleader for all the antics that had left one of the two bars in River's Bend in such a state.

He was propped up in a booth, his big, bulky hockey player's body pinned between the table and the wall.

And he was singing.

Loudly and off-key.

The song of choice?

Diamonds by Rhianna.

Unfortunately for Billie's ears, he wasn't nearly as talented as RiRi.

"Shine bright like a—" He belched, stepping on the gemstone in the lyric, and then resumed singing. Even louder, and somehow even more off-key.

Good lord.

The man might be talented on the ice, but his singing skills rivaled nails on a chalkboard.

And the nails would win the talent competition.

Wincing, she glanced over at Barry, the owner of the bar, and somehow heard his sigh over the noise. He was polishing what looked to be one of his few remaining glasses.

"I'll get you sorted, Bar," she said, stifling her own sigh as she crossed to him and held out her hand. "Keys?" she asked.

He put down the glass, tossed the towel over his shoulder, and reached into his pocket, slapping the set of bronze and stainless steel into her hand. They were each topped with colored rubber covers. "Blue still for the front door?"

A nod, anger drifting into his eyes. "Not that it'll make much sense to lock up with that window."

"I'll get you sorted," she repeated.

And she would.

Before she kicked some hockey player ass.

"I know," Barry told her, patting her on the shoulder. "You're a good woman, Billie Rose."

She smiled and then made it her mission to shoo him from the bar. His night had been long enough, what with the entire Rush hockey team deciding to go on a tear through River's Bend. Which, unfortunately for Bar, meant they hadn't had many places to "tear" to. They'd started the night at Monroe's, the other bar in town, and when they'd gotten sloppy, they'd strolled down to the other side of Main Street and came here. To Haggarty's.

Where havoc was wreaked.

Barry dragged his feet, and she knew that part of him still saw her as a little girl, still worried after her, especially when he peppered her with offers to stay, or to come back in the morning, or to call someone to come assist her. Knew it when he paused at the front door and asked, "You need help with *him?*"

But she was an adult now, no longer the shy, quiet girl who had been picked on at River's Bend Elementary, or the wild child teenager who'd pranked and drank—and, *cough,* other illicit things —her way through River's Bend High School.

She was a grown-ass woman—one who had absolutely no patience for bullshit, no matter the form it came in. But she *especially* had no tolerance for bullshit if it came courtesy of a pretty boy hockey player.

The Rush were the scourge.

A *necessary* scourge.

But still a scourge.

Her lips curved, thinking her English teacher of a grandmother would have given her a gold star for using the word *scourge* three times in as many sentences.

Hell, probably not.

Billie Rose's English teacher of a grandmother would have told her to expand her vocabulary.

Bane. *Eh, no.*

Pestilence. *Better.*

Curse? *Best.*

Because the Rush were both the life's blood and the curse of River's Bend.

A curse she was determined to break.

She spoke, and if her tone was deadly, if it made Barry shudder; made him pale slightly, grab his coat from the hooks just inside the door, and slip out said door; if it made him realize that the rest of him knew her as a grown-ass adult who took no shit from anyone when she said, "No, I'll take care of him," then so be it.

And if it made him cross himself...then heaven help Axel Finnegan.

Because she was done with Axel's particular brand of bullshit.

She'd been born in this town—*literally* in town, along the side of the road, her parents not having even made it to the highway that led to the next city over, where the only hospital around was located. She'd been too impatient to wait, too grounded to River's Bend even then. The town was in her blood. She ate and drank, slept and bled and cried to make it the best it could be for everyone who lived here. River's Bend was the most important thing in her life, and she *would not* allow these...these...

"Fuckboys," she muttered.

Right. She wouldn't allow the fuckboys of the Rush to continue their reign of terror.

She wouldn't let them ruin it.

Not *her* town.

If she'd had her way—and she had to be frank, as the newly elected mayor, she got her way a lot of the time (and if she had to be truthful—*blegh*—she'd gotten her way most of her life)—she would have gone along with the Chamber of Commerce's recommendation to not renew the Rush's contract with the town.

She'd reclaim the ice rink, take the town back, kick the fuckers out.

But the Rush were a large income source for the town (including taxes that had just funded a new elementary school), and that wasn't even taking into account that the organization employed hundreds of River's Bend citizens.

No jobs.

No income.

No *good*.

Which meant River's Bend needed the Rush.

But they didn't need them like *this*, didn't need them drinking, fucking, and smashing their way through town. Hell, she knew for a fact that Barry had struggled to get insurance after being dropped from his previous provider.

If he had to pay out of pocket for the repairs...

If the town continued to bear the brunt of the team's antics...

If the gamble she was taking didn't pay off...

River's Bend wouldn't survive.

She blew out a breath, turned to that drunk, singing hockey bastard, and battened down her resolve.

Billie Rose was just going to have to take the team in hand.

Axel Finnegan was the ringleader.

The problem child. The poster boy for fuckboys everywhere.

So, her lips curved, she would begin with him.

And she knew exactly where to start.

ONE

AXEL

I groaned and tried valiantly to open my eyes, but my head was pounding, so the moment light passed my lids, I slammed them closed again.

"Fuck," I muttered, running a hand over my face—

Or trying to.

Because it was impossible.

No, not *impossible*. I frowned, forced my lids open, ignoring the sunlight stabbing at my brain.

Only *one* was impossible to move because...it was handcuffed to some sort of rail above my head. The other hand was at my side, pinned half under my ass. *That* one was just numb, and I moved it carefully, nerves prickling, tingles shooting up my arm.

What kind of freaky shit had I gotten into last night?

I squinted, trying to remember, but not able to recall anything more than swatches of noise and things breaking and booze going down smoother and smoother.

Until it had tasted like water.

That's probably why it hurt so much to open my eyes today.

A foot kicked mine, and not lightly either.

"Ow," I muttered, glancing up and squinting at the sun. Someone was standing there, not that I could see more than a wavering black silhouette.

"Whatcha doing down there?"

Female.

My mind perked up. My brain focused enough for the wavering shadow to steady, to turn into something...delicious.

Small. Curvy. *Delicious*.

"Depends," I said, curving my lips into the smile that had successfully gotten me pussy from the time I was fifteen. "You coming down here to experience it?"

Silence.

Long and quiet enough that I could hear the birds chirping and the insects buzzing, and seriously, what the fuck time of the day was it?

I hadn't been up this early in...

I couldn't remember. Or maybe I *could* have remembered if the woman standing over me hadn't started laughing. Not a gentle, quiet, tinkling laugh like so many of the puck bunnies that hung out at the rink and wanted a piece of me before I hit it big, but a loud and hearty guffaw that shouldn't have been sexy and yet somehow was.

Roughened velvet.

I wanted to fuck her, and I hadn't even seen her face.

But hell, the way the shadows had coalesced into something curvy and petite paired with that sexy unhindered laugh, and I was hard.

"Baby—" I began.

The *click* of a shotgun cocking had my mind rocketing well away from my dick.

Okay, this wasn't nearly as amusing.

Or sexy.

"Hold on a—" I tried.

The laugh had disappeared, taut intensity had surrounded him. "I'm going to talk." Deadly words. "And you're going to speak when I give you permission to do so."

Ice. Orders.

They both began prickling down my nape, curling in my stomach like a venomous snake prepared to strike.

Meh.

Just call me Steve Irwin.

Of course...there was also that sting ray.

And I had a shotgun pointed at my head.

So...right. I kept my snark locked (albeit loaded, *heh*). The sun, on the other hand, was a total bitch, and since I was tired of squinting against it, I dropped my gaze to my feet.

The woman nudged me with her foot again—this time hard enough to hurt. "I'd advise that you keep your eyes on mine."

"I would," I said, getting frustrated now, that snake darting forward and baring its fangs as I stupidly reached out to grab it, "if I could fucking see you instead of burning my fucking irises by staring into the *sun!*"

Silence.

Shit.

I clenched my teeth against an apology and waited, trying to hold back a wince, expecting the shotgun to go off.

Instead, she surprised me by stepping to the side so that I could look up at her and see something besides blinding white light.

Blinking a few times to steady my vision, I felt my cock get even harder.

Fuck.

She was a porn film star come to life.

A cowboy hat on her head, a low-cut white tank covered by a flannel only halfway buttoned up, skintight jeans, and boots.

Not cowboy boots, but sturdy, brown leather boots with bright red laces.

They were well-worn. They were dirty.

They did *not* fit with the curvy little woman in front of me.

"Baby—"

The gun leveled at my chest.

"I don't believe I gave you permission to speak," she gritted out.

Probably, I should shut up, but I'd never been great with authority or people telling me what to do. "I don't believe I asked *you* to wake me up and point a shotgun at me," I snapped.

Slowly, she lifted one hand and tilted back her hat.

That snake coiled again.

Only this time, I could admit it was coiled in the corner in fear, hoping to not be provoked, because it wasn't sure it would survive if it struck again.

"Well," she said lightly, "I normally point shotguns at people who show up unwelcome on my porch, but I *especially* point shotguns at those who show up unwelcome *and* spend their free time tearing up my town." The gun didn't waver, not in the least. "So, what the fuck are you doing here, Axel Finnegan?"

Come to think of it, I didn't *know* what I was doing here.

Last I remembered, I'd been cuddled up to a rather tall blonde, and her hands had been sliding beneath the waistband of my jeans.

Had I fucked her?

I couldn't remember.

And it hurt too much when I tried to, so I just let it go. The blonde wouldn't be the first girl I didn't remember sleeping with. If I was being truthful—something I despised—she also probably wouldn't be the last.

"I don't know," I said, squinting against the sun and trying to actually see where I was. I should also probably be sorting out how I'd become handcuffed to the railing, but...meh.

I'd been in stranger scenarios.

One time I'd woken up floating in a pool, naked, sunburned to hell and precariously perched on one of those inflatable rafts shaped like a giant pineapple. Another time, I'd woken up naked and with half a watermelon (half-eaten to go with the theme) over my junk. Still once more, I'd peeled back my lids and woken up between three nude people—*people* because only two of them were female.

The common theme was nakedness.

Yeah, yeah, I liked to take off my clothes.

But I had a nice body, and *people* didn't seem to mind.

Not to mention, I grew up in locker rooms, grew up with stall showers where shyness and covering my junk wasn't necessary. I'd seen more dick than most porn stars, but it was part of the game—well, not the game so much as the cleaning up process afterward.

As was the partying and the waking up naked—and sometimes still drunk.

Not much fazed me. Not the dicks or the nakedness or the women and booze. Every time I'd ever woken up in a pesky scenario, I'd just shrugged, dragged my sorry ass out of there, and stumbled home.

Sometimes remembering (the watermelon had been a joke by my linemate). Sometimes not (like not remembering if I fucked the blonde from last night).

But I'd never woken up like this.

First, I wasn't clothed—which I supposed, wasn't the unusual part.

Second, I was handcuffed. This was out of the norm, but not unheard of.

Third, I was staring down the barrel of gun, the other side held by a gorgeous woman who appeared to be looking for any excuse to pull the trigger.

That was a little strange.

"You don't know," she said slowly, as though I were an idiot.

And maybe I was. I hadn't gone to college. I'd barely graduated high school. I was good at exactly three things—hockey, fucking, and drinking.

The middle skill was what prompted my next reply.

"Do you have a bondage fantasy?" I asked, rattling the cuff. "Because I'd be happy to oblige."

The gun dropped further...pointing at my dick.

I watched her finger tighten on the trigger, and I felt fear—*real fear*—for the first time in a long, *long* time.

But I couldn't even push out the request for her not to shoot me.

All I *could* do was sit there and watch and cringe and...*wait*.

Just when I thought she was definitely going to fire, she spun on her heel, stomped back across the porch, and disappeared into the house.

The door slammed.

And silence descended again.

Two

This was some bullshit.

Some complete and utter bullshit.

First, I'd been up half the night dealing with a cow in labor because the baby had been breech and mama cow had needed assistance—which meant I'd been armpit deep in said mama cow's uterus (or I suppose, if I were being technical, I had only been *elbow* deep in her uterus. The rest of my arm had become intimately acquainted with mama cow's birth canal).

The second piece of bullshit?

The man on my front porch.

Axel Finnegan.

Player—both on the ice and off. But, more importantly, Axel Finnegan was trouble.

Trouble that had somehow ended up on my porch—*handcuffed* to my railing—after I'd gotten approximately two hours of sleep.

I let the front door slam behind me, stashed my shotgun on the rack in the hall, and stomped over to my phone charging on the cradle in the kitchen. There was one person who would know —read: who was *responsible*—for Axel Finnegan being handcuffed on my porch.

My aunt.

One Billie Rose.

I jabbed at the screen, pulling up her number, and hit the green button to connect the call. It began ringing...and then immediately went to voicemail.

"Fuck," I hissed, dropping the cell on the counter.

I did *not* have time for this shit.

Grabbing my jacket off the hook—and leaving my shotgun in place, much to my chagrin—I shoved my cell into my pocket and headed back across the porch, clomping loudly and not giving two shits when it made Axel lurch up to his feet.

I kept walking.

"Hey! Where are you going?"

Not bothering to answer, I kept walking, heading to the barn where I dropped a leaf of hay into each of the horse's feeders, and then prepped the rest of the animals' food—pigs, goats, and a couple of sheep.

All were rescues.

The only working animals on the farm were the cows, and they were out grazing, the mama who'd given birth to the last of the few off-season calves that had been born the last couple of weeks having joined her brethren (or sister-ren?). Thankfully, though, there weren't any more pregnant cows who'd be keeping me from my bed.

I'd trudge through, like I always did, and tonight, I'd get some rest.

Right.

Because running a dilapidated cattle ranch on my own meant that I got *loads* of rest. Sighing, I waited for the horses to finish eating then let them out to pasture before beginning one of my many tasks that meant rest was truly only for the weary—mucking stalls.

Which meant it was a good hour before I emerged from the barn and headed toward my truck.

"Hey!" Axel called again, still handcuffed to the porch railing.

Did I feel a tingle of guilt?

Yeah.

Did I let that tingle change my plan?

Nope. The petty in me was happy to make him pay.

He scrambled to his feet again, crouching since the cuffs meant that he couldn't stand fully erect—

And hell, I did *not* need to think about Axel and erect things.

Not when he was the town bicycle.

Town hockey puck?

Town—?

"You can't just leave me here!" he shouted. "I have practice and—"

I yanked open the door, turned on the engine, drowning out the sound of his further protests, and drove off to fix the section of downed fence I'd spotted the previous day.

That took a couple of hours, and I was hot, sweaty, and cranky as fuck by the time I got back to the house.

I wasn't a breakfast girl, so I usually ate an early lunch, and as much as I was hoping that whatever fucked-up fairy had dropped off Axel on my porch—and my suspicions pointed to only one person, good ole Auntie Billie Rose—had picked him up, alas, it was not to be.

He was still there. Still handcuffed. Still naked.

He stood, as much as he was able to anyway, when I pulled into the drive.

Was silent—miracle of fucking miracles—as I got out and walked up to the front porch. *Stayed* silent as I moved back into the house, made myself a damned sandwich, and called Billie Rose. Well, I don't know if he stayed silent as I was in the kitchen, making that sandwich and phone call, but if he *did* talk, he wasn't loud enough for me to hear him.

Also—no surprise—Billie Rose didn't pick up.

Which was probably why I did what I did next.

I made the man a fucking sandwich.

Maybe someone might think it was a nice gesture.

It wasn't.

Neither was me grabbing him a bottle of water from the fridge. I didn't have keys to the handcuffs, and Billie Rose wasn't picking up her phone. I was fully aware that at some point I was going to have to call the sheriff to come get the trouble off my porch, but I'd rather not have everyone in River's Bend knowing what had happened, and everyone would know if I let the man die of dehydration on my porch.

The teasing alone would be unbearable.

Or not.

Because, smiling darkly, I thought that some of the townspeople might trade teasing for cheering, but...sigh. Neither of those was the point. I needed to make sure he didn't expire while I waited a little longer, crossed my fingers, and hoped that Billie Rose picked up.

But I *couldn't* have him dying of dehydration on my porch.

Too much paperwork.

"Then why the sandwich?" I muttered. It wasn't like Axel Finnegan was going to starve to death after a few hours. Or of dehydration, for that matter. It was just...my grandfather had ingrained a certain set of skills in me while growing up.

And one of those was being a good host.

Okay, so maybe being a good host didn't leave someone handcuffed to the porch railing, but...meh.

My hosting skills only went so far.

I pushed out the front door.

Axel was sitting on the porch, looking dejected, and I didn't feel a pang of remorse for leaving him there. I *didn't*.

I set the sandwich in front of him, the bottle next to it.

Silence.

"Is it poisoned?" he asked.

Amusement bubbled up inside me, but I didn't let it show. Instead, I turned on my heel, headed back into my house, and ate my sandwich, drank *my* bottle of water while staring at my phone, willing Billie Rose to call me back.

And then calling her two more times, just for good measure.

Then losing my temper on the last time and hissing out onto her voicemail, "You are so dead, Billie Rose. I cannot believe you would do this to me."

After jabbing at the button to end the call, I tossed my cell on the counter, sighed, and got back to work.

"Wait!" Axel called as I pounded down the stairs again.

I spun slowly and turned to face him, lifted my brows.

"You're really going to leave me here?" he asked, voice small. "Again?"

"You got a spare set of keys for those cuffs?" I countered, rolling my eyes at the innocent look.

He froze, frowning up at his arm. "Nooo," he said, drawing out the word.

"Exactly."

I began walking again, heading to the barn to bring the horses back in when Axel spoke again.

"But...you got a saw?"

Three

She was going to kill me.

Or I was going to lose an arm. Or—I lurched back—my dick.

"Jesus, watch where you're aiming that thing!"

"What?" she asked loudly, flipping the switch so the saw revved, drowning out anything I might say. Then she lifted it, holding the sharp, spinning blade casually, like it wouldn't just slice to shit anything that got close. "Sorry, I can't hear you."

And then she brought the blade down.

"Fucking hell!" I scrambled away, trying to get my feet under me, knowing it was a fucking lesson in futility since the saw was descending.

A loud whirring noise. A sharp, piercing sound.

Heat.

"Oh fuuuck," I groaned.

The wood vibrated, the cuffs heated, tiny metal shards flew into the air, swirling around me like snow, burning my skin as they landed on it—dangerous, probably, but it wasn't like she'd provided me with eye protection—and then—

I was free.

The saw turned off, dropped to the porch, too fucking near my leg—and my femoral artery—for comfort, and then the woman, whose name I still didn't know, dropped a pile of clothes next to me—sweats, a T-shirt, and a pair of socks—headed to the barn. I jumped to my feet, scrambled into the clothes that were a bit tight but fit reasonably well, and trailed after her, my entire body stiff from being chained to the railing.

"Wait," I called. "I have to get to practice."

She kept walking.

It took me a few strides to get my legs to loosen up, but then they were ticking, and I caught up with her just as she pushed into the barn, snagging her arm and dragging her to a stop.

"Get your fucking hand off me," she gritted, eyes flashing.

"I have to get to practice," I said again, not letting her go.

Which was a mistake.

"*Don't* touch me."

My fingers tightened. "But I need to go, otherwise I'll be fucked."

I might be a mess, but hockey came first.

Always.

"Fucked?" Her eyes narrowed, and she snorted. "Yeah. I know the feeling. Now, *let go.*" She grabbed my thumb and yanked it back, sending red-hot pain splintering up my hand and arm. I had to drop to my knees so I didn't break the digit, and then she shoved me back.

I ended up on my ass.

"You're free." A wave of her hand. "So get the fuck out of here."

Except I had no shoes, no car, no phone, and no clue where I was. I only knew that the apartments I lived in were nowhere in sight and that Main Street was real the fuck far away. "I—"

"Road to town is a mile up the road," she said, pointing and effectively interrupting me before I could really get going.

And then turned away.

What the *fuck?*

No one interrupted me. When I spoke in the locker room or at the bar or anywhere, really, people listened. They didn't try to break my thumbs or turn away from me. They certainly didn't leave me handcuffed to porch railings.

"How far out of town are we?" I asked, standing up and rubbing my sorely abused thumb.

She stopped, spun to face me. "*We* are not out of town. *You* are out of town. And including the mile you need to walk to the road," she said, "*you* are six miles from the ice rink. If you start running now, I suspect it'll be the perfect warmup for practice."

"I don't have any shoes."

"You're a big, tough hockey guy. You'll survive."

"I—"

But she'd given me her back again.

I'd said it once, I would say it again. People did *not* ignore me.

"Look, baby," I said, moving in front of her, forcing her to stop. "If you give me a ride, I'll make it worth your while."

Silence.

A long beat of quiet.

A long, slow breath.

Two things with this woman that I was coming to realize would bring nothing good.

Though, I supposed this scenario was different from before. It didn't involve a saw or me being handcuffed, so one could argue that it was actually *better* than the previous times.

Go me.

Plus, instead of pulling a shotgun out of nowhere, she just snorted and went back to walking away, sidestepping me and moving farther into the barn, moving across the space and entering a room at the far end without another look back.

Less, *go me.*

"Fuck," I muttered, knowing that I wasn't going to walk six-plus miles into town.

Maybe I could find a phone inside the house?

There had to be one.

Right.

Except, I'd taken exactly one step back toward the exit when the woman stuck her head out of the room and said in a cool, dead tone that had the hairs on my nape prickling, "And if you're considering what I think you're considering, know that I have shotguns in many more places than my house."

I froze.

Then I remembered myself.

I was Axel *Fucking* Finnegan. I wasn't scared of anything, least of all a tiny, curvy female with brown curls and a body that was dwarfed by a plaid flannel.

Straightening my shoulders, I strode to her, not stopping until my toes were lined up with those incongruous brown boots, and absolutely willing to sacrifice a few toes if need be.

And my pride might make that a necessity.

"You got a shotgun in that room?" I nodded toward the space she'd previously disappeared into.

Her brow furrowed. "No."

"Good."

"Why?"

"Because it means you won't shoot me when I do this." I moved into her, bodies brushing close as I pushed forward, herding her into the room, forcing her to lift her chin in order to continue looking at me.

Which she did.

Because *of course* she did.

I caged her in against the wall, putting one hand by her hip, the other by her head. She was tiny, so I had to bend pretty far in order to meet her eyes, chin lift or not.

"Do what?" she asked, markedly calm.

I leaned closer. "What's your name, baby?" I asked, staring deep into her eyes.

Her lips parted and need exploded through me. Tons of curves to worship, pretty brown eyes to watch as I made her come. I felt her breath on my mouth, so damned close and yet not nearly close enough. I wanted to taste her, to get my tongue in her mouth, her pussy. My cock twitched and I leaned a little more heavily against her until my pelvis was lined up with hers, my chest only a hairs-breadth away.

White teeth digging into a pink bottom lip.

Pupils dilating.

A body softening.

And...

Then she started laughing. At me. *Again*.

What. The. Fuck?

She shoved me back and slid to the side. "Does that actually *work?*" she asked between giant guffaws, bending at the waist. "Oh, my God. *What's your name, baby?*" she added in a poor approximation of my voice. "That can't actually work on women. No fucking way."

It did work.

It *always* worked.

And I'd thought it before, but seriously, I was thinking it again. What in the actual fuck was wrong with this woman?

"Here," she said, straightening and coming back over to me. "Let me save you the trouble, Lothario."

Her hands clamped onto my face and...she kissed me.

Fuck, how she kissed me. Her tongue slipping into my mouth, sleek, hot darts making my cock go instantly hard. Her lips pressing into mine, a little rough and all too tempting. Her body and those fucking curves coming flush to mine.

She kissed me until I forgot that I was trying to kiss *her* into submission—or at least into a ride to town.

She kissed me until my cock ached and my hands found their way to her body.

She kissed me until I forgot all about practice and six miles to the rink and the fact that I'd woken up handcuffed and naked on her porch.

She kissed me until—

I reached for her, and she broke away.

"Phone's in the tack room," she said, voice so fucking neutral it sliced right through the haze of arousal. My cock deflated. My lungs seized. "You've got an hour to get off my property, or I'm introducing you to my other shotgun."

Then she was gone.

Four

Oh hell, I thought as I stormed away, leaving Axel Finnegan and his problems behind me, but—unfortunately for my psyche—not leaving behind the feel of his lips, the brush of his tongue, the way his hard body had felt against mine.

"I shouldn't have done that," I whispered, channeling my inner Hagrid. "I should *not* have done that."

It was a quintessentially stupid thing to have done.

Kissing the sluttiest man in River's Bend?

Enjoying that kiss more than I'd enjoyed perhaps any other kiss in the entire entirety of my life?

See? Really fucking stupid.

I hadn't slept with anyone in a long time, *too* fucking long, clearly, as I'd wanted to jump the bones of *fucking* Axel Finnegan.

But it wasn't like I wanted to be in a relationship. I didn't. I was unattached, not because of a lack of attention—not to sound cocky, but I'd had steady company when I wanted over the years, hookups when I hadn't, and interest expressed when I wasn't down for either of those two. However, running a ranch was exhausting work, and now running *this* ranch, slowly digging it out from the financial hellhole my parents had left for me—a double fuck you because I hadn't even wanted the ranch in the first place, and the debt on the land had been so *freaking* astronomical, that I hadn't been able to sell it and pay off those debts.

I knew Russet Ranch could be profitable. It had been when my grandpa had been in charge, but my parents weren't for hard work, and they'd slowly eaten away at the cushion until my inheritance had been less influx and more trying to get out from beneath this giant boulder with my credit score intact.

That had been two years ago.

Now, I was another year away from being clear and free, and...I kind of liked ranch work.

Okay, the last shouldn't be a surprise. I'd loved the summers I'd spent here, getting up with the sun and spending the day on horseback with my grandpa. He'd tell me stories of his younger days. He'd listen to me about my kid-to-teenager related problems (*e.g., "Sarah isn't talking to me anymore!"* and *"Mr. Watson is the meanest teacher EVER!"* and later, *"Bobby Mulligan is the biggest asshole on the planet!"*)

Then Gramps had died.

My parents had decided to sell their house and live on the paid-off ranch, not realizing that the profits from that property couldn't all go straight into their pockets, not if they wanted to keep enjoying those profits.

But...money flowed through their hands like water.

They didn't invest in a new roof for the barn, and the hay got moldy and rat-infested, so they had to buy more hay at a premium. The fences weren't kept up as they should have been, and we lost several heifers due to auto accidents. The vet was too expensive, so we couldn't afford to call him out if a mama was struggling to give birth.

And pretty soon the business was floundering.

That was what I'd inherited.

That was what I might have sold, even despite the hit I'd take to my credit.

If not for...this.

I sighed.

Because *this* was the horseshoes nailed to the front door. Openings pointing up, held there by Gramps as I'd hammered them in place one scorching summer evening. *This* was the wine barrel planters lining either side of the porch we'd made one summer together. *This* was the tack room and the door to the barn with scratches from Gramps's knife, marking my increasing height year after year. *This* was the fences on the west side of the property we'd built together, the tractor with its peeling green paint he'd taught me how to repair on a whisper and a prayer and a roll of duct tape and a can of WD-40. *This* was the heavy gate that had given me more than a few splinters over the years as I'd opened and closed it to allow Gramp's big, old Chevy truck through.

History. Mine. Gramps.

Right here on this land.

Still, I probably should have let it go when my parents told me they were moving on when I'd bought them out. It certainly would have been easier than these last two years of working, hardly sleeping, and worrying about worrying myself into an early grave.

But all the worrying about worrying had brought forth a light at the end of the tunnel.

I could see it on the horizon—a time when I might be able to breathe, to not work every moment of every day. Where I might be able to hire back some ranch hands instead of relying on the type of trading help all of us ranchers relied on.

Eli's roof caved in? We all dropped everything to go over and repair it.

A fence at Tommy's was down? We brought supplies and got to work.

It was shipment day (read: my cows became someone else's steaks)? I had more spare hands than I knew what to do with.

My neighbors were the only reason I'd survived these last two years.

I would just like to...not need them quite as much.

Not have to worry about calling Eli away from his sick wife, or Tommy from his kids, or Hank from his preferred solitude.

They'd probably show up anyway because they were good guys and they'd been close to Gramps. I just...wanted to be able to do it by myself, to not be like my parents and mooch everyone into oblivion.

Which was why I didn't have an ounce of time for someone like Axel, who'd had everything handed to him, and he didn't even understand how precious that gift was. Instead, he kicked that gift horse in the mouth, knocked out the poor animal's teeth—like the fucking hockey player he was—and terrorized the town of River's Bend.

I didn't have time for his special brand of bullshit.

I had a mama and baby cow to check on, hay to plant, and hopefully dinner to eat and sleep to get.

Which was why I went straight to the counter for my keys, grabbing my coat on the way back out, because although I was sweating now, the moment the sun went behind the mountains in the distance, it would start to get chilly really quickly.

Axel was sitting on the fence as I pulled out, his ass on the top rung and his bare feet on the other.

He looked good.

Too damned good.

And unfortunately, now I knew exactly what was beneath his clothes, with confidence to declare that he looked good *everywhere*.

My lips tingled.

My fingers gripped the steering wheel tight, some insane urge encouraging me to pull over and offer him a ride, no matter how big of an asshole he was, no matter that his special brand of bull-shit would bring me no little amount of trouble.

Luckily for me, Gramps always said I was more stubborn than a turtle wanting to stay in its shell.

Because that stubbornness had me hitting the gas pedal instead of the brake.

It had me zooming by Axel Finnegan, leaving a cloud of dust in my wake.

It had me concentrating on mama and baby cow, on checking to make sure the field and equipment were ready for planting tomorrow, and it had me...looking for Axel when I eventually made my way back to my house.

He was gone.

That was *not* disappointment.

Fuck me, I was kind of worried it was.

FIVE

Axel

Fuck, I love hockey.

The speed, the rush of scoring a goal, the roar of the crowd, the thrill...of spying a pretty girl in the stands and knowing that she was going to go home with me.

Case in point, the gorgeous redhead smiling at me every time I went near the far side of the boards.

And considering that she was gorgeous, both in face and body, and that with every loop I made toward her side of the ice, her top seemed to move a centimeter lower, I figured it was a damned good bet she would be in my bed that evening.

I smiled in her direction.

Her top slid another inch lower, revealing navy lace and the tops of dusky pink nipples.

My cock twitched in my cup.

Not super comfortable, for those wondering in the peanut gallery. But damn if it wasn't worth it. My mouth—

"Ow!" I hissed, jerking my focus away from the woman and rubbing the side of my neck as I glared at my teammate.

"I think you focusing on tits too much is why you ended up naked on that farm this morning," Joel, my left winger, said on a smirk, having shot the puck—albeit without much more force than to make the impact sting—at me.

"Fucker," I muttered, shooting the puck back—only a *little* harder since Joel could really let it fucking rip, wasn't great at letting things go, and I didn't want to get a harder puck in return. "And technically, I wasn't naked when you got me."

Just had been naked *previously*.

And had been wearing too tight, borrowed clothes that had screamed about my previous, unclothed state.

Not ideal.

Which was why Joel grinned as he caught the puck easily on the end of his blade and messed around with it on the ice. "Just saying, keep being an asshole and next time, I won't pick your naked ass up."

"Not naked. Plus"—I waved a hand at myself—"Not too many people have been gifted the naked goodness of all *this.*"

Joel froze for a heartbeat.

Then busted out laughing.

"Dude," he said through his obnoxious chortles, "half the fucking planet has seen your naked ass."

"Or at least half the fucking *town*," Ryan said, his tone dry. Ry was the right winger on the line I centered of him, Joel, and myself.

And also, *such* a fucking comedian.

Talented player.

But total douche canoe.

Mainly because he was the only guy on the Rush who acted like he was too good to hang out with the rest of the team. Probably couldn't wait until he got out of this Podunk town and had his chance at the big leagues.

Fucking loser.

Or maybe that's you.

I blinked, started to push the thought away, but then Coach blew his whistle and yelled, "Quit talking and fucking skate!"

Aw.

That brought forth such good memories over the years. So many old, slightly overweight, white men yelling at me. And yeah, I was white, too, but I wasn't old and definitely wasn't slightly overweight...my body was a temple of liquor, meals at 7-11, and a shit-ton of hard work in the gym—in other words, I was hot as hell.

Bam.

Take that strange, curvy ranch woman with the shotgun and balls of steel.

"Finnegan!"

Right.

The point was that I'd gotten so used to my coaches yelling at me over the years that I didn't much give a shit when they did it now.

I just rolled my eyes and started skating.

One, to impress that redhead with her tits hanging out.

Two, because I didn't want to play on this fucking team forever.

I wanted to make it in the big time, and I was getting too fucking old—sad that at twenty-five I was getting too old to get a real shot at the NHL, but true—to find myself permanently on a roster of an NHL team. I was tired of this bouncing up and down bullshit like the last two seasons had been—one game in the minors with the Rush, one game up with the Gold. I worked my ass off on the ice both here and there, but I wasn't ever going to be one of those flashy guys leading the league in points.

Grinding, fighting for an ugly goal, *that* was my style.

And funny story, most of the big-league teams wanted goal-scorers.

Still, being here was grinding on me—no pun intended—and

the only way I knew to blow off steam was to play hard and then drink and fuck harder, to blank out the memories, the disappointment...and then to get the hell back on the ice and do it all over again.

So that was what I did.

I blanked the woman, the naked, handcuffed shenanigans, and I worked my ass off.

We ran through drills as a team and then broke into smaller groups for more drills, more personalized attention (read: more getting yelled at), but through it all I worked my ass off and was dripping sweat by the time I smiled at the redhead through the glass one final time and made my way off the ice.

I went to the workout room, did my cooldown, stretched, met with the trainer, talked to Coach briefly (I'd probably be playing a game up with the Gold the following week if I continued having good showings in *our* match-ups). Then I took a shower, not bothering to hurry.

I knew the redhead would be waiting.

And I wasn't disappointed.

She was standing outside the back door, along with a brunette and a buxom blonde—a trifecta of femininity that any straight male would be hard-pressed to ignore. The last one, the blonde, had been around a lot, so much so that the guys called her Glitter Tits because her lotion left sparkles behind.

Her personal calling card as she banged her way through the roster.

And one I wasn't going to play with.

Fucking glitter. Herpes of the craft world.

And also of the hookup world.

"Oh, thank you, Jesus," Joel muttered, coming up behind me. "I call—"

"The redhead is mine."

Joel grunted, clearly not as perturbed by the glitter. "I wanted

Candi anyway. Bitch sucks like a fucking Hoover. But I'll take two." He moved toward the blonde and brunette. "Ladies," he said smoothly, wrapping arms around their shoulders. "What are we doing tonight?"

"Haggarty's?" the blonde offered.

Joel winced. "Don't think we're allowed there for a while."

The blonde, Candi apparently, giggled.

And that was as much as I heard. Because I sidled my way over to the redhead. "Hi, honey," I murmured.

She blinked up at me, her lips curving as she stepped up to me, close enough that her breasts rested against my chest. They were large, but not natural and soft. Instead, they were hard globes.

Good thing I was an equal opportunity breast man.

Fake. Real. Big. Small. Barely there.

I liked them all.

"How about Monroe's?" she asked, nibbling at her bottom lip. She shifted and trailed a finger down my abdomen, heading for the waistband of my slacks. "Then my place?" A beat. "*With* my girls?"

I grinned.

"And your friend?"

My grin faded as I wrapped my fingers around her wrist, stilled the movements. "I like Joel, but I don't share."

Much, anyway.

Or rather, any*more*.

And as gorgeous as the redhead was, she wasn't pretty enough for me to be sharing a pussy or to start fucking sword-fighting.

Been there, done that.

I preferred my own All-I-Could-Eat Buffet.

She smiled up at him. "Okay. Monroe's. My place. No sharing." She rose on tiptoe and pressed her lips to my ear, tongue flicking out. "Unless I can convince you otherwise." A beat. "And I bet I can."

I laughed, slid my hand up her side, my fingers grazing the underside of one breast. "I'll take that bet."

———

Groaning, my head pounding, my ass sore as hell, I started to roll over.

Then stopped.

Or...I *was* stopped.

By—

I peeled my lids back, the morning sunlight blinding me, and groaned again, this time louder and filled with fury.

I was handcuffed to a railing.

Again.

I was naked. *Again.*

I was—

A door opened. Footsteps echoed across the wood, started to fade as they moved by me.

Then stopped, echoed again, this time louder, and they came close.

Then, "Seriously?"

I glanced up at the brown-haired woman from the day before, her legs encased in tight denim, her curvy ass on display, her breasts pushing against a blue tank, revealed by a half-zipped hoodie, her hair tucked under a worn baseball hat.

"Um, hi?" I said, going—and failing—for casual.

She closed her eyes, tilted her head back, staring up at the ceiling of the porch, her long, drawn-out sigh raising and dropping her shoulders.

My gaze followed hers, saw nothing aside from wood panels with a few recessed lights and peeling paint.

Then she dropped her head back down, her nostrils flaring on the sharp inhale she took.

She whirled on her heel, started for the barn.

"You're not going for the shotgun, are you?" I asked, my free hand unconsciously covering my dick.

Her eyes went to the ceiling again.

Then she sighed again, shoulders slumping.

"I'm getting the fucking saw."

Six

Bailey

I was resting the blade on the cuff, Axel's wrist angled away as far as possible, and suddenly I realized something I hadn't the day before.

I could end the man's career with one wrong move.

Yesterday, I'd been furious, not thinking, whipping the saw around like it was a fly swatter.

Today...I was resigned.

And a little terrified that I might saw someone's hand off.

Saw *his* hand off.

A flick of the switch to turn it on, fingers on the trigger, and...

I sighed.

Dropped the power tool.

Blue eyes, dark brows gathered tightly together over them, confusion forming a frown.

I spun on my heel, headed to the barn, and went to the tack room, beyond the saddles and rope and other horse paraphernalia, all the way to the back, where my grandpa's tool bench had been moved.

By my mom.

Who'd turned the garage into a craft room.

Another thing Gramps would be turning over in his grave for.

Lace and gingham where there had once been steel and gasoline? He'd have lost his ever-loving mind.

I searched through the ancient, heavy drawers, the wood so worn that it was decades out from being able to give me a sliver and smooth as butter, until I found what I was looking for.

Then I closed the drawer with my hip, left the barn, and returned to the mini-hockey god on my porch.

He was pretty.

He was talented.

He was...totally out of control.

Luckily, the last wasn't my problem to deal with.

I just needed him off my porch so I could continue digging myself out of my financial hole, get myself into a position where I could sell the ranch...or, if I kept it, where I didn't have to work seven days a week, twelve hours a day, just to prevent it from sinking to the bottom of the ocean and dragging me down with it.

Maybe get laid.

Maybe spend a few months without my arm up a cow's—

I stepped out of the barn and saw those blue eyes on me, felt a shiver down my spine.

Dangerous. *Stupid.*

Fucking hell, I should have just risked the dismemberment —*his* dismemberment.

Instead, I'd gotten worried about ending a man's career...and maybe his life, since it was a decently long drive to the hospital, and I wasn't all that good with tourniquets.

And yet, I still carried the pipe saw across the yard, up the steps, and knelt next to Axel.

"You smell like you bathed in whiskey," I grumbled.

A flash of straight white teeth.

"*You* smell like shit."

That shouldn't have sliced.

I'd just been in the barn, after all.

And I'd spent the last two years elbow deep in shit.

It was probably bonded directly to my cells, my DNA. My perfume might as well have been called Manure. So, Axel had given me less of an insult than an observation...and it was an *observation* I was going to ignore.

Ignoring made the hurt go away, right?

I lifted the pipe saw, placed it on the cuff, and began sawing, its thin metal teeth struggling to find purchase on the cuff for a few strokes before getting into a groove.

I ignored the bitter tang of alcohol emanating from his pores, ignored that I was probably inundating him with the smell of *shit*, and kept working. This was a lot harder than just using the Sawzall, and I was wondering what in the fuck-all I'd been thinking, worrying about the man's arm when my own were on fire.

My arms were just as important.

My wrists, my elbows, my aching shoulder (that I'd had surgery on just before I'd inherited the farm). They were my livelihood, too.

He shifted, and my eyes slid down, and I...nearly sawed off both of our arms.

I should have gotten him pants first, I realized, steadying myself.

The man's cock was...well, I hoped to fuck for the girls he boned that he was a *show*er and not a *grow*er because...sweet baby Jesus.

Axel cleared his throat.

Probably because I was staring.

Probably because—fuck me—*No.* Not *fuck me.* No *fucking* me. There would be no *fucking*, period.

"Baby—"

Right. The man didn't know my name, immediately defaulted

to endearments, had a big dick...and I unfortunately knew that because he'd blacked out and ended up on my porch. Twice.

I went back to sawing.

Luckily, the sound drowned him out when he tried to talk again, and I sawed faster...because avoidance was a great strategy when a girl had been caught drooling over a penis.

Saw. Saw. *Saw*.

Saw. Sawing. *Sawing* some more.

I was *all* about the sawing and thinking about sawing and sawing was life and—

Thunk.

The blade made it through the last of the metal. I caught it before it did damage to his leg...or his cock...or any of *my* respective parts, and...

He pulled his arm free, wincing as he rolled his wrist. "Thanks."

Right. Stop staring. *Focus.*

I hopped to my feet, and if it was fast and abrupt then...it was fast and abrupt.

Shit.

He dropped his arm to his lap, drawing my eyes down and—

"I'll get you some clothes," I said quickly, whirling away and thinking that if this kept happening, I needed to invest in more sweats...or bigger sizes or...more obviously, to get the clothes I was loaning this man back. It would probably also be prudent to invest in lock picking classes, or maybe a skeleton key for handcuffs.

Did they make that?

I hoped so. Because Billie Rose was relentless and the Rush didn't seem to be inclined to stop partying, and a skeleton key would save my saw...*and* my arms.

Fingers on my elbow, a big, strong body hovering over mine.

"I—" he began.

I jerked away, spun, and walked into my house. Was it fast? Yes.

Did it border on running? Yes. Did I stop to lock the door behind me? Also, yes.

I wasn't stupid.

I knew Axel's reputation.

And I knew my own...or rather my own *body*. A body that had experienced a serious lack of orgasms over the last few years. Yes, it was sad that my life had gotten so exhausting that even the act of pulling my vibrator out of my bedside drawer and using it had seemed like too much effort.

But that didn't mean I was going to leave my front door unlocked and risk tripping and falling onto Axel's dick.

Unlikely? Maybe.

Unlikely when I'd gotten a glimpse of that dick and my body had gone all puppy-wiggling-as-I-waited-desperately for a treat? Nope.

Hence the door-locking.

I hurried to my closet, yanked out my final pair of fat-time-of-the-month sweats, a T-shirt that I wore as a nightshirt, and then I headed downstairs...

To find a naked Axel standing in my entryway, back to me, gaze seemingly on the door.

That I'd locked.

I *knew* I did.

I must have made a noise because Axel spun...and sweet Jesus... my eyes slid down again.

Seven

Axel

The door hadn't latched properly.

I'd heard the lock *click*, turned to the door wanting to get a glance at that lush ass encased in tight denim, and then...the wind had picked up, and the panel of wood that had seen better days about two decades before had swung open...

Like a gift from the hockey gods.

So...I'd walked in.

It was like stepping into another world.

The eighties had exploded. Hell, the seventies and the sixties had exploded right along with it. The kitchen was that avocado green, and gold shag carpeting was in the family room, and pale blue curtains patterned with roses hung over the windows.

It was a visual assault on the senses.

The keyword being: *assault*.

Then my gaze had caught on a picture. Of the woman, of the woman whose name I still didn't know wearing a white dress and heels, her arms around an older man. Their eyes too similar to not be family. Her eyes filled with warmth, her smile wide. None of the shadows present in her chocolate brown gaze that had glared down at me.

And I'd frozen.

Beautiful.

Young.

Warm.

And where had that woman gone?

"What. The. *Fuck?*"

My eyes darted up to the stairs, and seriously. Where. Had. That. Woman. In. The. Picture. Gone?

There was no makeup on her face—not that she needed it. She was fucking breathtaking without that crap slopped on like so many of the women I interacted with wore. It was just...like something had changed from the woman in the picture, and not just that I'd seen her twice without a stitch of makeup on. But there wasn't any time to pinpoint exactly what had made the change, nor truly how it manifested in her eyes and face currently. Because she was bearing down on me, her expression furious, those eyes... they were about as far away from warm as I had ever seen.

Glacial.

Icebergs.

No, shards of ice hanging from the ceiling, preparing to fall and impale me.

I turned, watched her come down the steps holding a pair of cream-colored sweats and a tie-dye—yes, seriously, a *tie-dye*—shirt in her hands. She walked right up to me, slammed them against my chest, and snapped again, "What *the* fuck?"

Then she shoved me.

Hard enough that I stumbled back a step.

Luckily, I was used to skating around the ice with blades on my feet.

I could take a shove and keep on ticking.

"What the fuck, *what?*" I asked, glancing down and seeing that she'd provided a pair of socks, too. Thick and wooly, something that would protect my feet better than a thin strip of cotton. I tugged on the sweats, the socks, started to pull the shirt over my head when she spoke again.

"What the fuck are you doing *in my house?*"

I shrugged and yanked the shirt down, my head popping free, the material tight on my torso. "Wind blew the door open."

"The wind," she began in disbelief.

I stepped closer. "Yes. The wind."

A huff. "Right." She strode for the door, strode *out* the door, boots slapping on the front porch.

I was bending, tugging on the socks when I heard it.

A sharp inhale of breath, the absence of footsteps.

Straightening, I headed for the porch, pushed out the screen door, hearing it slam behind me. I didn't bother with the wooden one that had blown open earlier, just went to investigate that sharp breath.

And found it.

Or rather, found *her*. Because she was down on her knees, fingers wrapped around the narrow-bladed hand saw...and not moving.

"Baby?"

She jerked, and I heard that noise again, realized what it was, why it sounded familiar. Because I'd made that sound before, many times over the years. Because I'd heard countless teammates make the same noise.

In pain.

She was in pain.

Why did I care?

I *shouldn't* care. She didn't give a fuck about me. She'd nearly sawed my nuts off, for fuck's sake. But...she'd gotten me clothes twice and made me a sandwich the day before. She'd freed me from her railing without dismemberment—or undue attention from the sheriff.

And there was sad in her eyes.

I'd seen the happy in that picture, and I was curious. What had happened to *that* woman? Why did I have the prickly beast in front of me?

I dropped my hand to her shoulder.

She jerked again; the hiss of discomfort more audible.

"Let me help you."

Her fingers wrapped around the saw and with a grimace that had pain shooting through *me*, just in solidarity, she pushed to her feet. "I don't need help."

I raised a brow. "Oh?" I eyed the other saw that still sat by the railing. "So you can grab that one, too?"

She'd been turning for the three stairs that would lead to the path to the barn, but my question stopped her.

Slowly, she spun around, her gaze going to the porch—presumably to the saw—and then back up. I wasn't so self-centered (and look, I was *plenty* self-centered) to miss the agony that crept into her eyes. I *was*, however, enough of an asshole to call her bluff.

Evidenced by me staying still as she moved stiffly back to me, not saying a word as I watched her brace herself and bend.

Slowly.

Stiffly.

Painfully.

A hissed-out breath...then her fingers closed around the saw, and she straightened. Just as slowly. Just a stiffly. Just as painfully.

"Call your ride," she said, making her way to the stairs.

Both the saws in one hand.

The other on the railing.

A slow step down.

Another.

One more.

I moved, trailing her, some instinct inside me telling me not to grab the saws from her hands. Even though the urge was real, which was more than a bit disconcerting.

I didn't have a chivalrous bone in my body. I wasn't going to start now.

I did, however, walk next to her, and no, it wasn't because her stiff gait as she made her way down the path to the barn had me worried that I might need to catch her.

It was...because it was easier to annoy her that way.

"What's your name?"

"Fuck off," she snapped.

"Baby," I began

"Not *that* either."

I caught her arm, and, fuck it, I took the saws. Just to annoy her, not because I'd reached my limit of watching her uneven and painful stride and *had* to take the saws because I couldn't watch her limping again.

She glared.

Nope. Definitely *not* struggling to watch her in pain.

I stepped out of reach, tightened my grip on the saws.

That glare intensified.

I kept walking, into the barn, into the room where I'd used the phone before. It sat on a squat workbench in the back, several of the drawers open and rifled through. I saw the one that seemed to have other similar tools in it, shoved the little saw in, then turned and noticed the hooks on the wall, found the spot where the other electric saw belonged.

Then I should have used the phone, should have taken the shit-giving Joel was going to dish out and call my teammate.

I *should* memorize the number for the taxi company in town.

River's Bend, California was a small town, adjacent to several bigger ones in the Sacramento Valley. It had boomed during the Gold Rush (hence my team's name...and its convenient association with the NHL team the San Francisco Gold), but River's Bend was tucked more into the foothills of the Sierras and hadn't seen the same growth as some of the other cities in the area.

The people of River's Bend preferred it this way.

Hell, they'd probably prefer it if the town had never built— and then subsequently retrofitted and modernized—the rink, thus drawing in the Rush...and all the trouble the team brought.

See?

I wasn't unaware of the ill feelings the town had for the team.

Yeah, we'd broken a few glasses, the occasional pool cue, and one window. But we needed to let loose, and there wasn't much to do in River's Bend except for drinking, carousing, playing pool, and fucking on the Ridge.

We were just doing our civic duty.

Supporting local businesses.

Plus, I always cut a check for any damage done.

Which was probably the only reason we were allowed back in town—and in the few bars that were in residence on Main Street.

I was an asshole.

I drank too much, fucked too much, lost my temper too easily.

But I paid for my mistakes.

And I was good at ignoring the voice that said, maybe if I drank less, kept my temper more, focused on my game, then I might make it out of the minors.

I'd tried that before.

It hadn't made one fucking bit of difference.

Now I was going to make it *my* way—and that included plenty of booze and pussy and living the small part of my life that I could control my fucking way.

It didn't include curvy, acerbic brunettes.

Or feelings.

I reached for the phone, considering the distance to town—I knew my way now thanks to the pickup yesterday—and how fucked up my feet would be if I walked.

I had the rest of the day off.

I could ice them, pop the ibuprofen.

And save myself the trouble of Joel and his smirks.

That was so tempting that I actually stepped away from the phone, walked out of the room, and—

"What. The. Fuck?"

Eight

I'd hauled my ass up the ladder, each step more painful than the last...because I was an idiot who didn't pay attention to my tweaky back, because the lightbulb overhead was out, because the farm was barely in the black, and I still had a shit-ton of debt to pay off so I couldn't hire any hands to help.

Because...I'd overdone it with a hay load six months before and had strained something.

Then had continued irritating it, over and *over* again, because I couldn't stop working.

Repairing the fences on the west side near the highway. Trying to change the oil on Gramps' ancient trunk. Pulling out the Halloween decorations from the attic.

Bending over to pick up a saw, or to put on my socks, or to snag something I'd dropped, or to shave my ankles, or—

Bending over.

Period.

It hurt like hell. Which was why I tended to assume the squat and commence with activities stance.

Unfortunately, Axel Finnegan had the annoying tendency to scramble my brain.

So I did things like look at his penis (again, dammit!!). And, hell, it wasn't just his penis either, which sucked. It was...all of him. His body was gorgeous. His face, which came in regular contact with sticks and pucks and other hockey players, was even more so.

I wanted to write an ode to the lines of his jaw, so defined, so crisp, so...nibble-able.

Which wasn't a word, but I was hauling my broken self up a ladder, changing some bulbs that had gone out the day before, after having dragged the old wooden ladder from the corner and painfully wrestling it in position...

So, I was giving myself a break when it came to making up words.

By climbing up a ladder and reaching uncomfortably to unscrew the bulb over my head.

Ah, the life of a rancher.

Some girls liked to get pedicures and their hair done.

I was a stickler for LED bulbs, which meant I wouldn't be changing this damned thing in six months or a year or however long normal lightbulbs lasted.

I was just screwing the bulb in when—

"*What the fuck?*"

And *that* was the moment I lost my grip on the bulb...and the ladder.

The bulb miraculously stayed in the socket.

My body, however, didn't stay on the ladder.

My fingers scrabbled at the step, nails breaking off—and *that* was why I didn't splurge for manicures. Splinters jammed up into my skin, and, in the absolute worst-case scenario, despite all my scrabbling, I didn't manage to stay on the fucking ladder.

One second of free fall.

One second to know that no matter how much my back had

hurt before, it was going to hurt a hell of a lot more after hitting the ground.

I watched the ladder teeter.

Felt the ground get closer.

Knew I'd hit it, and then the ladder would hit me.

Joy.

I closed my eyes, braced, and—

Impact.

But not with the hard, compacted earth of the barn. With a set of strong arms and a muscular chest.

For a moment, my brain locked onto the fact that his exhale was louder than made a girl feel good. Because, seriously, was it really necessary to "*Oof!*" that loudly?

I wasn't filled with cotton candy, but hell, I wasn't made of bricks either.

And then I wasn't thinking about the volumes of *oofs* or what I was filled with, whether that be cotton candy or bricks or bowling fucking balls because pain radiated up my back, down my legs, burned all through my body.

It was much less pain, I knew, than if I'd hit the ground without Axel below me, taking the brunt of my fall, but it still took my breath away, had tears forming in my eyes.

His body jerked.

He *oof*ed again and then...we were moving.

Faster than I could track.

I caught a glimpse over his shoulder of the ladder wavering, tipping over before he moved again, hopping to his feet and—

"Fuck," he hissed, jerking again, the ladder having hit him square across the back.

"Are you o—?"

He began shifting, moving the ladder off him.

But he didn't move fast enough.

Because the bulb that I'd been screwing into place chose that moment to fall out of the socket, dropping down, and hitting Axel on the shoulder.

Glass exploded, tiny shards shooting outward and slicing us both. He cursed again, kept walking, and then we were out in the daylight, the sun blinding me as I bounced in his arms.

"What—?" But I stopped when his gaze jerked down to mine, eyes blazing.

And for the first time in my life, I didn't say anything, didn't come up with something snarky or sarcastic or bristly to say in response. I just clamped my lips together and let the man carry me up the porch stairs and inside.

He didn't stop until he'd entered the family room—an uncomfortable combination of blond wood and pale blue with shag carpet that my grandmother had decorated the space with before she'd died.

The only reason that Gramps had never changed it.

It was my grandma to a T—soft and warm, but on closer inspection, loud as fuck.

Case in point, the couch that looked blue, but when we got near, the solid blue became a tangle of azure flowers—bluebells, roses, irises, tulips, more that I couldn't identify.

Axel set me on the couch.

Gently.

Gently enough that I was surprised, shocked really, that a man of his size could be that gentle. "Stay," he muttered, slipping his arms out from underneath me. Then he straightened, whipped off his shirt.

Ho, mama.

I'd missed the tattoo before, but holy shit, that was glorious, a swathe of black lines twisting and folding together, starting in the middle of his back and wrapping forward, drifting around to his ribs. Those lines were strong and brash, inviting fingers and tongue to trace.

"Glass," he murmured, probably because he caught me looking—okay, *staring*.

Right.

I glanced down, lifted my hand to begin plucking the shards that had stuck to my shirt, were jabbing into my skin.

"Stop."

I froze.

He bent, carefully dug into the shag carpeting to extract a shard, then crossed to me, leaning close and doing it fast. So fast that my snark and sass and sarcasm stayed banked, that I just lay there staring up at him, my eyes wide.

An inhale, my lips parting.

But Axel didn't acknowledge the parting, my breathing accelerating.

He just leaned close and began picking the shards off, one after another, carefully folding them into his borrowed shirt. A couple of them stung, burning slightly when he tugged them free, and I knew I'd have a few places like he did, like the small cuts dotting his chest.

My hand lifted, touched the skin beneath it.

His eyes came to mine again, hot and warm and...gentle.

"I'm sorry," I whispered.

His brows dragged together. "For what?"

My brows lifted. "Um, the lightbulb and the fact that you've spent the last five minutes picking glass out of my shirt?"

Contrition across his face, trailed by fury.

Both of which confused me.

Until I heard his words.

"Um," he said sarcastically, albeit that sarcasm was coated with plenty of gentle, "how about I'm the one who says I'm sorry considering that I lost my fucking temper and made you fall off a tall ass ladder?"

I lifted my brows, a flicker of amusement sliding through me. "Just saying, my lightbulb is what made you bleed."

"Just *saying*." He smoothed back my hair. "My yelling at you is what caused you to fall off the ladder." His fingers brushed over my cheek. "I'm sorry," he whispered, his eyes drifting from mine. "It's lucky I was able to catch you."

A warm tendril in my stomach.

The silence stretched.

I stared into deep blue eyes.

My tongue darted out, wet my bottom lip.

He leaned in—

Oh fuck.

Fuck.

Then he froze, straightened. "Right." He cleared his throat. "Where's your vacuum?"

NINE

AXEL

The vacuum was mostly metal, puke green, and it went without saying, was absolutely ancient.

It had also puffed out smoke when I'd first plugged it in.

But I dutifully did something that I hadn't done in a good ten years, probably since before I'd moved away from home, during the times that my mom cared enough to pretend that she gave a damn about me.

Usually when I had a new surrogate dad and he made some comment about needing to teach me responsibility.

Then I'd be running a vacuum, dusting, scrubbing toilets.

Days, weeks, months later, he would leave, and she would disappear into a bottle.

Sometimes that bottle was filled with pills, sometimes it was filled with alcohol.

Either way, it meant that she forgot about me, and I could do what I wanted. Which was to get the fuck out of the house, get to the rink and beg for as much free ice time as possible, and when no ice was available (or I couldn't smile, charm, or beg my way into it), I found any flat surface I could to practice stick handling.

With a tennis ball and a hand-me-down stick.

Then running or doing push-ups and crunches and squats because they were good for building strength, and I could do them without any extra equipment.

Without needing any money.

Boyfriend time had the side benefit that I could usually scrounge some money from the men fucking my mom and could squirrel it away so that I had enough when it came time to pay for the season.

Boyfriend time also meant that I might be able to get the next size of skates, usually used. Very rarely—*very* rarely—new. But those new times were...fucking chef's kiss. To not have my toes scrunched up, to not have skates that weighed what felt like one-metric ton when the rest of the guys on the ice seemingly had every bit of new equipment, was amazing.

None of them could run a vacuum like I could, though.

Even a bellowing, smoke-producing one.

And miracle of miracles, the woman—whose name I somehow still didn't know—had stayed where I'd put her on the couch, eyes still wide, watching me like she'd never seen a grown-ass man vacuum.

So maybe I hadn't vacuumed the entire time I'd *been* a grown-ass man (one of the perks of playing hockey—even if I wasn't in the big leagues—meant that I could afford a maid service to come clean my rugs and toilets and dishes once a week).

Best money I ever spent.

Though some part of me had to wonder if seeing her look at me the way she was might mean I was willing to trade vacuuming duty for sexual favors.

Newsflash, I was *totally* willing to trade vacuuming duty for sexual favors.

Especially if it meant that I got my hands on that hot ass of hers.

I finished the path between the door and the couch, glanced down to shut off the vacuum, then saw a shard glittering on the too-small sweats she'd loaned me. So, I clicked the back of the vacuum in place, hit the switch to turn it off, and tugged off the borrowed pants.

A choking sound had me whipping around.

She was staring at me again, this time in a hot way that told me *she* might be all in for trading those sexual favors for housecleaning.

Maybe I could dust the baseboards for a blow job.

As though reading the thought on my mind, she scowled and looked away, starting to sit up. Quickly, I shook out the sweats, ran the vacuum over a large enough area to ensure there were no more tiny little pieces of glass that might remain and hurt her.

Hurt *her*.

Huh.

That was a new concept.

Usually, I didn't care about that. *Usually*, I was all about protecting myself. I had to, after all. I was the only person in the world who'd ever done any *me-protecting*, and I couldn't trust anyone else to do it. Not if I didn't want to get thrown to the wolves.

Me first.

Always.

It was the only way to survive.

I shut the vacuum down a second time, wrapped the cord, and glanced back at the couch.

Sure enough, she was on her feet. Hobbling forward. *Hobbling*.

Fucking hell, save me from stubborn women.

I shoved the vacuum to the side, stifled a sigh. Then I walked over to her, scooped her up, and set her down onto the couch again, this time holding her in my lap.

"What the fuck?" she snapped.

"The cactus is back, I see." I bent, inhaled, noting that beneath the horseshit, she smelled faintly of apples.

That was a definite step up.

"Let me go you—" She started to struggle against my hold, pushed against my hands then immediately paused, her breath hissing out.

"And so is the pain," I added. Carefully, I hefted her, shifting and flipping her so she was face down on the couch.

"What the fu—"

My fingers found the taut muscles that had spasmed on her back, digging in and massaging them in the way that the trainers for the Rush always did. Just on the edge of too painful, but with purpose that would ultimately be for the better.

She groaned, every muscle in her body going tense.

And then she melted, relaxed under my ministrations—and fuck, I might actually be losing it if I was using dumbass words like *ministrations* when I was just kneading a few sore muscles on a woman's back.

And *then* I paid attention to what I was doing, what I was feeling—and it wasn't that I was stroking a woman's back who I was trying to get into my bed (though, no surprise, I wouldn't turn that down). Rather, it was that I was feeling a slew of tight muscles that were riddled with knots. Absolutely *riddled* with them.

Her trapezius muscle was clenched tight.

The space on either side of her spine, curving around her shoulder blades felt like bubble wrap, knot after knot after knot present.

Her middle and lower back weren't much better.

So instead of it becoming an invitation, a coaxing, my touch stayed focused, kept that trainer-esque purpose as I diligently worked on those knots.

She didn't move, didn't fight me, and after a few moments, I heard it.

The softest moan.

My dick twitched.

That trainer-esque purpose disappeared like a fucking puff of smoke from the cigars Joel snuck in behind the rink.

My hands began moving with a different purpose then, kneading gentling into caresses, fingertips grazing. I watched goose bumps lift on her skin, listened to her breathing speed up, and I leaned a little closer.

She smelled like sunshine and flowers on a warm spring day.

My dick twitched again.

"You know," I said, ignoring the slight husk to my words, attempting levity, keeping those touches going, hoping to snag one piece of information from the mysterious woman beneath me. "I still don't know your name."

She went still.

Stiff.

Fuck. Too fast. Too much.

You have your fucking hands on her, bro. Just take the fucking win.

Her head shifted, turning to the side, her chocolate eyes coming to mine.

Then she shocked the shit out of me by giving me something wonderful.

She burst out laughing.

It was...beautiful.

It...stunned me to stillness as I watched those walls fall, as I saw a bright, beautiful center I wouldn't have expected from the prickly, stubborn woman I'd known so far.

It was...the woman from the picture I'd seen.

Warm and open and...so fucking intoxicating.

And I got to soak in all that beautiful for all of one heartbeat before I heard,

"Yoo-hoo!"

The front door swung open...and I realized I was on top of her, of this woman whose name I didn't know.

Naked.

TEN

 "Yoo-hoo!"

Kill.

Me.

Now.

I bucked like a pissed-off mama cow, attempting to launch Axel off my back, but he was tall and strong and...heavy.

Which meant that he was firmly on top of me when my aunt made it down the hall and into the family room.

Naked and on top of me.

The key word being...*naked*.

Or maybe *on top of me*.

Or maybe—

Fuck.

"Get off," I hissed, bucking again. A pained grunt escaped my lips, but at least I managed to dislodge the brute. Except...maybe that was worse?

Because now the naked Axel, in all his glorious nakedness, had been knocked off me and—

"*Oh!*"

Billie Rose, my aunt, even though we were only two years apart in age, skittered to a stop and her mouth and eyes went wide, feigning shock at the sight of a naked Axel Finnegan. As if she hadn't handcuffed him to my freaking porch.

"I'm sorry to interrupt," she said, clamping her hands over her eyes and starting to turn for the front door. "I'll just—"

"Stay right where you are," I ordered, pushing up off the couch, biting back my grimace, and finding my feet.

I turned, found that Axel had procured a throw pillow—pale yellow with more of the floral upon floral upon floral design—and clamped it over his pelvis.

Somehow still sexy, even with an ugly as sin pillow held over his nether bits.

And *nether bits.*

Seriously, I was *losing* it.

Which was why I marched over to Billie Rose, wound my fingers around her elbow, and did some clamping of my own, holding her tight when she would have escaped, and guiding her into the kitchen.

"What the fuck, Billie?" I said once we were out of earshot.

"The door wasn't shut," she said, deliberately tugging her elbow free and making herself at home in my kitchen, opening the cupboards and pulling out mugs for coffee, filling the pot with water, adding grounds, setting it to brew.

"Let me guess," I muttered as she moved to the fridge, tugging the door wide, "it was the *wind.*"

Billie Rose turned to me, her blond curls bouncing. "The wind?" Her brows drew together before her head whipped back to the fridge. "God, Bailey, it's like a wasteland in here. What do you eat? Do you need your Auntie Billie Rose to pick you up some groceries?"

"Ew, stop it, Bill," I muttered. "You know it's weird you call yourself that when you're basically my age." I sighed. "I'm fine. Just busy and haven't had time to go to the store."

So yeah, the pickings were a little slim.

It was tough to get to the grocery store when I worked so much and lived far from town. I'd used the last of my bread and lunch meat the night before for my dinner sandwich.

Which had been after my lunch sandwich.

And yeah maybe it lacked creativity, but sandwiches were easy and cheap and there were a ton of different varieties.

Last week it had been cheddar and salami.

Maybe this week it would be turkey. Or roast beef. Or PB and J.

God, it had been a long time since I'd had peanut butter and jelly.

Just the thought of it had my mouth watering.

See?

Variety. Delicious, delicious variety.

"Is there any fruit in here?" Billie Rose tugged open a drawer. "What about vegetables?" Plastic scraped as she opened another drawer. "Found— *Ugh*. I found *one*." The door slammed and she held up a carrot that, admittedly, had seen better days.

Just as Axel walked into the room. He was wearing the sweats I'd given him before, and I sent a prayer up to whatever gods were out there that a shard of glass would impale itself into his femoral when he headed for the coffee pot and asked silkily, "Do you want a cup...*Bailey?*"

Fuck.

He'd been listening to our conversation—or to Billie's prattling, rather.

And...hell. Why was a small part of me disappointed that he knew my name? That the weird little game we were playing at had ended, and—

"I had a dog named Bailey once," he said affably.

Except for the slice of devil in his eyes.

Fucker.

I narrowed *my* eyes, showed him the slice of devil *I* could have.

Axel put his palms up in surrender. "What? She was loyal." A shrug. "A bit dumb and slow, of course. But a good old girl." He grinned, ran his hands over his jaw, the bristles of his beard making a scratching sound that filled the kitchen. "I once threw a ball and it bounced off the fence, but instead of her stopping and turning around, she bounced off the fence, too." He chuckled. "Poor, dumb girl."

*Mother*fucker.

"I need to get back to work." I slanted my stare at Billie Rose, expressed every bit of displeasure I had for my *aunt* and her interfering tendencies in that one glance. "Enjoy your free coffee and then"—I widened my eyes deliberately—"take out the trash."

Not the slyest of insults, and as I turned for the front door of the house and caught sight of Axel's face, I knew he'd picked it up loud and clear.

Normally, I might feel a little guilty, especially when he'd stopped me from getting seriously hurt.

But he was grinning.

And an ass.

Loyal. Dumb. Slow?

He was the reason I'd fallen off the ladder.

Yelling at me.

Startling me.

So yeah, he could be *trash*.

Hell, he'd proved it time and again with his antics in town.

So, I held on to my fury, tucked that rage close to my heart—and admittedly, I'd become very good at that, at holding tight to my anger. Focusing on it. Living it. Breathing it in until it had burned its way onto my lungs, until it boiled its way through my veins.

Asshole.

He was an asshole.

And...I had work to do.

Starting with cleaning up the barn.

Ending with the planting.

There were always fences that needed to be repaired, stalls that needed to be mucked, horses that needed to be exercised and brushed down. Tack to be organized. The hydraulic fluid on the tractor refilled, the loose connection that was the cause of the leak and the regular need to refill changed out.

Then the sun would go down.

I'd summon the energy to go to town and shop for groceries, for the supplies for those peanut butter and jelly sandwiches.

Maybe I'd even treat myself to some ice cream.

See?

I'd really live it up. Peanut butter and jelly and ice cream. Quiet and solitude and peace.

What more could a woman want?

What more could *I* want?

Nothing.

I'd tried to have more once, and it had led me back here. That was the universe telling me to not reach for big dreams, to live and breathe small, to take comfort in the familiar, in this home, in this ranch, in the...

Peace.

But when I saw the ladder on its side, the shards of glass all around it...

When I remembered the gentle way that Axel had pushed back my hair...

When I remembered the desire that had weaved its way through my body when he'd been on top of me, hands moving over my body...

I'd felt alive.

Ever since Axel had showed up naked on my porch, I'd felt

alive. More in these last few days than I'd felt over the last two years.

And that had me...worried.

What had me even *more* worried?

Part of me wanted to see what might happen if Axel appeared on my porch for a third day in a row.

ELEVEN

AXEL

Billie Rose filled a mug with coffee, set it on the worn wooden table. "I don't know if I should be relieved or disappointed that you've put on clothes," she said, eyeing me closely, lips tipping up at the edges. "No one can say that you don't put the work in for your beach bod."

I picked up the mug, took a sip of the strong, black brew. "Can never be too on top of the beach bod."

A chuckle. Then, "I have your clothes in my car, by the way."

"I—"

I'd been prepared for another quip about beach readiness—maybe some reference to my pasty-ass skin since the majority of my naked time happened in the locker room or the bedroom—but that was the last thing I'd been expecting her to say.

"M-my c-clothes?" I sputtered.

Fuck.

Had I slept with *her?*

With *Billie Rose?*

Wasn't she...the mayor? And apparently Bailey's aunt, which

was a weird twist of...weirdness because I was creeping on her niece, and while sober I could appreciate she was an attractive woman, I didn't want to fuck Billie Rose.

Not in the least.

Billie Rose lifted her mug to her lips, sipped. "Yup. Because when you're drunk and I'm taking you home, you like to get naked."

I couldn't lie.

That sounded like me.

Except...home meant that I'd—

And she was the mayor and Bailey's aunt and...*fuck*.

"We didn't have sex, if that's what you're worried about." My eyes shot up, hit Billie's. "You're pretty, but I don't fuck drunk guys." She huffed out a laugh before her expression went abruptly serious, eyes narrowing. "And I *don't* fuck drunk guys who seem to have made it their duty to fuck up my town."

"I didn't mean—"

"To deface public property and sex your way through town and to make it extremely difficult on the people whose livelihood depends on the team?"

Was that a trickle of guilt?

Fuck.

Ever since I'd spent two mornings getting splinters all up my ass, I'd been feeling too fucking much.

Guilt.

Desire. Okay, *that* was familiar.

But the guilt, the empathy...yeah, those weren't comfortable or *wanted*, really.

"Fuck," I whispered.

"Yeah," Billie Rose muttered, taking another sip of her coffee. "Tell me about it." She leaned against the counter next to me, sighed. "The council voted to not renew the Rush's contract."

That jolted through me. "What?"

If they cut the contract...

If the Rush couldn't stay in River's Bend and it was made known that it was because of the team's behavior, because of *me*...

Fuck.

As in, my career would be *fucked*.

She smiled, and it wasn't the least bit friendly. "You heard me. And the thing is, *I'm* the one who can decide to accept that vote and nix the contract." The mug hit the counter. "So, the way I see it is that you have two choices. I can get you your clothes, I'll drive you home, and you can stop being an asshole by fucking with my town." Her finger jabbed at my chest. "You can keep your focus on your career and the ice, and I won't terminate the contract. Or"—her voice went sickly sweet—"you can keep fucking around, keep fucking with the town, and I will make it so the Rush *never* have a home in River's Bend again."

A bright smile.

"Now"—she drained her mug, rinsed it in the sink, then set it on the drying rack—"shall we get you dressed and home?"

————

I thought I glimpsed Bailey atop a horse, but Billie Rose was turning out of the driveway, speeding like a fucking maniac, and by the time I got over my whiplash to look again, the horse—and rider—were gone.

Sighing, I sat back in the seat.

Clothed.

With another pile of clothes folded in my lap.

Both smelled like shit.

Obviously, Billie Rose hadn't bothered to run them through the wash—not that I'd expected her to (though I couldn't deny that it would have been nice)—so I'd chosen the slightly less fragrant option.

It was still bad.

Whiskey and stale sweat and the cloying odor of something female.

I should have kept the sweats and T that Bailey had given me.

Yeah, they were too tight.

Yeah, they were tie-dye.

But they smelled like Bailey—well, the Bailey beneath the horse shit. The Bailey I'd smelled on the couch. Soft and floral with a hint of apples.

That was much preferred to the manure version.

Billie Rose swung her little sedan so rapidly around the turn that I ended up plastered against the door, head banging off the glass.

"God," I muttered.

"Yes?" she quipped, winding the car the other way, so quickly this time that I nearly ended up in her lap.

"Hilarious."

"I do try." A shrug, one of her hands coming off the wheel and shoving me, none too lightly, back into my seat. "Now, I'm not saying that my problem with the Rush might be solved if you weren't around to froth the waters of debauchery, but...I'm also *not* going to tell you to be sure to buckle up..."

She let that trail off, a hint of malice hitting the interior of the car.

Not that I was fearing for my life—well, that wasn't true since apparently the woman drove like a fucking nut—but I also didn't think that she'd purposely kill me, if only because that would create bad press for the town.

I reached behind me and buckled my seat belt anyway.

"Froth the waters of debauchery?" I asked, going for cool and collected, because minus the whole being-launched-from-a-moving-vehicle thing, the woman was funny.

Inappropriately.

Meh.

That was the best kind.

A shrug. "If the bad descriptor fits."

"If you say so."

Billie Rose didn't seem to have a reply to that, and since I was concentrating on trying to stay in my seat, I didn't add any further snark. Just shut up, held on, and hoped I would make it back to my apartment in one piece.

"It's weird not having you undress yourself as I drive," she murmured as she turned down Main Street.

I glanced at her, lifted my brows.

"You don't remember?"

My gaze went back to the street. "I don't remember a lot of things."

"Including the window? And the glasses? And RiRi?"

"RiRi?"

"RiRi," she repeated.

I shook my head. "Still not ringing a bell."

"RiRi," she repeated, this time with a huff, then added, her disgusted eyes slanting toward me for a second before flicking back to the road. "*Rihanna*. Your rendition of my favorite song of hers?"

"No," I said. "Not ringing a bell."

A beat. "Pity. Your voice is..."

She let that hang.

Hell, I knew my singing voice was awful.

I frequently tortured the guys with it.

But I didn't recall singing to *her*.

So...what the fuck?

She passed through the one—and only—signal downtown and turned right into the driveway of my apartment complex. Which took my mind off any Rihanna renditions and brought me face to face with something I should have recognized earlier.

Billie Rose had driven me home.

Except, Billie Rose *hadn't* driven me home.

She knew where I lived, but she'd driven me to Bailey's ranch, handcuffed me to the porch railing, and left me naked on her niece's porch.

What. The. *Fuck?*

The car screeched to a halt. She threw the transmission into park and turned to face me. "Time to go bye-bye." A finger wave before she reached across me, threw open the door.

"You know where I live," I said, rather stupidly.

A roll of her eyes. "Um, yeah. Everyone in town knows where you live." She huffed out a breath. "You've brought a good ninety percent of the single women here."

Okay, maybe that was true.

Maybe it wasn't.

Probably because the number was more like ninety-five percent.

Not the point.

I shook myself.

"But if you know where I live, then why'd you take me to Bailey's ranch?"

Her brows dragged together. "Why do you think *I* did that?"

Now *my* brows dragged together. "Um, because you showed up at Bailey's place with my clothes and told me I like to get naked when you drive me home?"

White teeth into a pink bottom lip. "Ah. Right. The fatal flaw in my plan—giving too many details." A shrug, her shaking that off as casually as she'd whipped her car through back-country roads. "Yes, I dropped you at Bailey's."

Dropped.

Now that was a euphemism.

"Why?"

"I have my reasons." A shrug, her lips tipped up into a smirk that told me I really wouldn't like those reasons.

"And the handcuffs?" I pressed, deciding to let those *reasons* go for the moment.

She blinked, expression going innocent (and completely unbelievably so). "What handcuffs? Oh"—she glanced away—"that's my phone. Probably important mayor business."

"I didn't hear your phone ring—"

Hand darting down, she unclicked my seat belt, shoved me hard enough that I nearly toppled out into the parking lot. Then once more, and I was falling out of the seat, catching myself on the frame, my clothes hitting the pavement. I gave in to the inevitable, got out, and stood.

"Gotta run!" she called.

The car moved forward.

Paused.

"Can you shut that?"

Right.

Stifling a sigh, I closed the door.

The window whirred down and one shoe then another flew through the opening. "Don't forget these!"

"I...uh...thanks, I guess."

She started to pull forward again. Stopped. The smile faded. "Seriously, Axel. Stop fucking with my town, or I'll do worse than handcuffs."

I faltered, having bent to reach for one of my shoes. "Wait, what?"

A wave. A beatific smile that didn't reach her eyes. "Bye! Have a great day!"

Billie Rose screeched out of the apartment complex.

I thought of the mayor and that beatific smile, of her hard blue eyes.

And I knew that handcuffs were the least of my worries.

Twelve

Bailey

Horses and cows. Planting and fences.

Shit. Lots and lots of shoveling shit.

Sandwiches.

And two weeks without Axel Finnegan on my front porch.

I was feeling strangely disappointed that he hadn't been there in all his naked glory.

No one had been to the ranch.

Not *one* person.

I'd come home from riding my horse, Data, to find my fridge and pantry stocked.

Billie Rose.

From the outside, it probably would seem like it was her way of apologizing for the naked delivery, but more likely, it was Billie Rose just taking care of me. Because she was nosy and pushy and used to getting her own way, and I knew it wasn't the last time she'd be interjecting herself into my life.

Regardless, she'd saved me a trip to the store *and* I'd had a variety of sandwich options that week.

Yeah, my aunt knew me.

Not all that surprising considering that, growing up, we spent most summers of our lives together on the ranch.

Billie Rose was my dad's much-younger sister. A native of River's Bend, she'd been a frequent visitor to Gramp's house. Even though Gramps and Gran were my maternal grandparents, they'd always been welcoming to everyone, whether they were biologically related or family through marriage or otherwise. More times than I could count, I'd come into the house to find someone from town in Gran's kitchen, eating her cookies, gossiping and laughing and—

I swallowed the bolt of grief, breathed it out through my nose, and knew I would probably always miss them.

Billie Rose had spent a lot of her time in the kitchen with Gran before she'd passed away when I was twelve. The two of them had been River's Bend's welcoming committee before, always fluttering around, always connected, always volunteering at school or organizing meal trains or raising money for a youth soccer team. Rooted in the town. And I was more at home with the cows and the horses and out in the field under the sun and sky with Gramps. Of course, though, it had been impossible not to be pulled into Billie Rose's orbit when I visited.

The poor girl with the crappy, disengaged parents who was dumped with her grandparents every summer while they went on luxurious vacations.

Not that I wanted to be anywhere else.

I just...I'd seen a few too many pitying looks during the summer months.

Well, before Billie took me under her wing, that was.

And, truthfully, the times I spent on the ranch were the best of my life. Mostly, because during the rest of the year, I was in the Bay Area with my parents.

Until I was a senior in high school.

That was when Gramps had gotten sick.

Then he'd died.

And then *they'd* spent the time while I'd been away at college nearly running the ranch into the ground.

So here I was, having just turned twenty-five, with a reverse mortgage hanging over my head—nearly paid off now, thankfully —and a college degree in English Literature.

Once I'd dreamed of being a high school English teacher.

Now I dreamed of cows and calves and fence repair.

And my diploma probably dreamed of being dusted off and put to actual use.

But...the ranch.

My legacy.

My family history.

And...I loved it here.

Sighing, I walked out onto the porch—where there was no Axel Finnegan, bee-tee-dub, just like every other day of the previous two weeks—and stared out at the horizon, the sun setting to the west, thinking about all the time in front of me.

I was tired.

Then again I was *always* tired.

But normally the tiredness didn't stretch out in front of me like a giant yawning chasm, threatening to take me under and choke me in the dark, tumultuous waters—

Dramatic much?

Not normally.

But tonight?

Yeah, I was.

Which was probably why I went back into my house, got my keys, hopped in my truck, and instead of going to bed early, like I always did...I drove to town.

———

It was Friday night.

Which meant that Monroe's, as one of River's Bend's two night spots (minus The Ridge, where all the kids went to get busy), was slammed.

Luckily, I was by myself.

Because there was a single barstool in the corner that I could squeeze myself onto, have a couple of beers, socialize in the least *social* way possible (being around people without actually having to interact with them much), and get this itching, prickling feeling that had been making its presence known between my shoulder blades for the last couple of weeks *go the fuck away.*

Then I'd go back to the ranch, to my solitude.

That was what I wanted.

Right?

I—

"Bailey?"

I blinked, glanced up at the woman behind the bar, and for a moment my socializing without actually socializing went by the back burner. "Dessie!" I squealed, so fucking happy to see her. "God, it's been *years*! When did you get back to town?"

Desiree shrugged and rolled her eyes. "When did the claws of River's Bend mafia drag me back in, you mean?"

I grinned. "Yeah. That."

"A month ago." She pulled a beer, pushed it toward a man two seats down from me. "Roger needed some help with the bar, and since I'm a glutton for punishment, I decided to move home for a bit and help."

"But I thought you'd just made lieutenant at the fire department."

Her face went strange.

Maybe sad. Maybe mad. Maybe—

She turned away, grabbed a chilled glass, and spun back around. "Still an IPA girl?"

I studied her face, but the strangeness was gone, and this wasn't the place to press anyway. "Is there any other type of beer?" I asked lightly.

"There is according to the dumbasses in the corner." She tilted her head and my gaze followed hers...

To Axel Finnegan holding court in the corner.

A blonde I didn't recognize sat on his lap. Two men who were big enough that they were certainly hockey players were taking up large portions of the booth around him, more women interspersed between them. Pitchers of beer sat among the group in various stages of emptiness, cups and baskets of food following the same pattern.

"They've given the order for the cheapest beer with the highest alcohol count." Dessie rolled her eyes, turned back to the tap, and began filling my glass. "Though, from what I hear, I guess we should just be happy they're not busting out windows." A snort. "Anyway, you would think grown men would get tired of just getting fucked up all the time."

"Unfortunately, I don't think there's anything grown about them," I muttered, fiddling with the coaster that Desiree had tossed on the bar in front of me.

"That's not what you said when I was naked and on top of you."

Dessie's eyes bugged out of her head.

I spun, saw that one Axel Finnegan had dislodged the blonde from his lap and squeezed next to me, leaning against the bar with a devil may care smile on his face.

"*You*," I snapped.

"Buttercup." He reached forward and tugged lightly at a strand of my hair.

Desiree choked.

I batted him away. "Back up, you—you—"

"Bastard?" One dark brown brow lifted. "Asshole?" He leaned closer, breath puffing on my lips. "Cock-sucker?" He leaned in farther, until his mouth was very near my ear. "Only once," he murmured, "and I found it wasn't for me."

Heat blazed through me.

Why was the thought of him sucking off another man so fucking hot?

Probably because I was imagining him with an equally hot guy, and then I was *imagining* both of those hot guys with me.

At the same time.

Yum.

I shivered.

Fuck.

Not *yum*.

Shit.

A flick of moisture. A flick of his *tongue* against my ear. And then a rough chuckle, the fucker seeming to know exactly what I was thinking.

I brought my hand up, pressed it against his chest...

Then dug my nails in.

Hard.

He winced.

Then covered my hand with his own, squeezed lightly, and murmured, "I *don't* mind a little bit of pain, though."

My thighs squeezed tight.

But I managed to get my shit together, shove him back, and spin forward on my stool.

Clearly, talking to him wasn't getting him to leave me alone. I turned back to Dessie, determined to ignore him. Her lips had tipped up in the corners, and her brows were practically in her hairline.

"He's pretty, but annoying," I stage-whispered. "And he's *not* getting fucked." I glared over at him. "Not by me anyway. Not now. Not before. Not *ever*."

He smirked.

I lifted my chin toward the corner booth he'd previously occupied but deliberately kept my gaze from his. "And not by that pretty blonde in the corner if he keeps ignoring her."

He turned, spared a glance toward the booth. For all of a...*second*.

If that.

Then he was shifting closer, moving so that his leg was tangled with mine, so that his body was too damned near.

Hot and hard and...I knew *exactly* what he was packing.

"Newsflash, buttercup," he murmured. "I don't give a fuck about the blonde."

Why did that send my pulse skittering? My breath accelerating?

"Don't pretend that you give a fuck about me," I said, hating that my voice wavered.

Slightly.

But enough.

"I'm not pretending."

I sucked in a breath.

Because there was a vulnerability in his bright blue eyes. Because...he might be telling the truth, and I didn't know what *the fuck* to make of that.

Except, that it made me feel...*something*.

I felt Desiree move away, and whether it was to give me the privacy she thought I wanted (since Axel was still there and close, and I hadn't kicked him in the big ol' dick I knew he had) or because she had other customers she needed to serve, I didn't know.

But I really, *seriously* missed the shield she'd provided.

Because it left me unable to ignore Axel, left me all too vulnerable to the heat curling in my belly.

Not that Axel had been much deterred by her with all his ear-licking and thigh-pressing. Not that *I* was deterred by his nearness or his yummy smell or those blazing blue eyes or the fingers drifting slowly down my throat—

Wait.

My *throat?*

Next, they'd be tracing along my collarbones, potentially sliding down beneath my bra, grazing my nip—

What the fuck was I doing?

Getting lured into complacency by the sexy smile and the spicy scent and hard body and the huge dick and—

Being a complete idiot.

Case in point?

The buxom blonde making an appearance.

"Axel," she whined, draping herself over him. "I'm *cold.*"

He turned to deal with her.

And I used the opportunity...

To run.

Thirteen

Axel

The blonde with the big tits, whose name I could *not* remember for the life of me, had turned into an octopus. With like fourteen arms.

And giant-ass suckers.

And—

I managed to wrestle her tentacles free and turned back to Bailey—

Who was gone.

"Fuck," I muttered.

"Axel!" Another whine.

And I'd had enough.

"Take a fucking hint," I growled. "I'm not interested now, and I'm not going to ever be."

A wobbling bottom lip, but ineffective considering that I'd already witnessed her ability to produce tears on a whim multiple times that evening, including when Joel had accidentally bumped her arm and she'd let loose the waterworks. Oh, and when another of the girls had eaten the last mozzarella stick. And, come to think of it, when I'd asked her to get off so I could take a piss.

Tears weren't sexy.

Tears on command were even less so.

Even with the great rack and pretty face.

"But—"

I nodded to the booth. "Go find Joel. He likes emotional bitches."

A tear slid free.

"And I don't, so fuck off, Cassidy."

"I—my name is Candi."

"I don't care."

"I—" A sob hitched her chest, and I was too much of a man to not notice that the sob hitching through her chest also had her boobs jiggling.

Damn.

That was nice.

Not so nice?

The tears glistening in her eyes and those tentacles reaching for me again.

"Fuck. Off," I repeated, lifting her away from me. This woman had always struck me as slightly nuts, so there was no way I was letting her get any closer. I planted my hand in between those massive boobs when she reached for me again, held her off, bending slightly so I could meet those falsely watery eyes. "I mean it. *Fuck. Off.* Do you get me?"

I held her stare.

Finally, she nodded.

"Go find Joel."

Another nod.

Then she was spinning away on a huff, marching across the busy floor. I didn't spare her another look. Instead, I searched the rest of the space for the stubborn, pesky brunette who liked to laugh at my attempts at charm and pointed shotguns at my junk.

There was no sign of her.

"Maybe enjoy your beer on the back patio?"

"That's not my beer—" My gaze caught on the bartender's, who lifted her eyebrows and dragged her stare from the full beer on the bar to a door I'd never noticed before. "Right." I snagged the glass. "I'll just go...enjoy...um...*this* on the patio."

It was more question than statement.

Which was probably why she nodded and lifted her chin toward the door.

Since I wasn't a *complete* idiot, I shut up and hit the door.

The cool air tugged at my skin, making it tighten like it did when I first skated out onto the ice. It was a familiar feeling and one of my favorites—home and the only thing that had never let me down: the game.

But then I stopped thinking about hockey.

Because all I could think about was *her*.

She was standing against a wooden post, nearly hidden in the shadows of the pergola, only the hanging lights overhead and moonlight drifting through the clouds revealing her profile.

And she was beautiful.

And sad.

And there was something in her that drew me to her—a moth to the light, a bee to nectar, a big, dumb, horny hockey player to something steel...with something soft and vulnerable beneath.

That wasn't like me.

I didn't *do* vulnerable.

I didn't *do* women I couldn't do easily.

But...Bailey...

Fuck, I didn't know what it was about her. What had me moving across the empty space, the late fall air obviously too cold for most of the other patrons, especially without the outdoor heaters on.

"You forgot this," I said, holding the beer out like it was an offering.

For peace?

For mistakes?

For wanting something I shouldn't?

She jumped and spun around, her hand clamping to her chest. "What the fuck?" she snapped, her eyes narrowing. "Fucking hell, Axel"—she inhaled sharply through her nose—"can't you take a hint?"

"Cool."

That had her freezing, brows drawing together.

I took a long sip of the beer, felt the cool, bubbly slide down my throat. "*God,* that's good."

"Hey! That's my—"

"I'm taking a hint." I sipped again, turning away and moving across the space, stepping out from beneath the pergola and staring up at the stars.

So bright.

No smog.

Just cold, fresh air and the faint buzz of conversation and music and *people.*

There wasn't anyone out here—no one aside from me and Bailey, that was. But her presence was...unsettling. Muted and yet somehow still huge. An aura that sank into my bones, that quieted me, and yet something that also had my skin buzzing with awareness.

I didn't *like* awareness.

I liked to skate fast and crush people against the boards in pursuit of the puck. I liked to be surrounded by noise and activity and to let myself be swept along in it, to numb myself in sensation so I couldn't be quiet like this, couldn't. I liked to drink until I didn't remember, and I liked to fuck until it was all pleasure and no pain and—

My sigh bubbled up in my throat and I swallowed it down.

Awareness was something I tried to avoid at all costs.

But it was something that grew until it nearly encompassed me as Bailey stomped over, her rubber-soled boots clomping on the concrete.

One second, I was just listening to her footsteps.

The next her presence was *in* mine, scent tangling with that of the beer as she came close, her ponytail whipping me across the cheek as her hand swept down and snagged the glass out of my grip.

"This"—the beer sloshed over the rim, splashed along her wrist —"is *mine*—"

Whatever else she was going to say was cut off.

Because of me.

Mainly because that beer was dripping off her golden skin, making it glisten under the twinkling lights overhead, the sheen calling to me.

To my mouth, my lips, my *tongue*.

I grasped her wrist, wrapping my fingers around the slender strength of her.

And then...I lifted it to my mouth, flicked out my tongue...and *tasted*.

Her skin. The beer.

The sweet, fruity taste of her.

The bitter hoppy flavor of the beer.

The soft, breathy sound of her moan in my ears.

My jaw flexed, and then I was dragging my lips along her wrist, up the inside of her forearm, pushing the loose sleeve of her flannel up as I went, pausing at her elbow, and then—

I couldn't resist nipping at the silken skin.

"Ow!" she hissed.

I soothed the small hurt with my tongue, was rewarded with the sweet, fruity taste of her.

It was better sans beer.

It was *better* when she moaned again, when that sound rippled through me and she didn't resist me pulling her closer, didn't protest when I wrapped her in my arms, dragged my lips from her elbow up to her throat, pressing my mouth to the spot just beneath her jaw.

She shuddered.

I moved to her ear, tasting that hanging lobe, dipping down to kiss the spot behind it that was pure *Bailey*. Apples and sweet, floral and just the slightest bit of horse.

No shit.

Just...nature and outside and quiet and the bright sun and the blue sky and...splinters in my ass.

I huffed out a breath, leaned back enough to see that her eyes were closed, her lips parted.

I had to taste her.

So...I did.

Slanting my mouth across hers, dancing my tongue across her lips.

She exhaled, moan rumbling up through her throat, along her tongue, into my mouth. That heat and need arrowed straight for my dick, making it throb and ache as it hardened against my zipper.

I groaned.

She stiffened, went ramrod straight in my arms.

Curses blared through my mind, but though I paused, I didn't lift my mouth from hers. Just held still and my breath and waited and hoped and hell, I threw up a couple of prayers to the hockey gods that she wasn't about to dump the beer over my head or my crotch or my—

A feminine sigh.

Then...she melted.

Her body coming flush against mine. Her moan rumbling through my mouth again.

Plush breasts. Strong thighs.

I heard a clink, felt cold liquid hit my shoes, soak into my jeans.

But then her fingers were gripping my arms and she was crawling up my body, lips fusing to mine, one leg wrapping around my waist. I reacted instantly, driving my tongue deeply into her mouth, grabbing that lush thigh, snagging the other so she was straddling my waist.

Short.

She was too short. I had to strain to reach her—

But fuck, I loved having her curves beneath my hands.

Loved it so much that I spun, pinning her against one of the pillars of the pergola, seeing the shadows from the lights overhead dance across her body, her face.

I wanted to see it glimmer all along her naked skin.

I *needed*—

Her hands moved, sliding to my middle, dipping beneath the hem of my shirt. I sucked in a breath when they skated over my stomach then up, fingers gliding along my pecs, nails dragging over my nipples.

Need reached a boiling point, and I started to reach for the button of her jeans.

Flicked it open.

I had a condom in my wallet. I always did.

It would be so easy to tug down her jeans, to yank open the fly on mine.

Her teeth found my bottom lip, nipped, sending a bolt of pain through me. It barely hurt, the slight sting sending my control splintering.

Yeah.

I wanted to fuck her.

Right there.

Right *now*.

Hefting her up, I kissed her harder, grabbed the tag of the zipper—

And it was like someone had gripped handfuls of my hair and

wrenched tightly, dragging my mouth from hers, shaking me fiercely.

Not here.

I couldn't fuck her *here*.

Fourteen

Bailey

I was distantly aware of movement, of Axel taking his mouth from mine and carrying me somewhere.

Distantly because I was touching that chest I'd seen twice before, caressing the muscles, feeling them bounce beneath my palms, his nipples tightening under my fingertips. Then I was stroking across his stomach.

Hard abs.

Strong arms.

Down.

A hard—

Holy hell, the top of his cock was resting against his stomach and pushing out above the waistband of his underwear. Ignoring the fact that he was still carrying me—because his cock was like a hypnotist's pendulum, and my gaze couldn't go anywhere else—I licked my lips as I stared at the hardened tip, moisture beading at the top, the taut skin pulled tight over the blunt head.

If I was feeling insecure about what he wanted—or if he

wanted *me*—the amount of precum currently making my mouth water, not to mention the hard dick, would have made that clear.

This man wanted me.

But I *wasn't* feeling insecure.

I was on fucking *fire*.

I wanted him.

I *needed* him.

Stroking down his stomach, I shoved my hand into his underwear, wrapping my fingers around his cock.

He cursed, choking on a groan.

My pussy clenched, an empty, needy bitch, and I needed him. *Needed.*

In my mouth. Inside *me*. In my hands. Between my breasts. Hard and pulsing on my tongue as his cum slid down my throat.

One touch had struck the match and I was burning, desperate, ready to fuck him right *freaking* then and there. His arms were still around me, his mouth on mine for another searing taste before drifting to my cheek, my jaw, my throat, nipping and licking and kissing as he continued leading me toward...somewhere I hoped would lead to his hands coming back to my pants, only dragging them down this time instead of stopping.

And the focus on my pants being solely a prerequisite to getting them out of the way so that he could push that giant cock inside me and fuck me into oblivion.

"Killing me, buttercup," he breathed against my skin, his lips and tongue working there and slowly driving me insane.

"Why?" I murmured, stroking my thumb over a throbbing vein on his shaft.

"Because I'm trying to get you back to my place when all I really want to do is fuck you right here and now."

My heart thudded.

My breath caught.

Then I said, "Okay."

He dropped his forehead to mine then huffed out a laugh, nipped my lips, and I tasted his smile. "Okay?"

"If I'm pretending this is a moment of insanity"—which I was, mostly because I was suddenly dying to fuck Axel, and my fingers were around his cock, and I couldn't make sense of *why* I was going to do something so fucking stupid, so...insanity—"then I could go for a little public sex."

I'd deal with the consequences later.

I'd deal with *all* of it later.

Axel froze, eyes blazing as he looked down at me.

"My apartment is around the corner," he murmured. "Public sex later."

"Late—"

My words were cut off by his lips, his tongue.

And then he was moving again, or maybe it was that we never *stopped* moving, and I was just so enamored of those bright blue eyes and the muscled body and the hard cock that was currently pulsing against my palm that I hadn't noticed that he could walk and carry me *and* talk, and then kiss me and carry me *and* walk, all without bringing us into the path of a speeding car or running into a pole or something.

That was probably mostly due to everyone in River's Bend being either in their beds or inside Monroe's.

No cars on the road to be hit by.

But he was kissing me, and I was ending a long-held drought, and he was sexy and a good kisser, and I held the man's cock in my hands and—

I wasn't going to worry about cars or the population's sleeping habits.

Instead, I was thinking about the feel of Axel's tongue as it stroked against mine, how his arms were so strong as they held me seemingly without effort. How the cool air on my skin did nothing to cool the fire blazing through me.

How...I just wanted.

So, I kissed him back as he ascended the stairs, held tight when he shifted me to the side to unlock a door.

And then, when we were inside, I tugged at his shirt.

But I didn't get far, didn't get it much more than an inch up before he spun us, pinning me between him and the door.

One long, heated draw on my mouth, his tongue probing deeply, his lips fierce against mine.

Then my feet hit the floor.

A big hand pressing my back and shoulders against the door one more time.

And Axel...oh fucking hell...Axel dropped to his knees.

Oh, *fuck*.

He was tall, much taller than me, but that height difference hadn't seemed so great when I was in his arms, my legs wrapped around his waist.

But when he was kneeling in front of me, his mouth even with my breasts, his hands coming to my jeans, dragging the zipper down, yanking the material to my ankles, and his size was...absolutely intoxicating.

A tug at one of my boots had it sliding from my foot. He tossed it over his shoulder and was on my next boot before the first even thudded to the ground.

Then the second was gone, my pants were whipped from my legs.

"Fuck," he growled.

I jumped, confused by the rumble of sound, even more so by the hands gripping my hips, spinning me so I was face-first against the door.

"This *fucking* ass," he rumbled, his hand smoothing slowly over my curves.

A yank had one side of my plain cotton panties tugged up, my cheek exposed.

"I've been dreaming about this ass," he rasped.

A bite of pain...no, a *bite*, I realized as the sting had moisture pooling between my legs, gathering at the tops of my thighs. But it was quickly soothed by tongue and lips and then he was tugging up the other side of my underwear, kissing his way over, fingers drifting slowly up my legs.

"Fuck," he murmured, hand moving around to my front, brushing over the damp material of my panties, pressing lightly on my clit. "I've been dreaming about *this* too."

I opened my mouth to say...something.

But then he tugged my hips sharply back, making me brace myself on the wooden panel, and the words caught in my throat.

My underwear disappeared, and my gasp turned into a moan and then a squeal when his mouth took its place. Long strokes of his tongue that built heat in my center, nips from his teeth that sent shivers through me, a press of one broad finger inside then two, causing my head to fall forehead against the door, my hips to arch back against his mouth, his fingers, his tongue.

"Oh, fuck," I breathed.

"Mmm." A rough groan, the sound vibrating through me.

"Oh, fuck," I breathed again.

Another groan, another finger slipping into me, and then his mouth closed over my clit, sucking deeply, tongue flicking, and—

"Fuck. Oh, fuck. *Fuck*. I'm going to—"

I didn't finish the sentence.

Because his tongue began working faster.

Because...I was going to come, and I was going to do it right then and—

Oh my God.

I was coming and holy shit, it was a brutal pleasure. No coaxing. No gentle wave flowing over me.

It was a nuclear bomb detonating directly over me.

Pleasure exploded through my body, bursting from my middle, flaming through my limbs.

And he didn't stop, not as the pleasure began to fade, not as my body went limp. He merely wrapped one big arm around me, holding me close, his fingers still deep and moving inside me as he began walking.

Long strides down a dark hall.

My breath shooting out of me when a soft mattress hit my back, when those fingers slipped from my pussy.

The lights flicked on.

I blinked against the sudden brightness.

Then Axel Finnegan was on top of me, spreading my thighs, his eyes absolutely on fire.

And I couldn't wait to be reduced to ashes.

Fifteen

Axel

My hands trembled as they slid up her thighs.

Golden skin, strong legs...bare pussy.

That was a surprise, a good one, all those glistening folds on display for me.

Bending slowly, I pressed a kiss to one hip bone and then the other.

Then the area in between.

Then because she tasted like heaven and I needed her on my tongue again, I kissed her. Right on that bare pussy, avoiding her clit because I knew it would still be sensitive, delving into her folds and dragging my tongue through all that moisture.

Liquid heat.

Thighs trembling.

Her stomach clenching and releasing even as it was only halfway on display, because she still had her flannel and shirt and bra—I assumed—on. I needed to get to that, to get them off her, but how could I with the feast in front of me?

She hissed out a breath when I hit a particularly sensitive spot on her labia, so I focused there, sucking and licking until her moans came louder and faster, until she gripped my hair, until her thighs tried to close on me.

I pushed her legs farther apart, dipped my tongue deeply into her and redoubled my efforts.

A shudder. "Axel."

I kept going, using the pressure and pattern I'd learned that made her explode in my front hall. I kept going until she was shaking, until those fingers delved into my hair, dug into my scalp, held me to her.

I kept going until my name was a shriek on her lips, until she shook so fiercely that I half-worried she was going to fall to pieces.

Then she slumped to the mattress, her legs going limp around me.

I meant to keep going easy—or, well, not *easy* because I wasn't the kind of guy to fuck easy—but I'd intended to stay in control, to make this night the best ever for her.

To get her so addicted to me that she would come back and—

Wait.

What?

But before that thought could penetrate, Bailey *moved.*

Suddenly, I was on my back, and she was climbing over me, her hands on my shoulders and pressing me down into the mattress.

"Buttercup—"

Her mouth covered mine, tongue driving deep, hands gripping the sides of my face as she proceeded to kiss the fuck out of me.

I reached for the hem of her top, tugging it and her flannel off.

It bunched at her shoulders for a moment before she broke the kiss, and then she yanked the material over her head, tossing it to the side, leaving her in a plain beige bra that shouldn't have been sexy.

But it was.

Plumping those curves up until they threatened to spill over.

Then she was reaching behind her, arching back as she unsnapped her bra, and revealing...

Holy hell, she had great tits.

Big wasn't the half of it—because they *were* big, with perfectly-sized, puffy nipples. It was the way they bounced and hung and just fucking made my palms itch with the need to have them in my hands.

And my mouth.

I needed to taste her there, too.

She was reaching for my shirt, yanking *that* up, and since I wanted to be naked just as much as I wanted my mouth on her again, I let her.

And same went when she went for my pants.

I let her undo the zipper, drag the material down my legs.

She didn't get them far, but since my cock popped free, it was far enough, especially when she slid down my body and sucked my dick into her mouth.

Deep.

Wet.

A lot of suction.

A firm grip.

And...I lost my patience.

My hips jerked up, and I hit the back of her throat. Clumsy. Definitely an asshole move, since she wasn't prepared for it.

But...she was incredible.

She didn't cough or choke or push me away.

She just dipped down, sucked me deeper, gripped me tighter, and...*fucking* blew me.

Until my hips were jerking uncontrollably. Until sweat sheeted my body. Until my hands shook, and my thighs cramped and—

Fuck it.

I tore her off me before I exploded, tossing her up the mattress, barely having the presence of mind to stop her head from hitting the bedpost.

Then I was reaching for my nightstand, ripping the drawer open, rifling through the contents, desperate for a condom. Shit hit the floor, but I didn't care what it was, or that I heard shit shattering. *Nothing* was more important in that moment than getting inside her.

Finally, my fingers closed on the plastic square, and I lurched back, tearing it open with my teeth and rolling it down my cock.

Fuck.

It was hard.

I was shaking, my control on the precipice of snapping.

And...I was big.

And Bailey was small. So small that some of the need that had seized me waned. Because I was six-six, two hundred and ten pounds. She was...five-three? *Maybe* four. And though she was curvy, she couldn't have been more than a hundred and thirty pounds.

I was going to kill her, smother her, rip her to shreds, hurt—

"What?" she asked, chest heaving, breasts jiggling.

I wanted to not give a fuck, a worry. I wanted to shove her legs wide, to pound deep into her.

It was what I would have done with anyone else.

But...I was worried.

Which was why I snagged her and rolled to my back, bringing her on top.

Her lips parted, a gasp in the air.

I wrapped my hands around her hips, drew her down. "Ride me, buttercup."

Those lips went back together, curved into a smile, eyes dancing. "Yeah?"

I couldn't form words, so I just nodded, and thank fuck, she began to lower herself, notching my tip inside, and then, making my eyes roll back, curses litter the air, she sank down. Slowly, yes, but not stopping until her pelvis rested atop mine, until I was fully seated, until her tight, wet pussy was clasping my cock so fiercely that I nearly exploded before she even began moving.

"You're big," she whispered, shifting herself from side to side, making every single muscle in my body go tense, my orgasm already prickling at the base of my spine. "Fuck, you're *big.*"

She sucked in a breath, released it as a moan.

"Fuck," she breathed, lifting up and down slowly. "*Fuck.*"

Fuck was right.

She felt...perfect. Incredible. A fucking wet dream come to life.

I smirked, kept my hands on her hips. "Move, buttercup."

She *had* to move, or I might fucking die.

Dramatic? Yes. But she was clamping down on me like a vise and I was going to come, and yeah, she'd had two orgasms, but she hadn't had one with me inside her yet.

And I might be an asshole, but I always pleased my partners.

Which meant I didn't come without them. Or before them. Or—

"Fuck," I whispered as she rippled around me again.

But luckily, she started moving, and I got my hands on her breasts, on her nipples, rolling them lightly between thumb and forefinger, then harder when she moaned, arched forward, and demanded, "More."

Her head fell back, and she began moving faster, hips jerking, my name tumbling off her lips.

She was close.

Thank fuck.

I reached down between us, pressed my thumb to her clit, circling it firmly, grabbing at one of her hips when she bucked, holding her to me, making sure she didn't falter as she kept grinding me hard and deep and—

"Axel," she murmured, head snapping forward, eyes blazing when they hit mine. "I need—"

She was close.

But not *there*.

Flipping us, I started stroking into her.

"Yes. Oh, fuck," she whispered. "Oh fuck. Harder, baby, *harder.*"

That I could do.

I positioned her beneath me until I was hitting the spot inside her that had her gripping me tighter, and then I fucked her hard and fast, her pussy convulsing around me, her nails digging into my shoulders, her moans coming in quick succession.

"Oh, my *God—*"

She arched her neck back against the pillows, hips rising up to meet mine.

My name tumbled from her lips, the slick sounds of us coming together driving me closer to that edge.

But that was okay.

Because, thank fuck, she was there, too.

Nails digging deeper into my skin. Legs locking around my hips.

Pussy gripping me tight and—

She came apart, but I could barely watch her because my orgasm had wrapped around my body and yanked me roughly under. It exploded out from the base of my spine, shooting into my limbs, my movements going jerky as pleasure burst through me.

Nirvana.

The best fucking *ever.*

No.

The best *fucking* ever.

I collapsed down, barely able to catch myself so I didn't crush her and rolled us to the side, fingers stroking small patterns on the skin of her back, sending them through the strands of her hair.

My head was spinning.

Panic was chasing those tendrils of pleasure.

I was rocked to my fucking core and didn't have a fucking clue what to say.

Which was probably why I blurted, loudly and roughly, "I'm going to clean up."

Her gaze came to my face, but I didn't let it connect with mine.

"Right," she whispered.

And if my gait into the bathroom was more walk than run, then it was only because she seemed as rocked as I was—her eyes wide, her face pale, no more words coming.

I took my time cleaning up, washing my hands and dick and hands again because that shit should be done in the right order and I was so fucked that I was doing it wrong and—

I gripped the edge of the counter, hung my head.

"Fuck, Axel," I whispered, gaze coming to the mirror.

Taking in my own wide eyes, my own pale face.

"What was that?" I asked my reflection.

Except, I thought I knew.

And it absolutely terrified me.

So much so, that it took me a fucking lifetime—or so it seemed —to force myself out of the bathroom, my hand shaking when I turned the knob, knees practically knocking together as I tried to steel myself.

I needn't have bothered.

Because Bailey was gone.

Sixteen

I brushed Data's flank, her soft chestnut hair shining in the morning light.

It was beautiful.

She was beautiful.

And normally, I'd be able to appreciate those things. I'd made an effort to find the beauty in the small stuff after coming home to find that my parents had fucked up Gramps' legacy, after working my ass off for the last two years, after digging myself and the property out of the reverse mortgage hole.

Because I'd spent too long in the dark to waste any more time not appreciating the light.

But this morning, like every other morning of the last couple of weeks, I was...unsettled.

And I was spending all my extra energy trying to pretend that I wasn't, or at least trying to pretend that the reason I *was* so disconcerted wasn't one Axel Fucking Finnegan.

"Come on, Bay," I whispered to myself, running the brush

along Data's side. "Head down, move forward. Meet your goal. Get the fuck out." Data whinnied angrily, as though she knew what I was saying and wasn't happy her built-in spa service was talking about leaving.

Either that, or all my *unsettled* was making me lose my mind.

Yeah.

Probably the second. Because I kept right on conversing with a horse.

"Or stay," I soothed, brushing Data in earnest now. "Maybe I'll stay when I can afford help and can actually live and travel and eat at the occasional fancy restaurant and maybe I can finish my teaching degree and get a pedicure or wear clothes that aren't at risk of getting covered in horseshit, or..."

I put down the brush, wove my fingers through Data's mane.

"Who am I kidding?" I whispered. "I would always come right back."

As much as I hated the burden of the farm, I'd always felt at home here. Even though I hadn't grown up in River's Bend, even though my parents had moved me all over the fucking Bay Area. So many schools that I couldn't count—or, rather, I *could* count (I'd been in ten of them). More places to live than that—and often leaving them in the middle of the night, our stuff shoved into the back of the car, searching out the next poor soul to mooch off.

River's Bend.

This farm.

Stability.

Warm. *Home*. A break from my flighty parents.

To Gramps and Gram and even fucking Billie Rose (though she'd been way less interfering back then).

Even without Gramps and Gran, the people in this town were more than just friends or acquaintances. They were my family.

They'd been there, a constant source of stability my entire life.

So, I might groan and gripe about having to put off getting my teaching credential, having to come back, to step in and save Russet Ranch.

But this was also my *place*.

Plus, it had been the perfect opportunity to escape from...

To forget about—

Gravel crunching.

I turned just in time to see a familiar little SUV tear into my driveway, spraying rocks in all directions—and I made a mental note that when it came time to spread fresh gravel in a couple of months' time that Billie Rose would be helping.

"I'll get her a fucking shovel with her damn name emblazoned on it," I muttered.

Of course, Billie would probably show up before the sun had risen with bells on and loving that she could help someone...which would make the punishment very much *less* like a punishment, at least in my mind.

Probably to truly have an effect on her, I should force her to sit and watch while the rest of us worked.

Which would defeat the entire purpose.

But then again, I often felt defeated when it came to Billie Rose.

Smothering a sigh, I braced myself for the hurricane that would be my aunt.

The mayor of River's Bend hopped out of her car, her curls bouncing, her slacks and blouse clean and crisp and yet, paired— some might say incongruously—with sneakers. This was only if someone didn't know her, because those who *did* know her, knew that any heels she wore were strictly for appearing put together and in charge during her daily meetings. *I,* for instance, knew Billie had a pair of pumps in her trunk for when she would head back to City Hall and start making her way through her agenda for the day.

So take that little tidbit and—

I shook myself, watched her approach.

Billie Rose *was* River's Bend, through and through, and that meant hard-working (and ever-ready to jump in with those sneaker-clad feet), down to earth, and with limited patience for fancy and high maintenance. It went without saying that my aunt was pretty and her makeup complemented that, but it wasn't heavy or overstated. Simple. Optimized for high performance.

River's Bend to a T.

This small town in one tiny woman.

"Bailey," she called, the door slamming behind her as she began to storm my way with all the grace of a cow being flung around a fictional tornado. "I need you!"

Okay, maybe I was wrong.

Perhaps her makeup and clothing style was actually optimized for pushiness.

Or demanding-ness? Or—

"Bailey!" Her sneakers crunched loudly over the gravel.

A smothered sigh as I set aside the brush, turned to face Billie. "What's up?"

Brows narrowing. "Don't take that tone with me," she clipped.

My own brows snapped down. "Don't take *that* tone with *me,*" I countered.

Her frown deepened. Then cleared, mouth tipping up at the edges. "You know normal people are afraid of me."

"You *know,*" I said (or rather, continued countering), "I once had to rescue you from a dress because you couldn't get out of it—"

"That was scary!" she exclaimed, smile dying. "It was too tight, and I couldn't breathe—"

"Or operate zippers?" I asked dryly

"It was *hidden.*"

I shot her a look. "Yup. *So* difficult." I lifted my arm, looked down at my rib cage, and mimed undoing the "hidden" zipper.

"Brat," Billie rose muttered.

"Yup." I smiled. "Now, what do you need?"

Billie's expression went down-to-business. "The harvest parade is coming up."

Oh, Christ. The harvest parade was hell in the form of orange and yellow and red leaves, plastic gourds, and leftover uncarved pumpkins (since our California heat typically turned the carved ones to mush in less than a week).

Was I a monster who hated Thanksgiving?

Fuck, yeah.

But there was nothing worse than sitting around with my parents on that holiday, especially when they usually failed to show up in the first place (which meant that I ended up sitting around by myself for hours), and on the odd times they *did* show up to the festivities, they created drama and then flitted out, none the more aware of the train wreck they left in their wake. *Or*— and this had been rare growing up—it was spent with my *other* family.

With Billie's lovely, well-adjusted, super sweet and rosy (*ha*) parents and siblings.

They didn't live in River's Bend any longer, her parents moving to Palm Springs because they loved the weather, and her siblings having scattered across the state and country for work, but growing up, and even on the rare occasions I saw them now, they made my parents look like...well, monsters.

So Thanksgiving.

I wasn't there for it.

But Thanksgiving in River's Bend was H-E-Double-Hockey-Sticks.

No. Not thinking of hockey, because that would bring thoughts of Axel and our night and—

Double no.

The point was that Thanksgiving meant there was a parade. I might be a monster who didn't enjoy the holidays, but parades were worse. They were basically writhing masses of snotty and screaming kids, parents who were determined to one-up each other with costumes and all too much togetherness for my isolated-ranch-loving heart.

But Billie Rose naturally liked—okay *loved*—parades. Because she loved all things River's Bend and togetherness and bolstering town spirit.

And never mind that I'd just been thinking about how much I loved it just before Billie had shown up.

I was a cranky rancher.

I didn't do parades or color-coded costumes and—

Billie Rose had been Miss Harvest Parade 2012.

I knew this because even though I hadn't been here for the parade that particular year, Billie had come down to San Francisco with her mom, and the three of us had gone shopping for her dress in Union Square. It was where the zipper incident had gone down and when I'd put my superior rescuing skills to work—here I mentally buffed my knuckles on my shoulder. *Go me.*

Of course—and this had nothing to do with my hatred of the Harvest Festival and its corresponding parade—but I knew about Billie's victory because I'd wanted to go.

Because my mom had promised to drive me up for the festivities.

And...

Then she'd flaked.

Surprise? No.

It was very much *not* a surprise and there was no point in being upset about it and—

Anyway, my past didn't change the fact that parades were the devil and I sincerely disliked that I was going to be helping with one. *Going to* because Billie was going to ask and I was going to say yes, and *yes,* there would be lots of grumbling and lots of sighing and lots of cursing under my breath so the snotty, screamy kids and their one-upping parents couldn't hear.

But I was going to help.

Because Billie Rose was going to ask.

"Horses," I said, focusing back on the issue at hand. "Is that what you want?"

Billie's curls bounced as she nodded her head, and then no joke —*no joke*—she pulled out a clipboard from her pocket. How? Where—? But Billie Rose was listing off more *wants*. "Friendly ones for pony rides. And I also need four dozen hay bales, three saddles, and a variety of farm implements—"

"Where did you get—?" *Wait.* "Farm implements?" Like pitch forks and shit that people might impale themselves on? I shook my head. "No, that's not happening. Yes, on the bales of hay and saddles," I added quickly as Billie's expression turned thunderous. "I can also provide a baby cow."

Yes, technically it was a calf (a steer, really, since I'd relieved him of his balls), but Billie was Billie, and a baby *cow,* even if that was the wrong technical term, would distract her from *farm implements.* God help me if Billie got it in her head to decorate the parade route with pitch forks or heavy tillers that might fall and smash into a toddler's head, or worse and yet still somehow in the realm of possibility for my aunt, rail posts with rusty nails in them.

Now *that* would be a theme.

This year's Harvest Parade—Tetanus for Everyone!

Okay, so it probably wouldn't be fencing. That was important to *me*, but it couldn't be to Billie. Plus, I didn't think she would categorize posts, nails, and barbed wire as farm implements.

So...what?

Those pitchforks? Corroded saw blades? Plows? Hoes? Horseshoes?

Okay, the last would be okay...unless one of those snotty, screamy kids decided to chuck one at my head and—

Right.

Enough with the snotty, screamy kids.

Luckily, my distraction worked.

"A baby *cow?*" Billie shrieked, making me jump. Her face lit up.

"Really?" The last was somehow even louder, and I resisted the urge to clamp my hands over my ears.

"Really," I agreed, nodding toward the barn and the stall I currently had the late-season calf in. Mama cow had rejected him, and so I was the softie currently feeding Picard three times a day by bottle.

Yeah, I was a closet Star Trek nerd.

No, I wasn't going to tell anyone that his name was Picard.

I led the way inside, opened the wooden door, and revealed the black calf.

Billie Rose's squeals of excitement got louder. So loud that she startled Picard, his cute (which was the reason I'd brought him down and was feeding him three times a day—though thankfully, the vet had said I could stop with the middle of the night bottles) head shooting up, his *cow* (okay, easy on the pun, *steer*) eyes going wide and showing off the whites surrounding them.

I swatted Billie. "Have you forgotten everything about working with animals?"

She wasn't listening to me. Instead, she was already moving into the stall and kneeling at Picard's side, her arms going around the little steer's neck and hugging him tight. He was a love bug and ate up any attention I'd been able to spare him so far, so it was no surprise that he cuddled right up into Billie's lap, getting hay and dust all over her clothes.

But I knew that she probably had a change of them in her trunk, next to those heels. Billie Rose was nothing if not prepared.

Annoying.

A busybody.

But prepared.

And, I supposed, lovable, loyal, hard-working, and persistent.

I hated that I was finding good things in her. However, I also knew all of my hate and annoyance and frustration with my aunt and her busybody ways was because I was *unsettled*.

Because of Axel Finnegan and his magnificent cock.

Because—

"I love you."

I blinked, brows drawing together, fear coiling in my stomach, fear and something else. The possibility of something, the *need* of something, the longing and—

"I love you, my little smuffikins," Billie Rose semi-repeated, hugging Picard tight. "Who's my baby?" She glanced up, her blue eyes locking with mine. "What's her name?"

"His," I corrected. "And his name is..." Fuck. What was something that was sensible and rancher-tough and—right, the tough ranchers probably didn't even name their cattle. Just marched them right up onto the truck and—

"Cow," I blurted.

"Cow?" Billie Rose asked incredulously and decided *that* was the moment she'd begin remembering her animal husbandry skills and bovine terminology. Not when she'd been shrieking her way through the barn. *Now* she remembered that a cow referred to a female. "I thought you said he was a boy?"

Well, I couldn't admit to having named him Picard now, could I?

I had *one* secret.

Well...a *few*. But the least toxic of those was my closet nerdiness.

"Cow," I confirmed, more firmly this time.

Her eyes narrowed, fixed me in place. "This is one of your stupid nerd names, isn't it?"

Okay, so maybe Billie Rose knew most of my secrets.

Well, I wasn't giving her any more fuel to dig deeper, to discover the ones I'd buried deep.

"I don't know what you're talking about," I said innocently.

Too innocently.

Billie's brows lifted. "Bailey," she warned.

Shit.

I straightened my shoulders. "The steer's name is Cow."

A sigh. "*Bailey.*"

"It's *Cow.*"

She just stared at me.

Christ. I plunked my hands on my hips, and then I did the only thing I could—

"What kind of farm implements do you want?"

SEVENTEEN

Axel

"Hey, man!" Joel called as I tossed my bag into my car. "They're finally letting us back into Haggarty's, and I've got a plethora of small-town girls who are bored and looking for a wild night coming."

"Go you."

Joel narrowed his eyes. "What's with you?"

"Nothing." I rolled my shoulders, the tension from the phone call that had premeditated me packing my shit already eating at me.

"Oh shit, you got a call up, didn't you?" Joel asked.

I nodded, went for casual. "Yeah."

A punch to my shoulder. "That's a fucking good thing, yeah?"

"Yeah," I muttered. "It's great."

Joel searched my face. "Doesn't sound like you think it's great. That's the call we all want to get, so why are you acting like someone cut off your dick?"

"I'm not. I just have a long drive ahead of me."

Silence.

Rightly reading that I was less excited and more...anxious,

regretful, trying to sort out a fucking tangle of emotions inside my head that had me really wanting to stay in River's Bend with this fucker and the guys and drink my way into oblivion.

But...I didn't want to be like my mother.

"I need to go. They want me there for practice with the Gold in the morning."

"You got this."

"I know."

Penetrating green eyes then, "Right, man. Whatever you say. You know, if you talked about shit every once in a while—"

I sighed. "Just back off, okay?"

"Same shit different day with you, isn't it?" Joel shook his head. "Can't get out of your own fucking way."

"Fuck you."

"Fuck *you* right back."

God, Joel was an annoying fucker. Especially when he cracked a grin.

"Do me a favor," I said, tugging my phone out of my pocket and ignoring the smirk. "Don't trash Haggarty's, yeah?"

"Yeah, we already talked about that," Joel muttered. "After the mayor from hell paid you several visits." He shuddered. "That woman is a fucking menace."

Yeah, I'd had to cop to the kidnapping when he gave me a ride.

But I'd also shared later that the team's contract was at risk, that we might soon be viewed as fucking lepers in the hockey world.

He'd agreed to help me get the guys to cool it.

Mostly because we'd been the ringleaders and if *we* were cooling it, then the guys would cool it.

Still, I reiterated, "No broken glasses or windows. No being dicks to the locals."

A scowl, his legendary temper sparking. "Like I *said*, we've already talked about this. I'm on board with you getting the guys on track. But that doesn't mean I'm not going to go out and tie one on when the fancy strikes."

I started to sink down into the driver's seat. "Yeah, I know."

"You go spend four hours driving and fucking with your own head." He tilted his head toward Main Street. "I'll enjoy all the pussy you're missing out on."

"Great," I muttered. "Have fun with that."

A smirk, his temper already gone.

Probably, because I *was* facing a long drive with a fucked-up head.

"Oh, I will."

————

I leaned back against the wall of the locker room and watched the people buzzing around—players, media, support staff. The same as the Rush, except magnified to an nth degree.

Like comparing small potatoes to...bigger ones.

And that right there was my high school education.

The point was, more money, bigger back office, more...opportunity.

Though not for me.

I'd played two games at the Gold Mine, and now...I was heading back to River's Bend.

Same shit, different day.

Up and down, back and forth.

Not finding my place.

Cotton candy in your head, boy. No point in making dreams. Not for a Finnegan.

And God, I loved hearing my drunk of a mother's voice in my head.

Especially when I'd been told before I'd even had a chance to get undressed that I was being booted right back down.

I'd made it to the third line.

I'd thought...well, I'd thought that this time was different.

Good plays, more ice time. I'd even made it onto the scoresheet —and not for a penalty this time. Instead, I'd made a great pass over to Ben who'd managed to sneak it in for a goal that had tied the game. Total clutch. And...it didn't fucking matter. I was going right back to Bumfuck, California, where I couldn't even drink my way into oblivion because then I might fuck up the small sliver of a chance I had at making it back here again and then a scary, curly-haired blond woman might handcuff me to the porch of a woman who pointed shotguns at me and nearly sawed my balls off with power tools, and—

"Hey."

I jerked, cracking my head against the shelving overhead, and reminding me that—in this case, luckily—I was still wearing my helmet.

Ripping it off, I turned to look at Brit.

The goalie—and first female player in the NHL—had played her ass off and still looked fresh enough to play three more games even though rumor had it she was going to retire at the end of the season when her contract was up.

"Hey," I said, plunking my helmet onto the bench next to me.

"You played great tonight."

"Yeah, thanks," I muttered. "You did, too." I bent, started ripping the tape off my socks, waiting for her to leave.

She would.

They always did.

Instead, though, she sat next to me.

Waited.

I needed to get undressed—or at least to get my gear off then move into the private locker room to shower.

Another difference.

No press in the locker rooms in River's Bend, no need to worry about scarring some child who stumbled onto a sports blog's live stream.

I could just dump all my gear on the floor, get naked, and then—

"What's the deal with you, anyway?"

I glanced up from my socks, saw her brows had dragged together. "What do you mean?"

"Talented player. No fucking passion."

Now my brows dragged together. "I—"

She shrugged. "You see glimpses of it on the ice, moments of greatness, and then..." A flutter of her hand. "It's just...*gone.*"

I yanked my jersey over my head. "Well, thanks for the pep talk."

"I've never actually seen someone so skilled just...*not* have it." She leaned back and crossed one ankle over the other. "Or not maintain it anyway," she said. "Because that pass to Ben was sweet. Same as your work in the defensive zone." Her eyes were considering. "So, the question is, where does that all go?"

I knew *exactly* where that all went, and that was down the fucking drain because I was a pathetic nobody who would never—

"Doesn't matter," I said, cutting the pity train off as I yanked my shoulder pads over my head, tugged my elbow pads down and off my arms.

"Except, I'd kind of think you'd be good on the roster."

One shin guard. Then the other. "Right."

She punched me in the shoulder.

Hard.

"Ow!" I exclaimed. "What?" I asked, getting to work on my skates.

A flash of white teeth. "You know what."

"I know that goalies are fucking weird," I muttered.

She snorted. "Original."

"And I know that I'm not ever going to be on the roster —permanently."

A pause. "Yeah? How do you know that?"

I sighed, but I didn't jump back onto the pity train, just

shrugged, dropped my dirty shit in their respective spots, and then moved into the private locker room. I'd shower. Drive four hours. Get up at dawn to get on a fucking bus to drive eight hours—and basically right past this arena—to SoCal to play with the Rush.

Work hard.

Head down.

Not quite ever enough.

I reached for the waistband of my compression shorts, started to push them down.

"You know—"

I jumped, not realizing that Brit had followed me into the other room, and halted in my undressing, fingers clenching on the fabric.

She smirked. "You ain't got nothing I haven't seen a hundred times before, Axel."

Right.

A woman used to locker rooms and nakedness and—

Still, she turned away when she repeated, "You know, I think I've got a bead on what's going on in that pretty brain of yours."

"Look," I said, pushing down my shorts and stepping into the shower. "We both know that my brain isn't in the realm of pretty."

"Ah," she said after a moment. Her tone went dry. "Because you're just a big, dumb hockey player, do I have that right?"

I didn't comment, just pumped some shampoo into my hair, washed it quickly. Then took care of the rest of my body. By the time I'd finished and wrapped a towel around my waist, Brit had showered, too. She rubbed a sheet of cotton over her hair as we both walked into the locker room to get dressed, but she didn't immediately go to her stall as I expected.

Instead, she sat down next to me and sighed.

"So," she said. "I've been at this a long time, you know that, Finn, yeah?"

"It's Axel."

A grin. "No offense, but Axel is a stupid name. Finn is..."

"A good name for a rabbit?" I offered.

"...a strong, powerful—" Her face clouded, and I didn't blame her. A *rabbit?* No. A fish. A shark. A dolphin, but definitely not a bunny. She shook her head. "Wait, what?"

"Nothing," I said as I tugged on my underwear.

"Right," she replied and shook her head again. "Um, anyway, my point is that I've been doing this a long time."

"I know."

"So, Finn, I've seen a lot of broody males come through this locker room, and I know their moods."

I shot her a look as I pulled on my pants.

She just smiled, wide and bright. "And *your* mood says either you're upset about a woman or you're torturing yourself because you don't think you belong here."

I'd been buttoning my shirt, but her words made me freeze.

Her smile sobered. "Or...both," she murmured.

Clearing my throat, I said, "It's fine, Brit. Don't bother with" —I waved my hand—"all this. It's not worth it."

"*It's* not worth it? Or *you're* not worth it?"

Those words were a fucking punch to the gut, but after a moment, I kept buttoning. "What do you think your chances are at the Cup this season?"

Silence.

A flicker of sadness in her chocolate brown eyes, but after a moment she said, "Good."

"Good," I repeated. Then I bent to shove my feet into shoes.

"Better, of course, with a full roster," she said, tugging the towel from her head and laying it across her lap.

I grunted, reached for my backpack.

"Right," she said and stood, but just when I thought she was going to finally leave me alone, she stepped close, dropped her voice. "Look, Finny. I'm not trying to be nosy here. Well, I mean, I'm *always* nosy, but in this case, I'm trying to restrain myself, so I'll just say that I don't bullshit about hockey, not to the media, not to my teammates, not to myself. If there's something that needs to be improved, I tell it like it is. And the problem with you—"

My heart began to beat a little faster.

"—isn't what's happening on the ice. It's what's happening in here—"

She tapped my forehead.

"The *only* thing that is wrong with you is that you need to get out of your own way." Her expression was fierce. "You do that," she said. "You figure out how to flush down whatever bullshit is swirling around in there, and you will be *here.*" A wave to the locker room. "Not just for a game or two. But *permanently.*"

I inhaled, struggled to figure out what to say.

But she was already gone—striding across the room to her stall.

Getting dressed.

Getting on with her life.

And leaving me...to go back to mine.

EIGHTEEN

The knock on my door wasn't surprising.

The person on the other side of the wooden panel was.

I'd been expecting another assault from Billie Rose because I hadn't been to town for a few days and the planning for the Harvest Festival was reaching its fever peak. There would be more asks to be made, volunteer slots to pick up (or be voluntold for).

And I'd say yes.

Because Billie Rose was Billie Rose, and it was impossible to say no.

Because I was me and I *couldn't* say no.

Because the Harvest Festival meant a lot to this town, and I wouldn't let them down.

So, all that being said, I did *not* expect Dessie to be standing on my porch with a bottle of wine in one hand and a plastic bag hanging from the wrist of her other arm.

I sniffed when a delicious scent hit my nose. "Is that Danika's?"

A wave, the plastic crinkling. "Would I take a drive down to Sacramento for any other food?"

Scandinavian and Mexican fusion shouldn't be good.

Danika's didn't follow the rules of anything that *should be*.

It was part bakery, part restaurant, part shop, and all tiny hole-in-the-wall, non-credit-card-accepting vessel of deliciousness.

"Tacos?" I asked.

Or maybe begged.

A nod. "Pork. And that smørrebrød you like"—an open-faced sandwich on homemade rye bread that was already making my mouth water—"*and* that beet salad you like, and—"

Lagkage.

Please let it be *lagkage*. I needed three layers of sponge cake, fruit, and pastry cream in my mouth, and I needed it now.

"Lagkage."

I did a happy dance, and I wasn't shy about showing it as I pulled open the door farther and let Dessie—and, it had to be said, *the food*—in.

"Did you just only let me in because I have Danika's?"

A grin. "Yup."

"Rude," Dessie said, moving down the hall, but she only made it a few feet because then she halted.

Presumably spying the mess that was my family room.

I'd hauled Gran's old couch to the back porch and would eventually get it into the back of Gramps's truck so I could take it to the dump. The carpet and some of the subflooring would be joining the party, along with some of the sheetrock I'd cut out to investigate the leak.

Investigate, try to cobble together a repair, and knowing that I was going to need more help.

"Told you I was busy," I said dryly, hitching my head toward the kitchen, considering that was the only place I currently had more than one place to sit.

"Yeah, I see now that you weren't lying." She set the bag on the counter, started pulling out takeout containers.

I moved to the cabinet and snagged two wineglasses, then snagged the opener from a drawer. Dessie had been here often enough to retrieve a couple of forks and paper towels (I hadn't bothered to buy napkins in years) and then we were both sitting down and digging in.

No polite offerings.

Just two forks going at it.

We'd dug into the lagkage before Dessie hit at the real reason she was there. "Axel Finnegan."

One name.

Not even phrased as a question.

"I'm not going to sleep with him," I said, not quite lying—since I'd *already* slept with him and wasn't going to make that same mistake again.

"Hmm."

"What?"

"He wasn't giving me that vibe."

I shoved a huge bite of cake (and it was extra delicious because they'd put a layer of dulce de leche in amongst that yummy pastry cream), mostly to buy myself time to come up with a response.

"What vibe?" I asked.

That wasn't much of one, but...Danika's food coma had my brain moving sluggishly.

Probably why Dessie had brought it in the first place.

Feed me.

Interrogate me.

They went hand in hand.

"You know you could use him to unwind a little, to get some unhindered adult contact, and hopefully a couple of orgasms and a hard dick."

I'd gotten that.

I'd gotten all three. *Fuck*, had I gotten all three.

And it had left me with...unease.

"I love you, Dessie," I said, "but this isn't a conversation I want to have."

My friend's eyes locked with mine, and I knew she was thinking of my past, of why I might not want to have this conversation. And...I held my breath, expecting her to push.

To my surprise and relief, she didn't.

"Tell me what Billie has commandeered you into doing for the festival," she said before taking another bite of the cake, lips clinging tightly to the tines in order to get every last bit of pastry cream.

I knew the feeling.

I was doing the exact same thing with every bite.

"What *doesn't* she have me doing?"

I was on setup Friday morning, and stations Friday night and Saturday, and cleanup on Sunday.

My weekend was living and breathing the festival, the parade, the snotty-nosed kids.

And...I was semi-looking forward to it.

Or at least, I was getting swept up in Billie's excitement, so it felt less like a chore and instead something fun I was doing for the people of River's Bend...and if I happened to be one of those people...

Then I was trying to embrace it.

"Word," Dessie said. "She got Barry and Roger to donate kegs and wine, so I'm on the first shift of adult beverage distribution, and then I'm doing something with candy corn, something with turkey feathers, and something that involves confetti."

I sighed, held up my fork. "Fucking Billie Rose."

"Fucking Billie Rose," she muttered, clinking her fork to mine.

Then I thought of my fridge filled without asking, how my aunt always showed up for River's Bend. I thought of the kids' excitement and the happy memories that would be made during the festival, and a tendril of guilt coiled through me.

I'd volunteer at a hundred festivals if it meant that I could play a small role in what Billie Rose had built.

So I sighed, shoved another bite of cake in my mouth, chewed, swallowed, and said, "But we love her though."

"Yup. We sure do."

"She might be annoying, but she's our special brand of it."

Dessie clinked my fork again. "Damn right she is."

Nineteen

Axel

I moved to the door of my apartment, a giant thermos of coffee in my hand.

My attempt at getting rid of the fuzziness in my brain.

But not from alcohol for once.

Okay, not *for once*.

It had been weeks since I'd been to the bars in town, weeks since I'd organized any time out with the guys, had allowed myself to be coaxed away from the rink or my apartment to hang with the puck bunnies, weeks since Bailey, since the games with the Gold, since...Brit.

It had just been me and the puck and the ice...and Brit's words.

Just me and *all* of Netflix and not making my way back up to the Gold.

Just me and the bus (and the team...and it went without saying, my noise-canceling earbuds) as we'd been traveling for a shit-ton of games. But even then, it still had been me and Door-Dash and going to bed early in my hotel room, earplugs in place because the fucking rookie I was paired with, Bennie, snored like a goddamned chainsaw.

But none of that was the cause of the discord in my mind.

Instead, all that spinning and feeling like I was on my back foot came from...a woman who'd gotten me off my game.

No.

Two women.

Though thankfully, that game had not been my *hockey* game.

I was playing the best I had in years—probably because I wasn't fucking and drinking and staying up all hours of the night. Probably because...Brit's words had stuck in my fucking head.

As much as I tried to ignore them.

And anyway, not staying out, not tearing through town, not drinking...none of that was rocket science. It was something I should have been doing. It was just...

What was the point of trying that hard if I wasn't going to hit my goal?

Stupid, right?

Defeatist for sure.

But I'd spent too many years on the bus, on this team, on others, getting called up for a game or two, enjoying those five-star hotels and the chartered flights and the food and trainers and all the perks that come from being in the big leagues. Then getting bumped back down to the minors, back to the hours on the bus and midlist hotels, the bringing lunch and dinner from home or stopping at some fast-food joint if our order got fucked, or splurging for DoorDash because the food the team provided for us wasn't enough. Then add in a dash of an occasional commercial flight—and all that limited leg room—if we were traveling far enough that the bus travel wasn't going to do it.

But that was rare.

Bus life was where it was at.

My biggest perk in years was that I'd finally been on the team long enough to score my own double seat.

Yup.

I was most excited because I had two bus seats to myself and didn't have to share an armrest.

Go me.

But...I'd been holding on for a while, battling and working my ass off...and for what?

A game with the Gold, maybe two. Hanging on the fourth line, and if someone was injured creeping up to the third, and then right back down with the taste of my dream on my tongue...

And—

The only thing that is wrong with you is that you need to get out of your own way.

Those words. Brit's fucking words.

"There's no point in continuing to try," I muttered, taking a huge sip of the caffeinated brew. "There's no fucking point because I'm never going—"

I froze, those words echoing through my head, the spinning and discord becoming a full-on tornado.

Because I'd heard them before.

Just not from my mouth, but...from my mother's.

Bemoaning the shit hand she'd been dealt. Blaming the universe for not getting what she wanted.

Acting like the world owed her something just because she had been born.

And yeah, I could get behind the world owing everyone equal rights and respect and universal health care and housing, but the world didn't owe me a spot on the Gold, didn't owe me a spot on any NHL team.

And for me to think it did...

Fuck.

That meant I was becoming like *her*.

Soothing the hurts, the disappointment, the hole inside me with booze and fucking.

Blaming everyone else. Being angry.

Being fucking *mean.*
You're a fucking failure, Axel.
You ruined my life.
You're pathetic and—
I Was. Turning. Into. My. Mother.

Letting the disappointments turn me into someone terrible, someone mean, someone...pathetic.

I'd never believed those words then.

But here—*now*—sitting in this empty apartment, feeling like *this,* reflecting on the last years with the Rush...what I'd done to this town, what I'd done to the women I'd been with, how carelessly I'd treated them.

Taking what they offered and then sending them on their way so I could move on to the next and the next and—

My feet slid to a stop, my lungs filling in one sharp inhale, and I blinked back against the sting of that...

That...

Fucking painful truth.

What I'd done to *myself.*

My mother.

I was turning into my *mother.*

I sank to my knees, yanked out my cell, fingers fumbling as I jabbed at the screen. Not her. Not her.

I might be an asshole.

But I couldn't be *her.*

The call rang—once, twice, three times—

And, fuck, what was I doing.

Calling my *mom?*

Sick as fuck.

I started to lift my cell from my ear to end the call when she picked up—

"Hello?"

Her voice was the same—a complete glimpse into her emotional state and...that of our relationship.

"Hello?" she asked again. A male voice in the background, coming closer. My mother's tone growing somehow even more chipper, a teenager-esque giggle coming across the airwaves. "Hello? I—" There was fumbling, like she was going to hang up.

"Mom," I said.

Silence.

That fumbling stopping.

"Axel."

Giggles gone. Icicles in every syllable.

"Mom," I repeated, and then, somehow, because I couldn't hang up, "How are you doing?"

Calculating.

Her voice immediately went calculating, "I've really been struggling."

Fuck.

"I'm sorry to hear that."

"*Really* struggling." A sniff. "I-I—" A wobble in her tone I was well familiar with. "I've been struggling to even buy groceries in this day and age."

"I can send you some."

"Really?" she exclaimed. "I think six hundred should cover it. Just the essentials, you know—"

I closed my eyes as she prattled on, letting my head fall back against the wall.

"So, when are you going to send it, baby? I've got Venmo now and my handle is—"

"Groceries, Mom," I said. "I'll send you groceries."

"What?"

"I can have groceries delivered to your apartment. Do you want 2% or fat-free milk?"

"I-I—*Axel*."

Little daggers of ice flying toward my eardrums. I'd stopped sending her money seven years ago because she'd lit a fucking stick of dynamite and tossed it at my career and hadn't given one fuck.

And because it had never been enough. She'd wanted me to become some version of The Boyfriends, giving and giving until I was sucked dry. Because...it was always about her.

"I'm fine, Mom," I said dryly. "Thanks for asking."

Silence.

Then she sighed. "Is that what this is about?" she snapped. "That I like to live my own life? I put *everything* on hold for you. *Everything* and you've never been grateful. *Never.*"

"I know it was hard to be a single mom," I said.

A scoff. "*Do* you?"

"I do."

"So, you'll send it?" she asked. "A thousand to make it a nice round number?"

I bit back a sigh. "No, Mom."

"I saw you're doing your same shit again. Never quite getting to the finish line, huh? Never good enough to—"

The male rumble grew in volume.

"What?" Noise through the airwaves, fumbling, and I knew the query wasn't for me.

Knew what was going to happen next.

"Useless."

A click.

Silence.

I sat there with my eyes closed and my head back against the wall and the thermos in my lap and—

"Fuck," I sighed, opening my eyes and shoving my phone into my pocket.

Same shit.

Different day or month or year.

But the phone call had done what I'd intended, had reminded me, fucking slapped me right back into reality. I couldn't allow myself to become like her. No fucking way. And that resolution, the absolute certainty that I was now desperate to cling to, had paired with the dizziness, the tornado. Brit and Bailey and my mother. The juxtaposition of a woman from my past and the good ones from my present were fucking with my brain.

Which was probably why I didn't realize I'd started moving again, had actually opened the door.

To *her*.

Another woman of my present.

Another good one—a blonde, curly-haired, meddling kidnapper who liked to handcuff me to porches.

Maybe that said something weird about me, that I thought she was good with all that baggage, but I couldn't deny that Billie Rose had a strong sense of conviction and loved this town.

So good, despite the kidnapping.

"The Harvest Festival and Parade!"

It was yelled.

Straight up *yelled* in my direction, and after the phone call and brutal truth I'd just come face-to-face with and the dizziness in my brain from these fucking women who kept making me feel shit that I didn't want to...

I jumped like a scalded cat.

"Fuck!" I cursed as my coffee sloshed out through the open top of my thermos and burned the back of my hand.

Billie Rose *tsked*, and the kidnapper extraordinaire quickly took action, pushing the door to my apartment fully open, moving with astonishing speed that I rarely saw any place outside of the ice and would have been thoroughly impressed with if it hadn't come with a side of *Burning My Fucking Hand Off*.

But it did come with a side of that, so instead of admiration, I just followed her cursing and muttering as she hustled into my space, heading unerringly for the kitchen.

As though she knew without a doubt where it was.

And considering this woman appeared to have super speed, maybe she also had X-ray vision.

Either that or she could see that my apartment wasn't huge and there weren't too many places for a kitchen to be located.

So, I didn't ponder on superpowers too long, just headed into the kitchen and stuck my hand under the faucet that Billie Rose had "helpfully" (yes, I mentally gave that air quotes) turned on for me, ignoring her when she grabbed my thermos, dumped it, rinsed it, and turned it upside down to drain.

She snagged the canister of coffee, brewed another pot, and, after drying it, refilled my mug. It also didn't miss my notice that she'd put in black, just like I'd taken it at Bailey's house.

Good God.

The woman had a mind like an elephant.

Then she turned to me. "So, as I was saying—"

I snorted. "*Saying* isn't screaming." A beat, my gaze locking with hers, watching hers fill with a scary sort of determination. "Just saying," I muttered.

She held my eyes, that steely, flinty focus locking me in place.

Then she smiled. Brightly.

And *that* was almost scarier. "As I was saying," she repeated, opening cupboards and grabbing a mug. She filled it before rummaging through my fridge and cabinets until she turned up some milk and sugar. Making herself at home, as though she hadn't startled me into spilling my coffee and injuring myself, hadn't then barged inside and helped herself to my fridge and pantry. "As I was *saying,* the Harvest Festival and Parade is coming up."

Another bright smile.

Yup. That was definitely more frightening than the steely determination.

"I have no idea what in the fuck-all that is," I said, still salty as I pulled my hand from the water, the back of it bright pink and aching.

"I had a meeting with Edward"—Eddie, our GM, because no one called him Edward...except, apparently, *Billie Rose*—"yesterday afternoon, and now that you've stopped leading your hooligan crew in wreaking havoc through my town, I want the team involved in the festival." She smiled, digging into the purse hanging from her elbow and pulling out a tube of burn cream which she plunked onto the counter. "And *he* wants the team involved, especially considering my decision on whether or not to renew the team's usage contract of city properties will be coming up shortly." A casual shrug...that wasn't casual in the least based on the look she slanted my way. "So"—a clap of her hands—"you're my Harvest Festival and Parade buddy."

Wait, what?

I turned off the water, grabbed a paper towel, and dried my hands, putting the buddy thing aside for the moment and asking what I thought was the most pertinent question to start, "What's a Harvest Festival?"

Her mug had almost been at her lips, but my question had her freezing and slowly lowering the mug, plunking it onto the counter before *plunking* her hands onto her hips. "*Excuse me?*"

"Um..." I cleared my throat. "What's a Harvest Festival?"

"What's a *Harvest Festival?*" Her sound of disbelief prickled down my spine as I picked up the burn cream. "Axel Finnegan, you cannot seriously tell me that you've been in this town for three years and you don't even know what River's Bend's biggest annual event is."

Fuck.

"Um..."

There didn't appear to be a right or wrong answer to that.

Only wrong and...*wrong*.

So I didn't answer. Just stood there like a lump and stared at her.

Her brows lifted to form sharp rainbows on her forehead. Then she sighed. "The Harvest Festival begins on the weekend after Thanksgiving"—her gaze held mine, pinning me in place—"coincidentally, a weekend during which the Rush have no games—"

And if she didn't orchestrate that, I'd eat my glove.

And since I didn't let anyone wash them if I scored in a game (and because I'd been scoring a lot lately, that had been a while), that would be disgusting.

But then again, hockey superstitions often were gross.

"It kicks off with the festival's pie-eating contest on Friday evening," she went on, gesturing energetically with her free hand, her excitement for the event in every syllable. "That is followed up with bingo, face painting, a cake boogie, and a local arts and crafts fair, and other fun events that will last the entire weekend, including a parade."

I rubbed the ache that was beginning to form at my temple. "A cake *boogie?*"

She smiled. "Yup."

"I'm—" That ache intensified. "I don't know what that is either."

Her blond curls bounced as she shook her head in disgust. "A cake boogie is quite simply an event where everyone dances until the music stops, and whoever freezes last gets to go get a slice of cake."

That ache intensified. "Doesn't that mean everyone wants to be last?"

Her smile widened. "Yes, *if* the prize for winning the cake boogie wasn't the most coveted trophy in River's Bend history." She pulled out her cell, swiped at the screen, and showed him a truly horrific trophy. Vaguely cake-shaped, half of the gold finish wiped off and...was that duct tape holding it to its base?

I didn't understand these people.

Truly. I did *not*.

"People want to win *that?*"

A nod sent those curls bouncing. "Yup." The P at the end was a *pop*. "Just like they want to visit the petting zoo on Saturday and the kids want a pony ride and the adults want to win the limbo contest and take a turn at the dunk—"

My brain had gone from spinning to tornado again. "Wait," I said, putting my hand up.

Miraculously, she shut up.

"So, the festival is a mashup of…" I trailed off, not wanting to insult her when she was armed with coffee, had handcuffed me to porches, and held the team's future in those tiny palms.

"Awesomeness, fun, and town spirit?" she supplied.

"Right," I said. I cleared my throat. "*That*."

"Exactly." Her eyes sparkled. "And it all culminates in the"— and no joke, here she did jazz hands—"Harvest Parade!"

"Wow." My tone was neutral. "That sounds amazing."

See?

That was perfect. Supportive and not insulting and—

Very *not* perfect.

Because Billie Rose said what she said next.

She clapped her hands together. "Great! I'm so glad you said that."

Okay, it wasn't *that* sentiment that was imperfect.

It was what came out of those pink lips next.

"So that means, you'll have no problem being my co-chair on the planning committee!" Her mug went into the sink as I processed the words that might as well have been in another language.

Co-chair?

Planning committee?

I—wait, what?

She turned, was heading toward the door by the time they *did* click.

"Wait—" I began, moving after her.

Her hand closed on the knob, began turning it, tugged open the wooden panel. "Our first meeting is this Thursday. I'll pick you up at six." A finger wave.

"I—*wait*—Billie Rose—"

She paused in the doorway. "Oh, and don't worry," she said.

"Edward gave me the entire team's schedule of practices, events, games, and travel. We'll work around it to make sure you don't miss anything!"

"I—"

Shit. Why did that sound like a threat?

I didn't have time to process whether it truly was or not.

Because the door slammed, and Billie Rose was gone.

TWENTY

I slid through the crowd—it was Wednesday night Happy Hour at Monroe's and that meant the place was packed—and waved at Desiree as I pushed through a cluster of women near the bar.

Puck bunnies and fuck boys.

Those fuck boys being *puck* boys.

Not that I was looking.

In fact, I was deliberately keeping my gaze from that corner booth, from the cluster of big, brawny, and it had to be said, sexy men sitting at the table.

Heaven help me if I saw Axel again.

I might...do something stupid.

Something *else* stupid.

Something else really *fucking* stupid.

A girl tottered toward me, and I knew with only a glance that she wasn't from River's Bend (because I pretty much knew everyone—small town and all). She was in full going-out mode—which, more power to her for being able to rock those heels and the crop top and the sheer amount of sparkles on her body in a small-town bar. The thing I *did* have a problem with was her tottering toward me unsteadily, two pitchers of beer in her hands, both filled to the brim, and small splashes overflowing with each step she took.

"Whoa," I said, instantly moving toward her, intending to take one and help her with the burden.

"Back off, bitch," she snapped, jerking them away from me, another splash hitting the floor...and my shoes.

And my jeans.

Fucking hell. Now I was going to smell like cheap beer all fucking night.

Glitter bitch marched by, and I bit back a retort, shaking my head as I continued to the bar, and took a seat on an empty stool on Desiree's side of it.

"We've got to stop meeting like this," my childhood friend said. "Especially when you only come in for Happy Hour and not for my precious good looks." She fluttered her lashes at me. "I'm pretty to look at, even when drinks aren't half off."

I rolled my eyes. "You know it's been busy at the ranch."

"I *know* that you've avoided me for weeks now. Ever since one hot hockey player trailed after you onto the patio—"

My eyes narrowed. "Tell me what happened in San Bernadino, you know, at the job you were supposedly incredibly happy at and had just gotten a big promotion and—"

She spun away, grabbing a pitcher, glaring at me after she'd turned back and started to fill it.

Point to me.

Now, hopefully, she'd leave all conversation about the hot hockey man to die in a small, empty grave...or handcuffed to my porch—

No.

That wasn't right.

Neither was me being a snarky bitch to one of my friends.

"Sorry," I muttered.

"Me, too," she muttered back.

"Avoid talking about topics we've been avoiding?" I offered.

"Seems wisest," she said, after passing the pitcher off to a waitress.

In truth, I'd been doing my best to avoid everyone—including hot hockey players—and the ranch had helped me accomplish that. Downed fences, sick animals, a barn door that had needed repairing. The leak in the house that had forced me to pull up the carpet in the family room and throw away Gran's blue floral couch that had gotten wet too and ended up damaged and musty.

And there went me moving into the black.

House repairs and new furniture were expensive.

But the expense—and even the smell—weren't why I'd resisted the repairs. That was the couch Gran had picked out, her curtains and throw pillows, and it was the carpet Gramps had installed.

The only gift my parents had given me was to have not bothered spending the money to update the rooms they considered useless in the house.

The master bedroom and bathroom? Freshly updated (the new pipes freshly *leaking* inside the wall and all along the floor of the family room).

The kitchen, the family room, the guest rooms? All had been left untouched when they'd dumped the ranch into my lap. Including the room I stayed in—because I couldn't stay in *theirs*. Their fancy-ass mattress had nearly killed me—and my back—and I'd taken the next best alternative.

A rock-hard, ancient bed in a rarely used room.

Of course, if I'd been staying in the master bedroom, I probably would have noticed the leak and thus, would still have the couch and the ugly carpet.

I couldn't decide if I was sad or relieved.

It was bittersweet, but...circling back to extremely ugly.

"So, avoiding the topics we've been avoiding," Dessie said, wiping up a spill before pouring cocktails. "How are you?"

"Fine."

Desiree narrowed her eyes. "Uh-huh."

"Seriously."

"I know you, Bay. I know when you're busy. Which is always," she added. "Or at least that's what Billie Rose says and how you were before I left town."

"That was years ago."

"My point," she said, dropping a coaster onto the bar in front of me, "is that I knew you then, and I'd like to think I know you at least a bit now because that expression you're wearing is classic Bailey." She turned away before I could muster a response to that, and when she turned back, my IPA in her hand, the glass plunking onto the coaster. "And it's classic Bailey because it tells me that you're putting on a brave face, but something is tearing you up inside."

Got it in one.

But fuck it all, I wasn't going to cop to it.

"This is us avoiding topics we should be avoiding?"

Dessie grinned. "Well, you know me. I'm a stubborn pain in the ass."

Sighing, I said, "Nothing's tearing me up inside." Then added, after taking a swig of my beer when her expression didn't relax, "I really just *am* busy. Especially, since Billie Rose is on a rampage about the Harvest Parade."

"Not just the parade," Desiree muttered. "It's the entire festival."

Another sip. "You're right about *that*."

Someone hollered for Desiree, and my friend slid a menu on the counter and started to move away. "I'll take care of Mr. Impatient, but figure out something to eat. It's on me tonight—"

"I'm fine—"

A glare cut my words off. "It's on *me*, Bay. And you'll shut up and accept it."

Dessie was gone before I could finish my protest. "Right," I whispered, taking another sip as I studied the menu. I was lowering the glass to my coaster when someone shoved into the space next to me, bumping my arm, sloshing my beer, and making it so that I was going to smell like beer two times over, though at least the second time around it was with better beer.

Gasping, I set the glass down and shook out my hand, turning to see who'd bumped into me.

It was another woman—this one with long, blond hair and wearing a crop top and sparkles that mirrored the first one who'd bumped into me. She didn't apologize, tell me to back off, or even spare me a look. Instead, she just glared down the bar and began muttering about the bartender ignoring her.

Given that Desiree had about as much patience as I did with rude assholes, that *was* probably the case.

Another bump.

Though this one, thankfully, didn't end up with me being covered in more beer.

Because it was safely out of reach when another woman squeezed in. "I can't believe Axel isn't here."

His name was...

Heat.

Sinking into my bones, prickling down through my spine, gathering between my thighs.

Fuck, even my pussy convulsed, remembering how good it had felt to have him inside.

Pathetic.

I'm not pretending.

His words from that night. Tickling across my nape, sliding down my spine—

"He *never* comes out anymore," the new girl complained,

thankfully drawing me out of my memories, stopping me from turning into a puddle of sexual need.

A lie.

Because I'd seen his face when he'd realized what he'd done.

When he'd realized he'd slept with *me.*

I'd seen the disgust and the remorse and...

I'd lived through that for two years. I wasn't going there again, least of all with a fucking puckboy who had slept with half the damned town.

The girl huffed and waved at Desiree. "Well, I don't know why he doesn't come out anymore. It's boring without him." The last ended on a whine and was punctuated with another rude wave toward Dessie.

Dessie's gaze glazed past the woman and locked with mine. She rolled her eyes.

Biting back a grin, I lifted my beer in salute.

Or maybe commiseration.

Then she turned back to the customers in front of her and began pouring drinks.

Meanwhile, I was stuck next to twin Crop Tops and trying to ignore their conversation, to ignore all mentions of Axel Finnegan. Hell, I was trying to ignore all mentions of any of the team, of hockey in general.

And I was failing.

Because I was listening to the gossip.

How Axel had apparently been killing it on the ice but avoiding any of the post-game celebrations, at least according to the Crop Tops and his teammates.

"We're probably just not at the right place," the first girl said. "I mean, not even half the guys are here."

"I've gone to three of their road games," the girl who had squeezed in said. "He didn't go out after those either. And some of the other guys have stopped going out, too. And the ones that *do* go out, end up going home early."

Silence.

From the women, at least. The background noise of the bar was the only sound, for a few moments anyway.

Then the first Crop Top huffed and waved at Dessie again. "God, this bartender."

Meanwhile, I was kind of obsessing over the fact that Axel had stopped partying...and he'd done it after we'd slept together. I mean, that probably had nothing to do with me. He'd already been slowing down after the whole naked and handcuffed incidents. Or more likely, Billie Rose had gotten to him and threatened him with more kidnapping and splinters in his ass if he didn't get his shit together.

Or maybe...I had a magical pussy.

One that turned a man from playboy to hard worker.

Ha.

My magical pussy with the rainbows and glitter and pheromone-producing clit that drove men *wild* was totally why he'd run from the room the moment he'd come, why he hadn't been out to the ranch or seen me since that night.

I'd told him to not pretend that he cared about me.

He'd told me he wasn't pretending.

And he'd proved that over the last weeks.

I needed to take his actions at face value.

He'd gotten what he wanted.

He was done with me.

It was sick—*I*—was sick in being so unsettled—in thinking about him all the time, dreaming about him—

Fucking hell, desperate for another night with him.

The sex had been good. Hot. The best fucking *ever*. But that was all it was, so I needed to stop hiding at the ranch, stop worrying about running into him in town, stop avoiding my life just because he might be around.

And I was doing that.

Hence, Wednesday night at Monroe's.

"Did you decide what you wanted to eat?"

Blinking, I glanced up at Dessie. "What?"

The Crop Tops next to me huffed.

"Food, Bay," she said, her brows drawing together. "Do you want something to eat?"

"Sorry." I laughed, tucked my hair behind my ear. "I was thinking about..."

Now Dessie's brows lifted.

"Fencing," I finished lamely.

Dessie shook her head. "I'm going to get you something so that you stop thinking about fencing."

How about something to stop me from thinking about Axel Finnegan?

Luckily, I managed to hold that back and just told her, "I trust you to take care of me."

A grin.

No. A *smirk*, mischief creeping into Dessie's eyes.

Uh-oh.

"I trust," I added quickly, "that *you'll* get me home at a reasonable hour and that you'll only bring me one more beer so I don't end up hungover and—"

Dessie tossed her head, her long black hair shining as it cascaded down her back. "Oh no, Bay," she said, lips twitching. "You said you trusted me to take care of you." There was that mischief again. "So I'm going to—"

"Dessie," I warned.

A pat to my hand. "I'll take care of you."

"*Des*—"

"I wish someone would take care of *me.*" From one of the Crop Tops.

Dessie glanced from me to the women, that mischief grew, and...I knew.

I was fucked.

TWENTY-ONE

AXEL

"Go, go," Joel called. "Take it."

He let the puck slide through his feet, leaving me to pick it up.

Unfortunately for him—or me, really—he hadn't considered what was happening behind him.

Unfortunately for *me*, he was a big fucker and I didn't see the opposing player barreling toward me until I was picking myself up off the ice, moving my tongue around the inside of my mouthguard-protected teeth, half expecting to find several out of place or floating around out of their sockets.

They were all in place.

And I was moving again, chasing down the fucker who'd laid me out, who was streaking toward our net.

I hauled ass.

And...didn't catch up in time to disrupt his shot.

Goal.

Cool.

Sighing as the whistles blew and the red light turned on, I

rolled my shoulders and tried not to glance up at the scoreboard as I skated back to the bench.

Because it would reveal...an eight-goal deficit.

Insurmountable.

Shitty as fuck.

But that was the breaks of professional hockey.

"Sorry, man," Joel muttered, squirting some water in his mouth and promptly spitting it on the skate mat in front of him. Pointless habit. Not hydrating and probably gross, but fuck if I didn't do that same damned thing when he handed me the bottle.

Needed to wet my mouth.

Didn't want a lot of water sloshing around in my stomach when I tried to skate.

Though tonight that didn't matter.

Skating hard, working hard, trying hard, not one was going to make a bit of difference. This game was in the books. The best we could do was try to pull some decent plays together, something we could focus on going into the next game.

Joel snagged the bottle back, dropped it into the holder on the inset shelf in front of us. "How bad is it going to be?"

"Coach?" I asked.

Another line jumped on the ice, and we scooted down as we spoke, eyes on the ice, moving into position to get ready to take our next turn at getting beat the fuck down.

"Yeah," he muttered once we ran out of scooting room.

I slanted a glimpse at our head coach, noted the apoplectic expression on his face. "Bad," I muttered back.

"Shit."

"*Same* shit. Different day."

A half-grin. "Yeah," Joel said, sliding down again.

I followed suit, along with the rest of the guys on the bench, and said, "So, we're gonna do what we always do."

"There isn't any pussy on the ice."

Fucker. Albeit a funny one.

"No, asshole." But my lips were twitching, and I tried to channel Brit when I said, "We're gonna go out there and do *one* good thing before we get reamed in the locker room."

"Same shit," Joel said lightly, lifting his fist.

I bumped. "Different day."

And, nearly as one—since he was a big fucker and took up more than his fair share of the boards—we jumped onto the ice.

And...eventually, we managed to do one good thing.

———

I slung my bag over my shoulder, tugged on my beanie, and slammed my car door.

It was late. My legs were on fire. My eyes were bleary.

Yeah, we'd played like shit that night, yeah we'd lost...because of the aforementioned playing like shit. And yeah, as expected, we'd gotten our asses reamed, Coach screaming at us, and look, I got that sometimes some yelling worked. The keyword being *some*.

It snapped our dumbasses to attention.

Refocused us.

But when we already knew that we'd fucked up majorly, and yelling for that long, after that shitty of a game...

Wasn't going to make one fucking bit of difference.

Me staying after the game, trying to focus on that one good thing Joel and I had cobbled together and failing. So instead, I spent hours trying to fix my fucking hands that hadn't done what I'd wanted them to in the game, might. If I practiced enough, maybe I could play better, pass better, shoot better.

Be fucking better.

Unless the problem was in my head, like Brit had suggested.

Like I was starting to agree.

Like—

"Enough," I whispered, bleeping the locks and letting my head tilt back, roll back and forth to ease the throbbing muscles in my neck.

The parking lot for my apartment was being repaved, so I'd parked on the street a couple of blocks away, and if I cut through the patio of Monroe's, it would only take me a few more minutes to get home, soak my aching bones, and drink...some water since I was no longer self-medicating with alcohol and fucking.

Not going to be my mother.

No fucking way.

Sighing, I started walking, and in my sober state, I couldn't miss that the moon was high in the sky, shining through the clouds like a horror film, making me half expect a fucking werewolf to jump out of the bushes and take me down. Maybe that would make me a better player.

Werewolves were fast, yeah?

I'd just strap on four skates, let my tail be my rudder, and—

A rush of noise startled me, and I jumped as the back door of Monroe's flew open, nearly wiping me out.

But hockey skills.

I dodged, danced back...and just missed being flattened as I snagged the edge of the door, catching it before it slammed back into the brick wall, intending to just close it and continue on to my apartment.

Except...

"I'm totally fine," Bailey said on a giggle. "I'll just walk to Billie's and get her to give me a ride."

The slender bartender with shining black hair and deep brown eyes who'd encouraged me to follow Bailey onto this patio a few weeks back said, "That's not going to happen, Bay. You're going to sit your drunk ass back at the bar and then I'll close up and drive you home."

Bailey shook her head. "I'm fine to walk a couple of blocks—"

She turned, threw an arm out, and promptly proved that she

definitely wasn't fine to walk a few feet, let alone a few blocks, stumbling backward and nearly ending up on her ass.

Dropping my bag, I lurched forward, caught her.

She smelled like sunshine and apples, like dry grass and cool summer evenings.

She—

Blinked up at me, and then she smiled and—

Fuck, she was beautiful.

Warm and soft and woman. Hot and uninhibited and incredible in bed. Spicy and fierce and could wield a shotgun. Tough and strong and worked her ass off.

I'd been sober a lot lately.

Which meant that I'd been listening.

And I'd heard the talk, how she'd dug the ranch out of a financial hole, how she hardly accepted help, how she barely took a break and was always working and...how she'd always been like that.

Even as a kid.

Earning her keep, working her ass off.

To prove herself? To prove that she belonged?

All that listening meant that it was getting harder to ignore the emotions blossoming in my chest, to stop thinking about her, to ignore the voice in my head that said I could be different with her, that I *was* already different because of her.

That I wasn't going to be my mother and could have something good in my life without fucking it up.

Bailey blinked, her brows drawn together as she started to sit up. I snagged her arm, popped her up to her feet, not missing that she wavered when I got her onto them, so I left my fingers there, trying and failing to ignore how good it felt to be next to her, to hold her.

"I'm fine," she said, trying to pull free.

My fingers tightened before I realized it. "Easy, buttercup," I murmured, catching a glimpse of warmth in her eyes before she turned her gaze back to her friend and repeated, "I'm fine."

"Nope. You're drunk," the bartender said. "After two beers," she added. "Which is a sad state of affairs about your social life, I think, but not the point at this moment. Come inside, Bay. Last call is in a few minutes, and then I'll get you over to Billie Rose's or drive you home."

"I don't *want* to go home."

"Okay, I'll take you to Billie's."

She made a face, and fuck, it was cute. "I don't want to go to Billie's either."

"You just said—" The bartender sighed. "Bay. My place, yours, or Billie Rose's. That's your choice."

"Fine," Bailey muttered. "I'll go home. You always complain I never come out, but then when I try to have a good time—"

"You don't come out," the bartender said. "And it's not a complaint of you tonight, sweetie. I just can't have you going on an adventure when I'm trying to close down the bar."

Bailey pouted.

She was still cute, even though I didn't normally like drunk bitches, even though I definitely couldn't stand those who pouted.

Except, for Bailey.

Which was probably why my mouth worked before my brain caught up. "I'll drive her home."

Two female heads swiveled in my direction.

"We've got it," the bartender said, moving forward and peeling my fingers from Bailey's arm. "Thanks for the save, but you can go about your evening."

An argument was on the tip of my tongue, a protest that *I* was going to take care of her, dammit. That she was mine to protect and get home.

But...

Down that path led...

"Okay," I said, stepping back and picking up my bag, slinging it over my shoulder. "Night."

A hand on my arm, breasts pressing into my back. "Don't go."

Apples and flowers in my nose.

Warm, soft woman against me.

Need burning through my veins. It had been weeks since I'd had her, had anyone, and I wanted—

Gently, I dislodged her, started to step away.

"I miss your dick."

I froze, air stuck in the back of my throat, making me choke.

The bartender chuckled. "I thought you weren't going to sleep with him."

My gaze shot to hers, eyes narrowing. "It wasn't like that, don't try to insinuate that she's—"

Bailey stumbled, and I caught her against me.

The bartender's brows lifted, almost in challenge.

And all I could do was finish lamely, "...that she's like *that*."

"I *am* like that," Bailey declared. She lifted a hand to her mouth, as though she were whispering to her friend, but the words were loud as hell. "But only for Axel."

I inhaled sharply.

The bartender laughed as she glanced up at me. "She's going to hate herself if she remembers saying that in the morning."

"But Dessie! He's got a big cock."

It was still an attempt at a stage-whisper.

As thus, it wasn't a whisper at all.

And paired with her burrowing into me, with her arms sliding around my waist, her breasts hitting my chest, and that need burning through me? It transformed my need into a fucking inferno, blasting through the trees, flaming high and hot, incinerating everything in its path. I was a pile of ash, being blown in all directions, not sure which was the right one.

Run, be scattered like the pieces on the wind.

Stay, and be burned all over again.

Run, like I always did, like my mother always did.

Stay, and fight for what I want, for what might be.

"Okay, never mind." Dessie's brows were nearly in her hairline. "She's going to hate she said *that* in the morning."

My fingers traced along the sides of Bailey's arms until my hands could dip in, cup the indent of her waist, and I embraced the only part of me I knew how to embrace.

The cocky, arrogant asshole.

But I didn't run.

Instead, I grinned up at Dessie. "Can't hate the truth."

"Oh, honey," Dessie said. "You can *definitely* hate the truth. And this one"—a nod toward Bailey—"saying all that"—she waved a hand in the direction of my pelvis—"she's going to have a ton of hate for these *truths* coming out of her mouth right now."

Bailey ran a hand down my chest. "He's wearing a suit." Still stage whispering. "He's yummy in a suit. I've only seen him naked and in a T-shirt. A suit is better." She smiled up at me dopily, and fuck, that was cute, too. "Well, naked is best," she said, ticking off on her fingers. "Jeans are yummy. A T-shirt is great. But a suit is the best."

"That's two *bests*, buttercup."

A shrug. "Meh."

Burn.

I was going to *burn*.

Forcing myself to not taste that dopey smile, I caught Dessie's eyes. "I'm taking her home."

Bailey smiled, nodded jerkily.

Dessie's amusement cooled. "That's *not* happening."

"I'm a dick," I said. "A dick who's slept with a lot of girls, but I don't do unwilling, and I don't do drunk."

Dessie's lips pressed flat, her eyes going fierce. "I'm still not letting you—"

Bailey wove her fingers through mine. "I'm going home with him, Desiree."

That felt...right. Her fingers in mine, her body close. The words.

I lifted my free hand, rubbed a spot over my heart that was twinging—fucking sore muscles from too much hockey. "I'll get her home safe and in bed. *Alone*," I added when Desiree frowned even more fiercely. "I promise."

The bartender's brown eyes locked with mine, but a shout coming from inside had her turning away. She called out that she'd be right there before whipping back to face me, lifting a finger and pointing it in my direction. "It goes without saying that if that changes, I'll cut that big dick of yours off."

Bailey giggled.

I glared down at her. "I thought you liked my dick," I told her. "It getting cut off should make you sad."

She blew me a kiss. "I'll tell you a secret." She leaned close, but the volume didn't decrease. "Dessie seems scary, but she's a big softie."

"I'm not," Dessie said.

"Noted," I told her, holding her stare. "And there will be no reason to cut off my dick."

"See, that is another truth spoken," she muttered, spinning on her heel and heading back into Monroe's, pausing only to toss over her shoulder, "Because don't forget that I have a kitchen full of sharp knives available for my use."

Bailey's hand dipped into the waistband of my slacks the moment the door banged shut. "She's all bark." A beat. "I promise."

I highly doubted that.

But considering I was fending off a woman who'd turned into an octopus as I shepherded her to my car (an octopus who was trying in earnest to get her hands down my pants), I didn't have any more mental energy to spare for Desiree the bartender.

Into the passenger's seat.

Belt buckled.

Door closed.

Her *eyes* closed.

Thank God.

I got into my side, quietly closing the door behind me, and turning on the engine, taking off along the quiet street.

A sleeping Bailey was a lot less dangerous to my fortitude...and the *thoughts* swirling through my mind.

"They said you don't come out anymore."

The words came as I'd pulled out of downtown.

Were said so quietly that I barely heard it.

When I chanced a glance at her, she was still, those lids still closed.

"What, buttercup?" I asked softly, turning onto the dark road that led out to her ranch.

"The women."

Sleepy words.

Ones I should have left to lie.

But I couldn't.

"What women?"

"The ones from the bar," she said, head rolling, those lids peeling back and her eyes hitting mine. "They said you don't go out with your teammates anymore."

I hadn't.

Not since that night.

My fingers clenched on the steering wheel, and I focused back on the road. "I don't."

"Why not?"

Because of you.

Because of *me.*

Because of that night and all the feelings I'd caught but was pretending I hadn't.

Because...I didn't want to be like my mom, avoiding hard work and drinking myself into a person I couldn't stand to look at in the mirror.

Because maybe I could be the man Brit talked about, the man I wanted to be.

I didn't tell her any of that.

"It got old," I said instead. Which was the truth. The barest bit of it. But still the truth, since I couldn't bring myself to lie to this woman. "And at some point I have to grow up."

She was quiet.

Then her lips curved, lids dipping again. "And Billie Rose got to you."

I chuckled. Because that was also the truth. She'd given me the shove up the mountain, before the push had come from Brit, bringing me to the cliff's edge, before the jolt of courage this woman was giving me to jump off and let the wind rush over my skin, the ground come up faster than it seemed possible, the trees and bushes and rocks flying by.

The better to impale me? To end me? To—

Maybe I'd have a parachute.

Maybe Bailey could be *my* parachute.

"Billie Rose *is* pretty fucking scary," I said quickly, pushing the thoughts aside.

A wobbly nod. "Yeah. And knows too much."

Now I laughed outright. "She does at that."

Her eyes opened again, and I had to force my gaze back to the road. So fucking pretty and captivating and...

I wanted her.

A *fucking* lot.

"Axel?"

"Mmm," I said, deliberately concentrating on driving.

"I want you."

The mirror of my thoughts had my dick going hard, my stare slanting to the side. "You're drunk."

A shrug. "Drunk *and* horny."

"I meant what I told Desiree. You're too drunk, buttercup. It's not happening."

Bailey made a face, reaching over the console, squeezing my thigh. "Dessie worries too much."

I returned it to her lap. "Dessie is a good friend to you," I said. "And I won't break her trust."

It was an excuse.

But it was also the truth.

And look who had fucking morals for the first time in my life.

A fucking miracle that was.

So was the silence that fell, the silence that was then followed by agreement. "Yeah," she whispered. "That's fair."

Thank God.

"But *I* never promised Dessie anything."

My gaze shot back to hers—

Just in time to see her whip her shirt up and over her head.

Twenty-Two

BAILEY

I rolled over in bed, my head pounding, the light shining through the window like tiny spikes that were cheerfully driving themselves into my brain.

For a moment, I thought I was sick.

My throat was sore, I felt like I'd been run over by a truck, and then there was that headache.

But then I rolled over and encountered...

Naked skin.

Tattoos I recognized.

Muscles I'd stroked with my fingers and my tongue.

I jerked my gaze up and fell right into deep blue eyes.

A handsome face. Hair that was just on the right side of long. Dark brown hair that had clearly been mussed by fingers. Scruff on a square jaw. Lips that were clearly meant to be kissed.

Axel Finnegan.

And all at once, the night came back to me.

The bar.

Too many beers. No. *Two* many beers.

I'd said...

Oh fuck. I'd said a lot. Too much, and I'd—

Axel was in bed with me.

Naked.

And *I* was naked.

And I'd—

A squeal welling up in my throat, embarrassment threatening to swell up and choke me. Violently.

Until it unalived me and the horror of reliving the events from the night before just freaking *stopped*.

"Buttercup," he murmured, reaching out a hand and—

I panicked.

Lurching back from that hand, even as I wanted it on my face, my skin, my body. It was need and danger wrapped up in a single body part.

"I-I—"

I scrambled away from him, getting tangled in the sheets as I tried to escape and...

That strong hand caught me before I ended up on the floor, fingers wrapping around my wrist, yanking me away from the edge of the mattress, stopping me from falling out of bed.

I was naked.

I'd been drunk.

He was naked.

The last thing I remembered was taking my shirt off.

"Not so fast, buttercup," he said, drawing me across the mattress, the tangle of sheets, the comforter bunching up between us, between my naked body and his.

"I need to go. I *have* to go." The arm he'd grabbed was trapped between us, but I used the other to push against him.

Fuck.

That was his *hip*.

All strong muscles and hard man and hot, bare skin.

Shit. *Shit.*

"I need to go," I said again. "I have to—"

He rolled us, his body pinning me in place, fingers still around my wrist, drawing that arm up and over my head. My other hand was somehow still on his hip, and with him over me, I found that instead of pushing him away, I was drawing him closer.

"First," he murmured, "you can't go."

My chin came up, and I jerked my hand away like it had been burned. "First," I snapped, starting to feel more like myself, even though he was still on top of me, making my body sing, my mind swim, "you can't tell me one fucking thing, Axel Finnegan. *One* fucking *thing!*"

His palm dropped to my thigh.

Hot and broad, squeezing a little roughly before sliding up, cupping my ass. Long, thick fingers drifting into the crack, dipping down, in, and brushing—

My breath caught.

"First," he said, swiping those fingers forward. "You're wet, and naked, and"—another swipe—"*that's* my favorite way to find you."

"Asshole."

Swipe. Dip.

"Correction"—one blunt tip traced my entrance—"*this* is my favorite way to find you—naked and wet and snapping at me."

A quiver ran through me. "You're sick."

His fingers released my wrist, coming up to cup my cheek, turning my face gently from side to side. "And you're beautiful when you're angry. When your eyes are full of fire and your cheeks go pink and—"

"Fuck. Off."

He dipped closer, brushed his nose against mine. "And I love to hear you say the word *fuck*." Another brush, his lips drawing close to mine. "Especially, when it's in regard to me."

I glared at him. "*First,* I seem to remember you promising

Dessie that you wouldn't take advantage of me, and yet, here I am, naked in bed, and you're—you're—"

"First," he said, interrupting me again. "You can't go because you're already home."

"I—" I stopped, glanced around, realized that we were in *my* bed, in my room.

In my...house.

Oh.

But that didn't change the other—

"Second"—he jerked me closer, wrapping my leg around his hip—"we didn't fuck last night."

"I'm naked and we're in bed together, I think it's obvious that—"

"I'd *think*," he said, shifting his weight and snagging my other leg, bringing it around his waist. "I'd think it would be obvious that you would be able to feel that I'm wearing pants, considering that *you're* naked."

Oh.

Now that he mentioned it, there was a bit of friction from his slacks rubbing against my...

"*I'm* still naked and—"

"Because you stripped down in my car, and when I tried to put your clothes back *on* you, you kept taking them off again."

"I—" Images of me taking my top off in his car, of unsnapping my bra, throwing it out the window. Then on the front porch, leaping up the stairs, yelling, "One, two, three, he, he, he!"

Like I'd done with Gramps when I was six years old.

Except, I hadn't gotten naked when I was six, hadn't kicked off my shoes, unbuttoned my pants, and dropped them on the porch.

Along with my underwear.

Hadn't then flounced through my house, tugged off a man's shirt he'd tugged over my head (twice), hadn't thrown myself at him, obviously (and *ew*), hadn't—

Begged him to stay in bed with me.

"Oh, God," I groaned, dropping my head back to the pillows and slamming my eyes shut.

"It was hot," he said softly, nuzzling my throat, lips pressing lightly to my skin. "Biggest case of blue balls I'd ever had in my life, having you rubbing against me, your naked body on display, you asking for me to fuck you." An inhale. "*Begging* me to fuck you."

My lungs seized. My thighs trembled—

Which he felt, if his smirk was anything to go by.

"But I promised," he said. "I promised, and I might be an asshole, but I don't break my promises."

A breath in.

A breath out.

Desire boiling in my veins.

His mouth dragged higher, drifting across my jaw, sending that heat boiling into steam, threatening to explode out through my skin. His lips reached my ear. "I've never wanted anything as much as I wanted you in that moment."

"But you didn't take me," I breathed.

"No," he whispered.

"Why?" I whispered back.

He stilled in my arms. Yes, *in* my arms because they'd come around him, had wrapped him tight, were holding him close.

"Do you really think so little of me?"

The question was so quiet that I barely heard it.

But I *did* hear it.

And it struck me hard, embedded itself in my heart, my gut... my tongue. Which loosened, my reply sliding off it, floating through the air even before I realized it. "In my experience, men don't care much for promises." A beat. "Or boundaries. Or—"

I clamped my teeth together.

Idiot.

I didn't talk about that. I didn't *think* about that.

His muscles bunched beneath my palms.

He was quiet for a long moment. Then, "What kind of experience is that, buttercup?"

Experience I wasn't going to talk about.

Not now.

Not *ever*.

I pulled my hands away from the warm skin and hard lines, dropped my legs back down to the mattress. "You should go."

Calloused fingertips on my cheek, drifting down my throat. "I *should...*"

I inhaled.

Silently, but sharply enough that it felt like a series of stab wounds through my lungs.

He lifted his head.

His eyes hit mine.

I didn't dare breathe again.

A thumb pressing lightly into my bottom lip, and the movement had my lungs unfreezing, the air trapped within them slowly hissing out.

His expression was gentle, those eyes soft and warm and—

Something unlocked inside me, and all of sudden there was a maelstrom of words swirling in my belly, crawling up the back of my throat, threatening to escape.

Too much threatening to escape.

Too many things that I couldn't afford to think about, that would tear me apart all over again.

And I'd just barely put myself back together.

That thumb slid to the side, traced the corner of my mouth.

His head dropped again, and his lips came close, near enough that I could feel the damp heat of his breath against my mouth... heat that inched closer, breath that kissed mine.

But his lips didn't brush over mine, didn't take mine, didn't coax mine wider, his tongue dipping into my mouth.

Instead...he kissed my cheek.

"I should go."

Then he was up and out of my bed, grabbing his shoes and bag and shirt off the chair in the corner of my room, heading for the door without a second glance.

I almost called him back.

Almost.

But, in the end, I let him walk right out of my room.

My house.

Presumably, my life.

TWENTY-THREE

AXEL

I waited until I saw her come out of the house, fully dressed (sadly) and heading for the barn.

I waited until she disappeared inside, knowing that she was taking care of the animals, knowing that she wouldn't dare to do anything other than fulfill the responsibilities that came with having them in her life.

Pft.

It was insane to think that I knew the woman at all.

She was a fucking mystery, an enigma, and yet, I knew that if I trailed my lips down her throat, her breath would catch. I knew that she liked her clit stroked firmly with my tongue. I knew how her hips felt beneath my palms, the sound she made when she came.

I knew...

Sex.

I knew how to fuck her.

Why did that thought have my fingers clenching on the

steering wheel as I navigated past the place she'd tossed her bra out the window?

Why did that thought have my foot hitting the brakes, stopping, retrieving it?

Why did the fact that I knew hardly anything outside of how to make her come sit heavy in my gut?

Why—

"It doesn't matter," I whispered.

I hit the gas.

None of it mattered.

I had practice to get to.

I had work to do.

I had to prove myself.

I had a life to live, and...that life didn't include a brown-eyed beauty.

Even *if* I knew how to make her come in at least a half-dozen ways.

———

The sweat was stinging as it dripped into my eyes, but I still pushed it on the treadmill.

I wasn't going to quit.

I wasn't going to end up like *her*.

I was going to flush the bullshit out of my mind, and I was going to do what Brit said and I was going to not be a total fuckup for the rest of my life.

My quads burned. My lungs felt like they'd been rubbed raw with rough-grit sandpaper.

But I wasn't. Going. To—

A hand reached over the top of the treadmill's control panel.

"Wait—"

It slapped at the red stop button, and I felt the machine slow down, the incline flattening out, the belt coming to a stop. I yanked the towel off the rail, swiped at the sweat pouring down my forehead.

"What the fuck?" I snapped, dropping my arm and glaring at...

Pierre Barie.

Shit.

My teeth clinked together so fast that I was surprised a few of them didn't immediately crack and drop out of my mouth.

This wasn't just snapping at my boss—one of my coaches or the head trainer or even the Rush's GM.

This was snapping at my boss's boss's *boss*.

Pierre Barie was the owner of the Rush. He was also the owner of the Gold, the much more successful NHL team, and the organization I'd been drafted by all those seasons ago (before I'd been traded to and played for the Rangers and their AHL affiliate and then traded back to the Rush). He was the owner of the team I'd been trying get a spot on for *fucking* years, and the owner of the team that I'd only gotten to play a total of eighteen games for *over* those years.

He didn't make roster decisions.

That was up to Charlotte Harris, the GM of the Gold.

But cursing out the boss's boss's boss (or maybe there should even be another *boss* in there) wasn't good form.

"Shit," I said, quickly stepping off the treadmill, wiping at my forehead again. Fuck. I was still cursing at him. "I'm sorry, sir, I—"

Pierre leaned back against the wall, his suit devoid of wrinkles as he crossed his arms and ankles and studied me. "I don't get you."

"I...well...there's nothing really to get about me," I said.

Silence.

Then a sigh.

"Talented young player," he said, pushing off the wall, uncrossing his arms and moving toward me. "Char was stoked when we picked you up, and that first season with the Rush? It looked like all the potential we'd seen in you was going to come to fruition."

Churning began in my stomach.

One season.

Then I'd crashed, burned, and been traded to New York.

Before that trade had gone through, I'd been eighteen, fucking stoked to have escaped the bullshit that was my life. And instead of flushing the bullshit down the drain, keeping my head up and moving forward, *I'd* been sucked in.

Sucked *down*.

The top, the pinnacle, every single thing I'd hoped for had been *right* there.

And then I'd been reminded of how easily it could all be torn away, how easily it could be reduced to ash and scattered in every direction on the wind.

"Something changed."

Not a question. A statement that told me he knew it as fact, and unfortunately...it *was* fact. I couldn't bullshit or bravado my way out of the truth, not with Pierre standing there, pinning me in place with his icy blue stare.

He didn't know that *everything* had changed.

I'd thought they'd wanted me, valued me as a player, had thought of me as—

I'd thought *I* was something.

In the end, it was the same old shit.

In an instant, the foundation I'd built was gone, revealed to have been built out of toothpicks and tissue paper, to be so fragile that it was almost laughable that I would have thought it might just hold its shape in the first place.

"The question is, where did all that potential go?"

I didn't reply.

What could I say?

My little house of toothpicks and tissue paper had fallen to pieces, and I'd lost it like a toddler having a hissy fit over being given the wrong color plate?

That I'd thought it would be easy?

After so long of having it hard, of fighting for every inch, I'd just hoped that I might get just a *little* fucking bit of easy.

But I hadn't gotten easy.

Same shit, different day. Same life. *Always.*

"Something changed, and the fire went out of you," he said. "That fire went out until..."

Until I'd fucked a woman who'd made me feel something.

Until Brit told me that I needed to be the one to see myself through this.

Until the fog in my head had cleared and I'd realized I was becoming my mother.

My. *Mother.*

Fucking hell.

"Now," Pierre finished.

I inhaled.

His head tilted to the side, studying me closely. "I saw a report, caught a game, then two and three, and even in the losses, I'm seeing that player Char had once been so excited for again." Pierre leaned back against the wall. "So, I'm wondering what has changed, and if it's here to stay."

My lungs were burning, the air held tight in them for too long. I released it.

"I'm getting older," I told him. "I know it's do or die time. That's a great motivator." I shrugged, my eyes drifting to the side, unable to hold his any longer. "There's not any deep reason."

A long moment of quiet.

Then, "Is that also why you're pushing yourself into oblivion after practice when you should be at home or with your teammates relaxing with a beer?"

I couldn't go home, couldn't remember Bailey, remember the man I was.

I couldn't go out, couldn't keep hiding from the man I was worried I'd become.

Not just because I had a fucking Harvest Festival planning meeting with Billie Rose, but because I couldn't...be *out* again, couldn't let myself be drawn into that trap of hiding behind the alcohol, my teammates, the women.

Not if I wanted to be...

Not *her*.

"No," I said. "I have a meeting with the mayor," I said.

Brows lifting.

"I'm helping at the Harvest Festival thing."

Pierre's brows lifted even higher. "What's a Harvest Festival?"

See? Exactly what I'd been thinking when Billie Rose had first brought it up, and now I was going to be elbows deep in fall vomit festival "fun." The parade, pumpkins, kids, and me being roped in by a curly-haired blonde with a penchant for organizing...

And kidnapping.

And handcuffs.

Po-tay-to. Po-tah-to.

"I'm still not entirely sure," I admitted, and Pierre's brows dropped, his lips twitching at the corners.

"Yet, you're volunteering?"

"Well, I'm thinking of it more like voluntolding."

A pause. "How'd Billie Rose manage that?"

Well...fuck.

I couldn't exactly mention that she'd threatened the team (and had done so because I'd been the ringleader of getting the boys into trouble because I was so far up my ass it took me being threatened with the final nail in the coffin of my career and then being drunk-napped and handcuffed twice for me to realize that I needed to turn some shit around).

That wouldn't exactly help my chances of securing a spot on the Gold...or any other team in the NHL for that matter.

Nope.

So...I did the smart thing for once and shut the fuck up.

Pierre cocked his head to the side. "Billie Rose *can* be persuasive, and a bulldog when she wants something."

That was something I could agree to without giving anything away. "Yes."

"Hell, she single-handedly took on the organization's lawyers during the initial negotiation"—he chuckled—"I swear we were lucky to come out of that with our shirts."

"Yeah," I said, not really knowing *what* to say.

Blue eyes on mine. "So, what does your voluntolding assignment include?"

"Apparently *all* of my free time outside of the team."

If the schedule and spreadsheet she'd emailed me was to be believed.

And how she'd gotten my email was as much of a mystery as how she'd managed to arrange my schedule with Coach without my permission.

The Power of Billie Rose.

I believed in it.

I was leaving it at that.

Pierre's blue eyes twinkled. "She why you stopped terrorizing the town?"

Yes...and no.

Brit had been the guide to the top. Billie Rose the impetus to jump. Her *niece* the person that actually shoved me off the cliff and into the fog...that had cleared, just in time for me to realize that the reflection that was staring at me in the pool of water at its base wasn't my own.

Instead, it was...my mother's.

And *that* had been hard enough of a snap to make me recognize that this chance was my last chance and I'd better get my shit together.

So here I was.

On the treadmill.

After practice.

After some extra time on the ice.

But—at least the last, the whole getting it together finally part, realizing it was my last chance—gave me a convenient shield to hide behind. All that hard work meant that no one was going to look at me too closely and—

That hopefully included the owner of the team I'd once thought was going to be my free ticket to the big leagues, to the future that would finally fill that void inside me, would prove to the world that I wasn't a complete and total failure.

Unfortunately, he was standing in front of me.

Seeing me.

Unfortunately, he didn't have, wouldn't ever have that golden ticket.

He didn't make roster decisions—not that I was naive enough to think that he couldn't influence them—but more than that, he knew exactly what was going on.

He saw too much.

He saw *me*.

Which was why it wasn't a surprise when Pierre pushed off the wall again, straightened the cuffs of his suit jacket, and nodded. "Well, I'm off."

Then the man who'd once held my dreams in his hands left.

He'd seen right through me.

Again.

Twenty-Four

The straw scratched my arms as I hefted it across the street, but I supposed I should feel lucky that Billie Rose was far enough removed from ranch life to not recognize the difference between straw and hay.

Hay—heavy as hell.

Straw—much lighter as I hauled bale after bale of it from the back of the truck and used it to line the street.

In what Billie would think were quaint lines of *hay* bales bracketing each side of Main Street, but what were, in actuality, straw bales that my arms (and back) were thanking me for.

Dessie—whose arms were full of plastic pumpkins—and gourds...yup, those were gourds—passed by me, slanting another curious look at me. *Another* because she'd been tossing them my way the entire time we'd been completing our Billie Rose assigned duties.

Me: hay bales.

Dessie: decorative gourds.

Me: avoiding my friend's curiosity post-Axel spending the night in my home.

Dessie: walking by at regular intervals, her expression saying that she was going to get it out of me.

Me: making those straw bales a perfect line.

Dessie: launching gourds left and right, losing patience by the second.

The only gift I'd received was that gourd-launching took less time than hale-bale-lining, so Billie Rose had commandeered Dessie for some other project.

A little relief.

At least for the moment.

Because straw bales were just the beginnings of my tasks.

Later, I was on twinkly light duty—and had express instructions to make sure they draped perfectly—before I needed to head to the auditorium to wrap treats for the cake boogie. Then tonight after the parade, I was on the face-painting booth for one hour, would be helping the kids make decorative frames out of candy corn (the only thing that blegh of a treat was good for, stale post-Halloween leftovers or otherwise) for the final two.

Tomorrow, I'd start early with chores on the ranch...and then I had a full day of volunteering.

Was I salty about it?

Outwardly, yes.

Inwardly, the little girl inside me who never got to come to the festivities was excited to be a part of everything—once I'd managed to swallow the bittersweet and moved on beyond my past memories, that was.

Because pouting about the parade made me...pathetic.

I couldn't punish everyone else just because my mom was a tool bag.

The kids deserved better, and their excitement made it impossible *not* to match their energy.

So, I would ignore what I missed out on and paint a bajillion pumpkins and butterflies and Batman symbols on adorable cheeks. I'd hot glue a shit-ton of candy corn to cardstock cutouts and use *all* the Polaroid cameras to take shots of the families and kids and cute little babies to fill those homemade frames.

I'd haul bales (of straw), and shake my butt at the cake boogie, and I'd—

"Whoa there."

My fingers clenched around the bale wire, the heavy-duty string that was keeping all the straw together, and it bit into my skin.

But that wasn't what took my breath away.

No, it was a male voice. Sliding down my spine, hot breath soaking into my skin, teasing fingers drifting up my thigh, dipping in through my silken, wet heat.

I spun and saw...him.

Axel Finnegan.

Standing there, black circles beneath his eyes, scruff on his face, short black bristles highlighting the strong lines of his jaw...and jumping back, dodging the bale of hay I was holding, lips tipping up when I gasped and jerked away, nearly toppling myself over in my attempts to not knock him to the ground.

One hand gripped the bale wire between mine, the other wrapped around my waist.

"Easy, buttercup," he murmured, his breath in my hair, his mouth near my ear.

I shivered, leaned into him, even though the straw bale was between us and he was bending over it like we were playing a weird game of reverse limbo.

I could swear that I felt his lips brush the top of my ear, but then he was slipping the bale from my grip, sliding his hand off my waist.

"This going in line with the others?"

My head jerked like a bobblehead doll. "I—"

But he was gone, walking across the street, his blue T-shirt straining over the muscles of his back, his biceps...

Holy hell, that cotton stretched to the max over his chest and arms wasn't *nearly* as good as his ass in those jeans.

That was a gift from the gods for women.

Two plump Christmas hams, strong thighs that I'd sat atop as I'd sucked his cock deep, legs that had flexed and contracted as he'd pinned me to the mattress, as he'd fucked me rough and hard...so that I'd come so freaking hard that—

"Need some help with the rest of these?"

I jumped again, spun to face Axel, and...braced.

To see *what?*

The sliver of hurt on his face that I'd put there the last time I'd seen him?

The slight hint of soft in his eyes that he'd given me that morning?

Panic? Derision? Anger?

Heat?

But none of those were present.

This was Axel Finnegan, star hockey player, former bad boy, but current town favorite because he'd been avoiding the bars, attending the Harvest Festival planning meetings, and because just two days before, he'd picked up Betty Harrison's unruly black lab who'd escaped the yard, returned Balthazar (yeah, really) home, and *then* had repaired the fence through which big, goofy Batty had slithered.

Pre-season—he'd been despised (and, yeah, that disgust had been warranted).

Today—he was revered.

He'd earned it, at least from what I could see, from what I'd experienced, from what the copious amounts—and it was *copious* —of town gossip had said.

Reviled to Golden Boy.

Quite the swing.

And yeah, so maybe I'd been paying attention to what he'd

been doing, what was being said *about* him...because I was pathetic and maybe I'd sent him away...

But I was still—

Staring at him.

My mouth unmoving.

The hay—*straw*—bales in the back of my truck.

I had shit to do, and that didn't include drooling over Axel, even *if* his ass was squeezable and those thighs had my pussy clenching, and his *eyes* were so fucking blue and pretty and pinning me in place.

"Bailey?"

"Yes," I said, shaking myself out of the Fuck Fog and whipping around so I could grab another bale. "This is the last load." I cleared my throat. "I just need to finish lining the block and then I'm on twinkly light duty."

Silence—or as silent as it could be with the hustle and bustle of the setup—fell between us.

Then he stepped close to where I was standing at the back of the truck, leaned down, and—*dammit*—I sucked in a breath.

Because his mouth was near, and his body was close to mine, and I wanted...

Him.

But all he did was lean beyond me, snag a bale, and turn away, carrying it across the blocked-off street and placing it in line with the other bales. Perfectly so, in truth, nudging it slightly with his foot after a glance that had his head tilting from side to side.

Then he turned back.

And all *I* could do was clench the bale wire tighter and start my feet moving, bringing the straw over, scuttling beyond him, plunking it down onto the sidewalk.

Did it land straight?

No.

Did I fix it, even knowing that Billie Rose might go full Harvest Fesitivazilla?

Nope.

I just hurried back, giving Axel a wide berth, snatching another bale, not acknowledging that he was doing the same. Definitely not acknowledging that he was helping me, that his scent was in my nose as we crossed paths in the street, that my gaze kept drifting to his body, remembering, *needing*.

I'd told him to go.

I'd *told* him.

So, head down.

Avoid.

Move shit.

Lunch.

Then twinkly lights and cake slice wrapping.

Avoid like it was an art form that I'd mastered. Because avoidance *was* an art form I'd mastered, ever since Colt—

The name drew me to a stop in the middle of the street, my empty hands—since I'd been heading back for another bale—clutching into tight fists.

I hadn't thought that name, hadn't allowed it to cross my mind, not since I'd signed the divorce papers. But today, his name whispering around my brain turned my blood frozen, set my heart to pumping tiny icicles through my veins.

His voice as frigid as a northern lake.

His fingers biting into my skin.

His fists lifting and then...coming down.

His body pinning mine into place, taking—

"Bailey."

I didn't jump.

Not that time.

Instead, my body reacted on instinct. I was back in time, during those two years with *him*. I was in my past, on that stormy night, firmly entrenched in the moment that *everything* had changed.

Where I'd reached my breaking point.

Where *I'd* broken—body and mind and heart.

Fists into my ribs, connecting with my skull, my jaw...my *soul*.

Pain tearing through me. Tears sliding down my face, a scream lodged in my throat. Trying to hold it together, to wait until he'd finished, until he'd gone, until...it was over.

Then running out into the night.

The heavy rain plastering my torn clothes to my body, my feet bare and cold, and then bare and cold and *bleeding* from the rough road.

All of those memories flashed through my brain like a slideshow of cruelty and violence and my body moved without my knowledge, without my permission.

I dropped to my knees, threw my hands over my head, and...

I braced.

Waited for the blows to come.

Silence again, only this time it held as the memories faded and the pounding in my ears settled to a faint drum of noise, as the street sounds drifted back in, and I became aware of the fact that I was on my knees, in the middle of the road, with my arms folded over my head.

Trying to protect my most vulnerable spots.

"Buttercup."

A whisper that shuddered through me with all the ease of a jackhammer.

But that wasn't what sent my heart hammering against my ribs.

I was on my knees. *Bracing*.

In the middle of the *fucking* street.

My eyes flew open—

And caught on Axel's.

Pity.

There was pity in those deep blue depths.

I pushed off the ground. I found my feet.

And...I ran.

Twenty-Five

Axel

One second, she was on her knees.

The next, she was up and running away from me.

Not toward her truck, not getting in and driving down the blocked-off street, but taking off down Main, making a sharp right, and disappearing into a narrow alley that was almost hidden between two brick buildings.

She'd dropped to her knees in a second, the move so rapid, it could only be instinctual.

Cowering, compressed into a tiny ball.

Covering her head and—

It's not your problem.

It wasn't.

She'd made it clear that it wasn't.

So, I should just let her go, give her the space to get herself together—and I had no doubt that she *would* get herself together because she was a total badass.

But she'd been cowering—

It's not your—

Fuck that.

I took off after her, not wanting to scare her, but also not willing to let her run off to who knew where, freaked the fuck out and—

It might not be my problem, but I needed to get my head out of my ass and stop pretending. I couldn't stop myself from caring about her, from thinking about her, from wanting her.

There was something about Bailey that...

We were connected.

We were...something that I couldn't just ignore.

Absorbing that, recognizing distantly that where that truth sat in my stomach and heart and mind was...terrifying.

Maybe it was.

But I was going after her anyway.

I hauled ass down the alley, turned to the right. *Nothing.* Turned left. *Nothing.* "Fuck," I whispered, pausing for a second and taking stock of my surroundings. The alley opened onto a narrow street, the backs of the businesses on the next street over close enough to create plenty of shadows, even in the sunlit afternoon. But the stretch of dark opened up beyond the buildings, the sunlight glowing through the end of another short alley ahead.

Old brick buildings.

Crisscrossed roads.

A small town that was full of sickeningly happy people who were setting up a carnival on steroids.

I shook my head.

Not the time, and anyway, I was trying to stay on the good side of this town, trying to not fuck my shit up for a change. *That* was why I was hauling hay bales and had crawled out of bed at six after being on the bus all night.

To get ready for the festival.

To spend the night painting faces and making frames out of candy.

Then tomorrow to tell fortunes if the fucking costume that

Billie Rose had showed me earlier was any indication. And when the guys caught sight of me in that dumbass hat and robe, sitting in front of a crystal ball, making predictions for kids...

The shit-giving would be immense.

Worse? Somehow, I didn't care.

The guys were...

I knew they didn't get it—my sudden change in personality, the loss of interest in fucking and drinking, in working hard and playing harder. Why my life was suddenly all about hockey and the town and about doing my job on the ice and then spending every spare moment off it that hadn't been taken over by Billie Rose living and breathing the sport.

My life.

My past.

My...failures.

Swallowing hard, pushing that away, I moved across the narrow street, slipped through the alley, and left the shadows and buildings behind. To the left there was a wide-open park, its huge playground filled with kids and parents, the younger subset tearing down and around the slides and across the monkey bars and just having a freaking ball while the older people set up more tables... and a balloon trellis that guided people from Main Street over to the park (albeit through a wider alley than the one I'd just come through). It was chaos and bright colors, but of the happy variety, the large trees dotting the perimeter of the park and giving plenty of shade for both young and old.

But Bailey wouldn't be there.

Not with how her face had been, how she'd run.

I turned, gaze searching.

And when I saw it...I knew exactly where she'd gone.

I still approached with caution, though, like she was a wild animal ready to swipe out with her claws if I dared to get too close. A breath and I rounded the back of the dumpster, sank down beside her. "Couldn't pick a nicer-smelling place to run off and cry to?"

Her shoulders jerked, head lifting from where it had been pressed to her knees, turning to look at me, and fuck if her damp brown eyes didn't have my heart squeezing. But since they also had my stomach churning, my feet wanting to get to work, to turn my body away and run from what was probably going to end in disaster—

Because it involved me.

Because my whole goal was to get out of this town when she had firm roots keeping her here.

Because my whole fucking life was built on tissue paper and toothpicks, and it always collapsed and—

"You are such an asshole," she snapped, drawing me out of my mental tailspin.

I grinned.

I was that.

And being an asshole was a hell of a lot easier than being in my head, so I'd take it.

Same as I'd take her being pissed at me because that was better than sitting here being sad with her, letting her sit in the embarrassment and shame, letting it roll over her, suck her down—

I was already there.

She didn't need to join me.

Her head dropped back to her knees, voice muffled. "Just go away, okay?"

Tempting.

It was certainly the safer option to leave, perhaps the smarter one, too. I should focus on the shit I needed to do, to concentrate on getting the hell out of this town and the havoc it was wreaking on my mind.

But this fucking woman had me...addicted.

I couldn't leave.

Which was why I plunked down next to her, bent my knees,

resting my elbows on them, and looked out on the park, to those kids playing and the parents setting up and the mature trees and open space and—

"This isn't you going away," she muttered.

My lips twitched.

Fuck, I loved it when she snapped at me.

"Nope," was all I said in reply, keeping my eyes on the park, on the kids running around. One of them was trying to corral a small dog who appeared to be determined to catch a squirrel running high through the branches of the trees overhead and failing miserably. The little pup had his paws up on the tree trunk and was barking like mad, its equally little human tugging on the leash and not making much progress.

Cute.

And hell, I didn't know what was wrong with me.

Or maybe I *did*. Maybe *she* was sitting right next to me.

Bailey sighed.

"You gonna cry or run?" I pushed.

Her head popped up, those pretty (and furious) eyes hitting mine. "You know, just when I was thinking that you might not be a *giant* asshole, you prove me wrong."

A shrug. "Well, you made that quite clear the other night."

Regret across her face.

A reminder of my weakness in asking her to see me differently than I see myself, than the world saw me, the town, my family—

Cutting that thought off right at the tracks, I glanced back at the park. "And anyway, being pissed at me is easier than being sad."

Out of the corner of my eye, I saw the stillness enter her body.

It called to a stillness in my own, one that had been there from the moment I'd seen her drop to her knees, her arms lifting to ward me off.

Fear.

Such solid, rigid fear that she'd been transported back to a moment in time, to a memory, to a darkness that engulfed her in just one millisecond.

I'd seen the horror on her face when she straightened, knew she'd forgotten where she was.

Forgotten *who* she was.

Or maybe that was just me projecting.

Or *maybe* that was what was happening to *me*.

"What are *you* pissed about, Axel?"

Or perhaps that was why her question threw me for such a loop.

Because I *was* pissed and hurt and scared and...

"Who hurt you?" I countered instead of thinking about any of the shit that was cycling through my mind.

Flush it down. Don't let it control me.

Move on.

"Bailey," I pressed, asking again, "Who hurt you?"

Silence was my answer.

Silence that was punctuated by the screams of kids, the conversations of adults, the hum of cars in the distance. I could *almost* hear Billie Rose directing people to finish setting up the hay bales.

Because she definitely wouldn't miss that it had been halted, that Bailey and I had dropped the ball.

The bale.

Whatever.

"Who?" I asked again.

Her voice slightly muffled again, head having returned to her knees. "What does it matter? It's over now."

Twenty-Six

Bailey

I realized I'd made a mistake the moment his hand came to the back of my neck, fingers threading up into my hair, lifting my head until I had to meet his gaze.

His *eyes.*

They were furious. "What does it *matter?*" he asked, completely aghast. "I touched your fucking arm, and you fucking fell to pieces in the middle of the street."

"It wasn't you touching my arm."

I shouldn't have said that.

Another mistake.

Kind of like fucking this man on an impulse, getting drunk on two fucking beers, and somehow ending up falling asleep in his arms, waking up naked, and wanting...

Idiot.

I should *not* have said that.

Great, now I was channeling my inner Hagrid.

"Who was it?" he asked, the question a shard of ice. "What happened?"

What happened?

Then or ten minutes ago?

Ten minutes ago, it had been me, remembering what it was like to want and need someone. It was my heart feeling vulnerable. The slight bite of cool in the air, clinging to my skin. A man who was bigger than me coming up behind me. The rumble of a male voice.

A male who was much, much stronger than me.

One who could hurt me—

"Nothing," I said, that fear beginning to churn in my stomach. "It *doesn't* matter. I'm over it and—"

His laughter was tinged with a sharp edge. "Yeah, sure you're *over* it."

The ridicule stung, I couldn't lie. But at least that helped me shove down the memories of the past. "Go fuck yourself."

"I'd rather fuck *you*."

Which was so ridiculous that I actually laughed. *Laughed* after making a freaking idiot of myself in front of half the town and what had most certainly been Billie Rose's watchful (and soon-to-be demanding) gaze.

I laughed because this man pissed me off so *freaking* much.

"Just like you're *over* trying to drown your worries in pussy and booze, so you don't have to think about how much of a fuckup you are?" The moment the words crossed my lips, guilt wrapped around me, tight enough to threaten my breath.

He reared back, eyes going wide for a heartbeat.

Then cooling, any emotion concealed behind thick, frosty ice.

"I *am* a fuckup," he said after a moment, shocking the shit out of me and making those ropes of guilt wrap even tighter. His voice dropped. "Or at least, that's the sentiment I can't get the fuck out of my head."

That was the last thing I'd thought he'd say.

Ever.

Fuck, I was an asshole.

"But that doesn't have anything to do with what happened out there." He glanced away. "What happened to you."

My heart began thudding, but I did my level best to cling to the topic at hand—that being Axel and not me. "You know that you're an excellent hockey player."

He snorted.

More guilt giving me fucking rope burns as it wrapped tightly around me. Part of me couldn't believe that this man was actually insecure. Except...I'd seen a glimpse of his insecurity in my bedroom, a glimmer of vulnerability before he'd left my bedroom. Oh, it had been there and gone quickly, masked by sexy words and a smoldering smile. But it had been there. "You are," I said softly. "I don't even watch hockey, and I've heard about how good you've been playing."

His gaze didn't come back to mine, but his tone had softened. "Who hurt you, buttercup?"

I inhaled, dropping my chin to my knees.

"My ex-husband."

I hadn't meant to admit that. To do more Hagrid-channeling and tell Axel about Co—

A breath. My eyes closing and then opening.

Swallowing down bile.

Pushing forward.

About Colt.

God, just thinking his name again had the bile threatening to rise once more, had panic itching down my spine, flexing and itching its way down my arms and legs.

A gentle hand settled on my nape, massaging lightly. "What's his name, social security number, and last known city of residence?"

I shouldn't have laughed.

Not after what Colt had done to me.

But, somehow, I giggled. "What are you going to do?" I asked. "You couldn't even take on Billie Rose."

"Well, I don't know who could."

"You have a good foot on her and outweigh her by like a hundred pounds."

"I have the same on you, and you scare the shit out of me."

I sucked in a breath. "Axel."

"And anyway," he said quickly. "I now can say that I both know your aunt *and* have experienced the Power of Billie Rose. A thousand pounds wouldn't make the least bit of difference in stopping her from getting what she wanted."

My lips twitched.

"No." I turned my head, resting my ear on my folded arms as I watched him. "It wouldn't stop her." Then I inhaled again, released it slowly. "The truth is," I whispered, "you scare me, too. I —" My eyes traced his profile, the strong lines of his jaw, his nose, the tiny scar at the corner of his mouth.

That moved when he asked, "Because of your ex?"

I nodded. "I trusted him, and he hurt me." His head turned, eyes blazing when they hit mine, and I struggled, not knowing if I wanted to be swept into the powerful whirlpools, to drown in Axel Finnegan's bright blue gaze, or if I needed to run, to throw up every barrier, cling to every bit of distance.

But I'd done that already.

I'd run.

And I was sitting next to him anyway.

"What's his name?"

"Colt," I said and sighed. "And that's more than I want to talk about today."

Another flash of blue eyes. "He hurt you."

He had.

Broke pieces of me into so many pieces I hadn't thought I would be able to move forward. But I *had* moved on. I'd healed and found myself, and did I still hide a bit beneath my protective layers?

Yes.

Did I still prefer my own company?

For the most part.

But not always. I might be more comfortable at the ranch with the horses as my only friends. I might use it as a shield. But I'd begun to inch out behind it. Coming to town more frequently, seeing my friends, rebuilding bonds I hadn't been capable of creating after Colt.

Opening up to this man.

Wanting him.

Sitting here.

I wasn't that broken woman any longer, and I was doing myself a disservice clinging to that notion.

"He did," I said softly. "But I'm not going to let him do it any longer." I released a breath, turned away from those blazing blue eyes, and stared out at the park. The scene of fun and togetherness, family and River's Bend, chaos and love settling me.

This was home.

And this man next to me...he wasn't a threat.

"Why do you think you're a fuckup?"

He moved—I felt rather than saw it since I was still watching the bedlam in front of me—but even as his hand settled on my back, fingers sifting through the ends of my hair, I didn't flinch again.

Because he wasn't Colt.

He was Axel.

Pleasure not pain. Respecting the boundaries I'd put in place. Coming after me, distracting me, going all growly and protective and—

He. Wasn't. Colt.

My chest rose and fell on a breath.

And when he didn't answer my question, I asked again, "Why do you think you're a fuckup?"

His fingers stilled for a heartbeat before moving again. "You know," he murmured, "you have the prettiest hair I've ever seen. I swear to fuck that I've dreamed about it sliding over my naked skin too many times to count."

Heat boiling up through my toes, skating up my calves, like roughened fingertips trailing along them, skating over my thighs, dipping between them.

My tongue darted out, dampening my bottom lip, remembering his kiss, how greedily he'd tasted me.

But he still hadn't answered my question.

"Axel."

A sigh, those fingers still running through my hair. "You're not going to give me an inch, are you?"

"No," I said. "That's not my style."

He went motionless again, and then to my surprise, he chuckled. "Fucking love that, too," he muttered. I opened my mouth to say...something, but his free hand lifted, thumb brushing across my bottom lip. "I am a fuckup. Not think it. I *know* it."

"I shouldn't have said that before. People make mistakes," I said, thinking he was referring to the town and his crappy behavior of the last months. "But it's the way they make them right that's important."

"Yeah," he whispered.

"You've changed," I said softly, not liking the thread of disdain in that word. "Seriously, I can see it. The whole town has."

He turned back to me. "Thank you."

My inner radar was pinging, a coil of unease settling in my belly. "Axel," I said, cupping his jaw, the bristles of his beard scrapping my palm. "I was feeling vulnerable before and trying to keep you away. I didn't mean it. It's just...easier sometimes to keep people at a distance so I can be safe."

A shift, his mouth coming to my palm, lips pressing lightly.

Making me shiver.

Then he gently set my hand back on my knee and turned back

to the park. "It's okay, buttercup. I get it." Not a whisper this time, the tone almost cheerful, but I could still hear the disdain.

"No, I don't think you do."

Twenty-Seven

Axel

Her brows were furrowed.

Her eyes sparked.

She turned and poked me in the arm. "You are *not* a fuckup."

Tell that to the man with all the potential who couldn't make it to the finish line.

"Axel," she said, and fuck, she was pretty with all that ferocity on her face. "You are talented and smart and have a soft side."

I snorted.

Her hand came to my cheek again, and, fuck, I wanted nothing more than to kiss my way up her arm, stripping her naked as I moved, getting my mouth on her skin, her breasts, her pussy.

A hint of funk tempering the flowers and apples in my nose, and I was reminded where I was.

I wanted her...minus the side of dumpster.

"Admit it," she said lightly. "You have a soft side that gets you roped into helping a drunk woman who's stripping off her clothes and gluing candy corn onto paper frames later tonight."

"*That's* what I'm doing?"

She poked him. "Nice try, baby. You know exactly what each task entails because Billie Rose does a good spreadsheet."

I laughed.

Because it was the truth.

The mayor had given me an exceptionally detailed spreadsheet.

"So," she said, "why do you think you're a fuckup?"

"Besides my attempts at destroying the town?"

A roll of her eyes. "Yes."

"Besides—"

She stroked her hand along my jaw, down my throat, and rested it on my chest, just above my heart.

It was gentle.

It was the slightest bit possessive.

It...made me unstick.

Made the words inside me unstick.

"—being unable to make it out of the minors, especially when I got a chance I shouldn't have and couldn't take advantage of it, and—"

I clamped my teeth together, cut myself off before I revealed anything else.

Her fingers dug in slightly. "Axel," she breathed.

"Ignore me," I said. "We should get back to those bales." I started to peel her hand away, but she moved closer, her curves pushing into my side, her scent all around me, her mouth close to mine.

"What are you talking about?"

And...the truth just...came out.

"I might have believed you seven years ago when I was first playing, when I was fucking tearing it up," he muttered. "*Before* I found out that the only reason I made it into the league was because my mom fucked my way into it."

She jerked back, her head nearly hitting the dumpster, but I shot out my hand, slipping between her skull and the metal, cradling it so it didn't collide with the hard surface, protecting her even though my mind was a million miles away, was back in the past, back when I found out.

"I know I don't know anything about hockey," she said, "but that doesn't seem right."

I blinked.

"I mean, there are lawyers and contracts and stuff," she said softly. "Right? I mean, one person doesn't make the decision. Doesn't it have to go through a whole chain of people before they decide to sign a player?"

She...was right.

It wasn't something I'd ever thought of before.

But it didn't change the fact that, "The scout only came to watch me play because my mom fucked him."

"What?" she whispered.

"I never would have gotten seen, gotten an offer, made it this far if it weren't for my mom." I turned my head away.

Bailey's hand went to my hair, ran lightly through. "What happened?"

The truth had begun pouring out of me, and I couldn't stop it. "She's...well, the fucking *furthest* thing away from a mother that you would want, and she...is the reason I get to live my dream." I laughed, and it was bitter. Because I *was* bitter about it. "And she fucking *loved* telling me that. I thought I'd finally gotten away from it all, from all the bullshit and drama and drinking and lies and lording every fucking thing she'd ever done for me over my head, when she bothered to remember she had a son, that was. But no, she waited until we were heading into the playoffs, until it looked like a contract with the Gold was a real possibility and then..."

"She threatened to go to the media, and to sue the scout for sexual assault, the team for harassment unless I paid her off—even though I was already paying for her apartment, her phone and groceries, and had bought her a car." I blew out a breath. "I fucking gave her *anything* she asked for and she still threatened me, threatened to take every fucking thing away from me." I dropped my head back, and it collided with the dumpster, the sharp *thunk* reverberating through the metal. "I cut her off. I tried to push through…but every day, there was a call or a note or a threat. A-and my game started suffering and…next thing I knew, we were fucking knocked out in the first round of the playoffs, and I was traded." I clenched my jaw. "I had my shot. I fucked it up. *I'm* a fuckup. Even with a silver fucking platter in front of me, I couldn't hack it, couldn't make it. I still can't—"

"No."

I blinked as her nails dug in.

"You are *not* a fuckup, Axel Finnegan."

I started to shake my head, but both her hands came to my face, cupping my jaw and holding me fast.

"You are *not* a fuckup."

The words struck me hard, settled somewhere deep inside me, somewhere…that had me making a joke because it was too fucking deep, too fucking vulnerable. "Okay, maybe I'm just a fuck-*her*."

She snorted and surprised the shit out of me by slanting her mouth across mine and kissing the absolute shit out of me.

There was tongue and teeth and lips and suction, and my dick went hard and my lungs seized and my hands cupped that glorious ass of hers and—

She broke the kiss, lips swollen, breaths coming in rapid inhales and exhales. "You are a good fuck-*her*," she agreed, mouth twitching. But her eyes were serious when she added, "but not a fuck*up*. Okay?"

Was I supposed to believe her, just like that?

Apparently so because she stopped talking and then leaned forward and kissed me again. And with her lips on mine, her hands coming to my shoulders, her tongue slipping into my mouth, tangling with mine; with her body close and her scent all around me; with the need for her filling me in a way that had become normal for me with this woman, I believed it.

In that moment, I believed it might actually be the truth.

In that moment, I believed in her.

In...us.

Twenty-Eight

BAILEY

We'd made out like teenagers.

Behind a dumpster.

Okay, so maybe that part was less teenager and more a bit icky, but I hadn't had the words to heal the hurt inside Axel. I'd just...wanted to make him feel something that wasn't the hurt written into his eyes, the stark lines surrounding his mouth.

He wouldn't have listened, not really, if I kept reassuring him.

I didn't know enough about what had happened, about the process for drafting a player, about the old wound that had sat unhealed and festering for the last seven years to be able to rid him of that burden.

Because he knew about my old wound.

Or part of it, anyway.

And even though some of the weight had been shed, the edges just beginning to heal, the rest of it wouldn't just disappear with a conversation.

It would take time and action.

So, all I could do was show him what it felt like for me to have lost some of that bulk, to show him all the things he made me feel.

To stop being so fucking afraid and to just...*do.*

And, truthfully, it wasn't a trial to kiss Axel, to have his hands on me, his body close. It *was* a fucking trial to have to *stop* kissing and touching him in order to go back to dealing with straw bales and twinkly lights and candy corn, but alas, he'd come to his senses with a rough curse (and this man growling, *"Fuck!"* with his hands clenching on my ass had made me want to forget about making out like teenagers and start fucking like grownups).

Unfortunately, he'd gently propped me to my feet and found his own, and when he'd smoothed back the messy strands of my ponytail, I'd nearly melted on the spot.

Hell, when he'd laced our fingers together, I'd stumbled.

He'd caught me against his side, and truthfully, I'd stumble many times over if it meant that he'd hold me like this.

Even if it meant that Billie Rose's expression went calculating when we walked by her (and her copious rolls of ribbon she was sifting through to choose just the perfect one to wrap around each of the many street signs and light poles lining Main Street) on the way back to my truck.

Somehow the bales hadn't been unloaded, and I was impressed by Billie Rose's self-control to have left the task unfinished (and unchecked on her spreadsheet) while I sorted myself out.

But she had.

Same as she exhibited that impressive self-control by not cornering me immediately for details.

Axel slowly released me then reached for a bale, but I caught his arm, halted him, the words welling up in my throat, floating off my tongue. "Not a fuckup."

Emotion in blue eyes, hot and heady and vulnerable and... squeezing my heart tight.

His palm came to my cheek, his lips brushed my forehead.

His exhale was shaky.

Then he straightened and mischief crept in, wrapping itself around the tenderness. "I think I liked you better when you were busting my balls."

I grinned. "Liar."

Another kiss to my forehead. "Yeah," he murmured. "You're right. I liked you better when I was handcuffed to your porch."

I turned away.

He caught my arm. "I'm kidding, buttercup."

"I know." I ignored all good sense—and the gossips watching—rose on tiptoe and pressed my lips to his. "I was going to find Billie Rose and another set of handcuffs."

I might not be able to make my baggage—or his—disappear with a few kind words, a single conversation.

But I could make something spectacular happen.

I could make this man laugh.

And it was like the world had suddenly come back into full color.

————

"That's not quite straight."

I narrowed my eyes at Axel over my shoulder. "Seriously?"

We were behind schedule.

My dumpster meltdown—and okay, probably our dumpster make-out session—had put us behind Billie's spreadsheet schedule. We'd been working double time at hanging the lights that would help illuminate the festivities in the park.

And we had only...oh, eight million more trees to go.

Exaggerate?

Me?

Nah.

But if this man critiqued my light hanging ability *one more time*, I was going to...something—

Oh!

I was going to get those handcuffs and...restrain him in my bed—

No. That wasn't right.

On the porch, so he'd get splinters up his backside while I had my wild way with him.

Better, minus the last part.

Because that wouldn't be a punishment for him.

Cocky much?

Cocky...time.

Heh.

"No," he said. "That loop isn't hanging the same length as the other."

His voice was a little closer, and I knew I was losing it because I was mentally waxing poetic about *cocky* time and my thighs were trembling and I really couldn't give two fucks about the lights and—

The ladder creaked, shook slightly.

"Here," he murmured, lips brushing my ear, body coming very close behind me, arms gripping the sides of the ladder. His front pressed to my back, and cocky time came right back into the front of my mind.

Mainly because his cock was hard and pressing into my ass and...I wanted him.

"Problem?" he asked, voice silky smooth, his hips flexing, making me shiver.

Punishment.

I needed a punishment.

I'd put him in the barn, hitched to the wall on the wrong side of Picard's behind and let him deal with all those cow patties.

Nodding, I slid up a rung, reached out to fix the "uneven" loop.

"Steady," he said when I wobbled slightly.

"Really?" I muttered, glancing at him...and then down toward his hands that had covered my breasts.

"You were going to fall." He tried for innocent.

"And this is the proper hero's way to save the damsel from crashing to the ground?"

"First"—his hands massaged my breasts—"no one would ever call me a hero."

"I seem"—my voice caught when his thumb slid over one nipple and then the other, hips arching back—"to remember you saving me from another ladder."

"Hmm." He pressed a kiss to my nape, slowly released my breasts. "It seems to me that I need to protect you from ladders."

"I—"

His hands went to my hips, a groan slid from my lips.

Then I was on the ground, slightly wavering from the sudden change in altitude, my next reply lost somewhere in the vicinity of that ladder.

He reached up, fixed the strand, then climbed back down and moved the ladder over to the next tree. I moved, realized he'd taken advantage of our brief moment of being blocked by a tree trunk to come up behind me.

The stink.

Now my nipples were hard and aching, my pussy wet and needy. "What's second?" I asked, tilting my head to the side to watch his ass flex against the tight denim encasing it.

Damn, that was a nice view.

He glanced over his shoulder, smirking when I jerked my gaze up to meet his. "Second, I can't stay on the ground, staring at your ass for much longer."

"Oh?" I asked, bending to grab another strand of lights and undoing a length of it, giving him another glimpse of my butt—which happened to be encased in some tight denim of its own.

His soft groan felt like a physical caress between my thighs.

"Third," he rasped. "I'm hungry and we're behind schedule."

I handed up another length of lights. "There's a table of food over there"—I nodded to the far side of the park, where we'd already hung lights through the trees—"I can grab you something—"

"I plan on eating you for lunch, buttercup."

Oh.

Oh.

I wanted that, too, as I watched him on that ladder stretching his arms overhead as he strung the lights through the branches and mentally calculated the now four million remaining trees.

He was suddenly on his feet in front of me, towering over me, a movement that was so abrupt I startled, jerked back.

"Sorry," he murmured, starting to reach for me, stopping just before touching. "Is this—too much?"

My throat tightened, heart pounding, that knot of my past heavy in my stomach.

"No," I whispered. "I've worked hard to get past what Colt did. I—" I forced myself to hold his gaze when I said the next because it wasn't shameful, because I'd worked hard to get where I was, because I was going to *keep* working, "I've seen a therapist for the last couple of years. Even when I could barely afford food and the ranch's mortgage, I made sure that I saw Jennifer once a week. It's...I don't think I could have gotten here without her."

His hand drifting forward, cupping my jaw. "You would have," he said, fingers drifting back, sliding through the ends of my ponytail. "But I'm glad you got help."

"It might help—"

Another kiss to my forehead. "A man who's luckier than a shit-ton of other kids I passed by on my way here?" He straightened. "Thank you," he whispered. "For—"

A shriek.

We both jumped, and as we did so, I saw Billie Rose barreling our way. "Uh-oh," I muttered.

Axel's hand rested lightly on my back. "Brace for impact," he muttered.

It was so absurd that I laughed out loud…just as Billie Rose reached us.

My aunt slid to a stop, her head tilting to the side, considering.

His arm was pretty much around me. I'd been ogling his ass all of a minute before. We'd made out behind a fucking dumpster.

There was nothing to consider.

I was one of the Finnegan Floozies.

Which…had me laughing again, Axel's eyes coming to mine. "What?" he murmured.

"I'll tell you later," I murmured back.

Billie Rose's brows lifted. "Care to fill me in on the joke?"

"Nope," I said, popping the P. "We've got lights to hang."

"And a pussy to eat."

The words were so soft and silken.

I rose on my tiptoe, mouth just barely able to reach his earlobe. "I'm going to lick your dick like it's my favorite ice cream cone."

He froze then turned to face me, heat in his eyes and mischief in his expression. "Okay," he rumbled, "now you're going to make me find a dumpster."

I giggled.

He tugged the end of my ponytail.

I turned back to Billie Rose—

Or started to, anyway.

Because the ladder and lights were gone, and a gaggle of high school-aged boys had taken our task over a respectful six trees over.

"You two!" Billie Rose bellowed. "Lunch."

She tossed a pointed look in my direction, but I wasn't able to focus on it before an arm slipped around my waist, tugging me back against a big, strong chest, a hard cock against my ass, a rasping voice in my ear. "I'm fucking starving."

TWENTY-NINE

AXEL

I shoved the door open so hard that it collided with the wall, denting the sheetrock, and I didn't give one fuck.

Not when Bailey launched herself into my arms the moment my key was clear of the lock. Not when I was doing my best to get those clothes off her, and the fucking tight jeans I'd been admiring all day were a pain in the ass to draw down that ass, those plump thighs.

Not when she was yanking at my clothing.

And look, I wanted to be naked, too.

But I had a pussy to lick, a woman to make come.

And a limited amount of time for "lunch" before we had to get back to it.

Dropping to my knees, I yanked at the laces of one boot, managed to wrestle it off, and chucked it over my shoulder. Then I went to work on the other, repeating the process and cursing the entire time.

Bailey reached for my shoulders, tried to tug me up, but I'd finally gotten the second boot off, was lifting her up enough to tear off her jeans.

They dropped soundlessly to the floor as I moved for her panties.

"There's my pretty pussy," I crooned, and didn't bother to set her feet down, just lifted her, tossing her legs over my shoulders and moving so that her back was against the wall. Then I did what I've been dreaming about since I'd had her.

I got my mouth on her.

Dipped my tongue through wet folds, finding that spot just to the left of her clit that made her cry out and arch against me, her fingers gripping my hair tight.

Then I set about finding *all* her spots.

Wet dripping down my chin, inner muscles clenching around my tongue. Her cries in my ears, her thighs squeezing me so intensely that I worried for a second I might not be able to breathe.

The worry faded because my name was rolling off her tongue.

Because her breath was hitching.

Because as much as I was tongue-fucking her, she was fucking my mouth.

Fucking, incredible woman.

"Axel," she hissed, arching back, her head bumping into one of the generic photos I had hanging on the wall.

It fell off its hook, crashed to the ground, probably breaking, but I didn't bother looking. Not when the tempo of her hips had changed, had sped, had roughened as she ground against my face.

She was close and I couldn't give fuck-all about the frame.

Then she was coming, and I still couldn't give fuck-all about the frame.

I just spun us, crashing into my coatrack, nearly knocking over the narrow table where I dumped my mail and keys. I needed a flat surface and I needed it now. The couch was closest, and I set her on the edge, helping her rip off my shirt, toeing off my shoes, shoving down my pants before I remembered the condom and had to dig out my wallet to snag the plastic square.

Her hands were on my chest, nails skating over my nipples, dragging down and wrapping around my cock.

Hard and sure strokes that did absolutely nothing for my control.

"Kiss me," she demanded, dragging my head down to hers.

Our mouths came together in a long, drawing kiss, tongues tangling, lips and bodies pressed tight.

Nothing better than my naked body against hers.

Except one thing.

I broke the kiss, sliding my mouth down her throat, worshiping the curve of her shoulder, the fragile collarbone, the hard buds of her nipples, the soft underside of each breast.

I wanted to taste every inch of her, to worship every centimeter.

But she had different ideas.

A shove had me sprawling back on the couch cushions, and then she was clambering on top of me, sinking down on my cock, her head falling back, her breasts jiggling as she worked her pussy on me.

"Fuck," she hissed.

I grunted, reaching for her hips, coaxing her forward.

She was tight and hot and the fucking view of her tits hanging down, so near my mouth that I had to lean up, to suck a nipple deep, had all my intentions of savoring disappearing.

Fast and hard.

Fast and deep.

Fast and...fast.

Luckily, she was right there with me, grinding on my dick, fingers digging into my shoulders, pussy clenching around me.

I snaked a hand between us, rubbed her clit, felt her pussy convulse even harder, even faster.

And thank fuck for that.

I needed her to come.

I needed to fuck *her*.

I needed—

"Axel!" she gasped, those contractions rhythmic and rapid, strong enough to nearly send me sailing.

But I held on, waiting for her to slow before I reversed our positions, before I pressed her back into the cushions, stroked hard and deep and—

"Fuck," I growled, way too soon.

I couldn't help it.

Stopping my orgasm would be like stepping in front of a train and expecting it to just halt on a dime. It was impossible with her milking me, with her tugging me close, her legs wrapping around my hips, her chants of "Yes, fuck. Yes. Keep going. Like that, don't stop. Don't—"

I groaned, my orgasm exploding at the base of my spine as her pussy gripped me even tighter, milking me.

A moan, her body relaxing, eyes sliding closed, legs falling from around my waist.

I slumped forward, barely able to get my elbows beneath me so that I didn't crush her, my heart thumping in my chest, sweat sheening my body, lungs and limbs burning in equal measure.

"Fuck," she whispered a moment, a minute, an eternity later.

"I know," I muttered. "I can't feel my legs."

Her hands slid through my hair, lightly traced my tattoo on my rib cage. I tensed, just slightly before I forced myself to relax. Yeah, I had the ink, but I didn't like to think about it, about what it represented—

And she fucking had the radar for that.

"Why the lines?" she asked.

I had a choice.

I could tell her the rest of it, sit in the past, let it shade this moment. Or I could shove it back down, know that she knew enough, knew more than anyone else besides my mother.

We'd both been rubbed raw that day.

I wanted to enjoy her.

Enjoy the peace of us being together before I had to glue candy on picture frames and dress up as a fortune teller.

I wanted...this moment.

"Another time, okay?" I said, smoothing back her hair.

Brown eyes searching mine for several long seconds. Then a nod, her hand moving away from the ink, down to my ass and squeezing tight. "Fuck," she breathed, "hockey players have the best asses."

I grinned, bent, and nipped her bottom lip, slipping my hand between the cushion and *her* ass. "I was thinking the same thing about ranchers."

Laughter on her face.

Joy in her eyes.

Then mischief.

"Should I tell you what else I was thinking?"

My dick twitched.

Her mouth curved.

And then she leaned up, her mouth coming to my ear, her words hot puffs of damp air as she told me.

And then because she'd told me I had to take her into the kitchen, bend her over until her breasts were flush against the pale gray marble of the island...

And then I had to fuck her until her legs collapsed.

Luckily, hers gave out before mine.

THIRTY

BAILEY

"Ow," I hissed, blowing on my poor, abused finger.

Hot glue guns were deadly dangerous.

"You know," Dessie said. "If you stopped staring at a certain hockey player with a big cock, you'd be less likely to burn yourself."

She had a point.

I still glared at her. "We weren't going to talk about that, remember? Plus"—I glanced around—"there are children about."

"Unfortunately, not any of them close enough at this moment to save you from this conversation."

I scowled because my glance had told me that, too.

It was just...I *was* distracted.

Because of my big hockey player with a giant dick.

Because he was being...cute?

More smoothing of my hair and kissing my forehead and holding my hand until we'd needed to go our separate ways to our respective stations. I'd painted faces for hours, and he'd brought me drinks and a plate for dinner when my station was slammed and I couldn't get away to take a break without turning away a line of adorable kiddos. Then I'd watched between bites when things had calmed down as he'd giggled with little kids when he'd taken his turn on the picture frame station, his big hands having no problem with the glue gun.

No burns on his fingers.

Probably because he wasn't remembering what it felt like to have his strong, hard body wrapped around me as he'd pounded deep and—

A candy corn beaned off my forehead.

I glared at Dessie again.

She smirked...then confiscated my glue gun.

"No crafting while under the influence of Axel Finnegan."

Rolling my eyes, I began sorting candy. But I didn't turn away from Axel.

Because I was considering returning the favor of providing food and sustenance.

Axel—a.k.a. the Fantastic Finnegano—was telling fortunes. In costume. With a hokey accent and a painted-on (okay, *I'd* painted it on) mustache.

And the line was out of control.

I could hear an occasional prediction and they had me cracking up.

But...I also kind of wanted to be close to him, even if just for a few minutes. A drug addict getting my fix. Dangerous and maybe stupid, but...he was...well, he wasn't Colt and I liked him and—

A hand on my arm.

I turned to Dessie. "He watches you, you know?"

"Because he's a fucking creeper."

Dessie smirked. "Because he's as into you as you're into him."

Okay, so maybe that was the truth. Maybe I needed to talk about Axel and me and pop the bubble that had surrounded us today, dissuade the hope cocooning me in safe, cotton wool.

But...I wanted this day.

I wanted *my* Harvest Festival.

The good memory to hold on to.

The joy of simple pleasures and liking someone who made my heart skip a beat.

So, I didn't walk down the obvious conversational path that Dessie was trying to lead me down. Instead, I said, "I like him. It's probably stupid and will implode"—oh, God, I hoped not—"but...I do, Des. I do like him, and I haven't had this in a long time. I know his reputation. I know *him*. So...let me have this, okay?"

Desiree studied my face, her lips pressing flat. "Okay," she said softly.

Then, miracle of miracles, let the subject drop as we worked to make extra frames.

Another round of cake boogying would be finished soon, and we'd have more pictures to print and cut and stuff into the frames, more kids who would want to put their own frame together, more busy work to fill the cool, fall evening with the twinkling stars overhead.

So now was the perfect time to bring him food.

Couldn't have my hockey player withering away now, could I?

I dropped the sorted candy and prepped frames in front of Dessie, nudged my friend's shoulder, and said, "I'll be back."

"Spring that man and go do something fun."

I waggled my brows. "Like a cake boogie?"

Dessie's expression went serious then softened, and she snagged my wrist. "It's good to have you back, Bay." A squeeze. "Just saying."

My heart thumped hard. "You too, Dessie."

A nod. Then her tone went brusque. "Go before I'm overwhelmed with little terrors who try to eat the stale candy."

I grinned but left her anyway, winding my way over to the food table, buying him a plate of food (and then a second because he was a giant hockey player and I wanted him to have enough energy for later). Then I snagged two beers, a couple bottles of water, and made my way back to the Fantastic Finnegano's tent.

The kids had cleared out.

The hockey players hadn't.

A gaggle of them had clustered in the entrance of the tent, their laughter booming.

I side-stepped a mountain-sized blond and, yeah, my heart skipped a beat when Axel glanced up and his gaze focused on me. His smile was a cozy blanket and the warmth in his eyes...well, it meant a lot.

"Who's this?" the mountain-sized man said.

"Back off, Joel," Axel snapped. "She's—"

I set the plates on the table, the beers and waters. Then I turned to the mountain, to *Joel*, apparently—and what a stupid name *that* was—and narrowed my eyes. "You here for a fortune?"

His mouth turned up at the corner. "You gonna give me one, sweetheart?" He reached forward like he was going to touch me.

I snagged his wrist, put just enough tension on the pressure point on the inside of it to halt his movement. "Yes, a broken wrist is in your future if you think about touching me."

"Should I point out that *you're* touching me?"

I released him. "There. Happy?"

"No," he said, stepping a little closer, eyes warming, voice dropping. "I *like* it when you touch me." A tilt of his head. "Want to get out of here, baby? I've got really big...fingers." The last was said as though he were imparting state secrets.

My lips twitched.

Laughter bubbled up in my chest, my throat, and, what the hell, I let it rip. Then let it continue flowing when his expression went completely befuddled. I laughed so hard I had to brace myself on my knees, that I couldn't catch my breath, that I barely felt Axel's hand on my back.

That I barely processed that it was his hand.

That it didn't make me panic.

Because my body knew his now.

Because his fingers had dipped under the hem of my shirt, the roughened tips brushing lightly over my skin.

"Brutal, buttercup."

I straightened, turned into his body, his arms coming around me. "God, I thought your lines were bad."

A snort had me glancing over my shoulder.

One of the guys—black hair, thick beard, chocolate brown eyes, all-around stunning—was smirking behind Joel.

The other was staring at his feet, but I saw his shoulders were shaking.

Axel tugged my ponytail, glanced up at his teammates. "Beat it," he ordered.

Joel huffed, but his mouth was still tipped up at the edges. "Rude."

"I mean, I'm not the one talking about fingers."

Joel chuckled. "Not you." He pointed one of those large digits in my direction. "Your smack talk is on point. You"—he jabbed it at Axel—"are an ungrateful teammate. We're all just here to show our support."

I squeezed Axel's wrist when he tensed. "Oh, you guys want to support the town. Oh my God!" I stepped out of his grip, clasped my hands to my chest. "That's so sweet."

Joel paled. "I—no— That's okay."

I giggled. "Oh now, don't be shy!" I moved toward the entrance and the fates were kind because my aunt happened to be passing by. "Billie Rose!"

She spun, brows together.

I waved. "Come over here."

For a moment, it seemed like she didn't want to approach, but then her face cleared, and she smiled, walking toward me.

"Hey, honey," she said, pressing a kiss to my cheek.

I grabbed Joel's wrist when he tried to slither away, and damn, the man was strong. But I'd wrestled cattle nearly my entire life. I could hold one hockey player in place, long enough for him to fall into Billie's snare, anyway.

"These *three*," I emphasized the last when the other two players tried to slink to the side, "were just telling me how they're quite desperate to show their support." My aunt began to smile. "I know that they're happy to jump in wherever, especially since it's getting late, and we always need more help at this time of night."

Considering.

Billie Rose's expression was considering.

No, *plotting*. Calculating. Like in a Pinky and the Brain, gonna take over the world type of way.

She smiled.

It was *awesome*.

"Fuck," one of the men behind me muttered.

I smothered a giggle. Just said, "Can you find these three some way to help?"

"Oh, I sure can, baby girl." She kissed my cheek again, waved at Axel, and said, "Close the flap on this tent and it's dinner break time for you." Then she turned to the trio of men and her voice was authoritative when she clipped out, "You, three, with me."

Joel shot me a glare over his shoulder.

I just finger waved. "Have fun and thanks for your...support."

A chuckle in my ear, fingers dipping into the cleft of my ass. "You know he's going to take a run at me the next time we're on the ice together."

I shrugged. "You can handle him."

"But can I handle you?" he murmured, nipping at the top of my ear.

"That's a nope." I reached out and snagged the edges of the tent, tugging them closed, then drew him over to the table. "Okay, Fantastic Finnegano, you need to eat dinner before the next rush."

"Hmm," he said, sitting on the edge and drawing me in between his legs. "I thought we'd already talked about what kind of food I'm craving."

"Well, *I* need you to have energy to satisfy that craving," I pointed out. "Otherwise, you're useless to me."

Without another word, he picked up the plate and began eating.

I giggled.

He offered me a bite of the pulled pork, and even though I wasn't really hungry, it was Dusty's pulled pork, so I ate it. "I like it when you do that."

"Do what?"

"Smile and laugh and relax against me." He popped another bite into my mouth. "Look happy and relaxed with a loser like me."

My heart clenched tight, and I ran my fingers through the bristles of his beard. "I thought we talked about this already."

"About what?"

I slanted him a look. "Don't play dumb."

"Then stop being so fucking sexy."

"Eat your food."

"Will you let me eat *you* later if I do?"

I rolled my eyes, even as a pulse of need slid between my thighs. "Didn't you already do that?"

He bent, pressed his nose to my throat, and inhaled deeply. "Yeah. So?"

"So that's the big, dark secret for the big, bad hockey player? You're obsessed with oral sex?"

"Is that a problem?"

"For me or you?" I teased.

Fingers in my ponytail, male laughter in my ears. "For you. Fuck knows it's not a problem for me."

"Hmm." I took the fork from him, started feeding him bites. If I had a night ahead of me with a sexy man who was planning to spend it between my thighs, then I'd better feed him.

And I was doing it purely for selfish purposes.

Not because I liked doing it, or because it felt intimate and I wanted more of these quiet, familiar moments, our bodies touching, our breaths intermingling, our hands brushing and stroking and—

The plate was torn out of my hands, plunked onto the table, rattling the crystal ball.

Hell, who was I kidding, I was *so* doing it because I liked all of that.

Almost as much as I liked him sliding a hand into my hair, tugging my head back, and kissing me senseless.

Heat, too much considering we were in public with only a couple of tent flaps between us and discovery.

Except, Billie Rose had told us to close them.

I knew that no one would disturb us.

I could get on my knees and—

A groan. "What are you thinking about?"

"Blowing you."

He choked.

I grinned.

"Trouble."

"So says the man who tore through my town."

"So says the woman who tore through my ego."

My grin was back, but all I did was say, "Happy to be of service."

His hand was bracketing my hip, long fingers digging into the top of my ass, drawing me flush against him so that I could feel his cock. It was like granite. It made my mouth water more than that pulled pork. But when he nuzzled the underside of my jaw, nipped lightly at the spot where it met my throat then inhaled deeply, he rasped out, "Apples," settling right in the vicinity of my heart, my grin faded.

"Are we doing this?" I asked softly.

I was scared and not. I was excited and hopeful and needy and weirded out and—I was, for the first time in a long time—looking forward to what the future would bring.

A future that wasn't just the ranch and the cattle, fences and horses and shag carpeting.

A future that involved this man.

His blue eyes, his words, his actions didn't prevaricate.

He didn't play coy, didn't pretend to not understand exactly what I was saying.

He just stroked back the wayward, uncooperative hairs that were escaping my ponytail and kissed my forehead, saying simply, "Yes, we're doing this."

Thirty-One

Axel

We were naked in Bailey's bed so we could be near the ranch and the animals that would need care in the morning.

We because I wasn't going to lounge in bed while she worked her ass off in the morning. *We* because I had ideas about that workbench in the barn and the fence near the empty stall, and the hay bales, and the walls with the old photos and tools and horse tack.

We because...I had *lots* of ideas.

I'd used some of them that evening, which was why she was naked and passed out, her arm around my waist, her soft, slow breaths puffing against my shoulder.

I was naked and staring out the dark window.

So quiet. So many shadows and secrets.

But it was peaceful rather than scary. I was with Bailey. *With* her in a way that wasn't dating.

It was more.

Maybe not my girlfriend, not yet. Not when I'd just barely

convinced her to take a chance on me, when I'd just barely convinced myself. But it was more than dating, more than a simple meal with a side of fucking afterward.

She was...*more.*

Just quite simply *more.*

And I owed her a fucking date.

I owed her candles and flowers and worshiping her body slowly, incrementally, beautifully, after the fourth date.

I owed her some time in her fucking living room that had been pulled apart because of a leak, helping her put it back together, even if she assured me that the contractors were showing up to fix the mess in a couple of days' time.

I owed—

My cell rang.

Her brows drew together, breath hitching, and I reached for the nightstand, wanting to shut off the call before it woke her.

But when I saw that it was Coach, my brows drew together, and I quickly swiped at the screen, lifted my cell to my ear, and slid out from between the sheets. "Hello?" I said quietly, moving into the hall and closing the door.

"Finnegan, did you see the game tonight?"

For a second, I was confused because we hadn't played.

Then I realized...the Gold had.

"Rogers got tagged with a cheap hit tonight and went into the boards hard," Coach said. "Broke his tibia and fibula. He's in surgery."

My heart began to pound.

"But he's out at least three months. Maybe longer."

I inhaled. "Oh?" I croaked.

"They want you in San Francisco in the morning." A beat. "I'd suggest you pack a big bag. If you play this right..."

He kept talking, letting me know the team had offered transport and already set me up with a room in a hotel, that practice was at 1:00 the following afternoon, that I needed to be at the arena before that to meet with someone from the back office to go over details, that someone was going to reach out in the next couple of days with more information about amending my contract for a long stay in the league.

Me.

A long stay in the league.

My chest went tight. My lungs refused to expand. My pulse pounded through my veins, and my throat had gone so freaking taut that I couldn't force out any sort of reply.

"You could make a go of this, Finnegan," Coach said. "Don't fuck it up, yeah?"

I cleared my throat. "Yeah," I managed. "Thanks—"

But I was talking to dead air.

Slowly, I lowered my phone to my side.

"Axel?" A gentle touch, slightly calloused fingers on my side. "Who was on the phone?"

"Coach," I rasped.

Her fingers tightened. "Is everything okay?"

"They want me in San Francisco in the morning."

Her brows lifted. "That's a good thing, right?"

I nodded. "I—" A breath. "Rogers, the normal center on the third line, broke his leg tonight. He's in surgery and will be out at least three months."

"Shit," she whispered.

"Yeah." My hand slid up her back, holding her to me like she was my lovey, and I needed the stuffed toy for comfort. And hadn't I just spent the last months realizing that I *did* need it, that I needed this woman in my life?

"But it's a good thing, right?" Her head jerked. "I mean, bad for him, but good for you, right? This will mean more time on the Gold, right?"

"Bad for him because it was a dirty play that led to him getting hurt." I swallowed hard. "Good for me so long as I don't fuck it up."

She went still. "Axel."

Clearing my throat, I lightly nudged her back. "Ignore me. You need to get back to bed, and I need to get packed and I, fuck, *I*"—I made a face—"need to text the tornado that is your aunt that I won't be able to take my shifts at the festival tomorrow."

Her hands came to my cheeks, and she turned my head toward hers. I hadn't even realized that I was staring down the hall, not looking at her, not *seeing* her.

Already, a curl of panic was coiled in my belly.

Threatening to expand, to fuck everything up.

I slid out of her hold, wanting, needing to go, to lock this down, to—

"Don't."

A sharp clipped-out word that had me blinking.

Those hands came to my face again. "Your mom didn't fuck the player who hurt Rogers."

"What the fuck, Bailey?"

"Don't," she said again, just as clipped out, gripping my biceps tight. "Your mom didn't do this. No one but *you*—" She poked me in the chest. "You did this. You got here. *You*—"

"And the fucker who hit Rogers."

Another poke. "Do people get hurt playing hockey?"

I knew where she was going with this. I knew what she was going to try and prove.

But none of that was going to make the coil of panic in my stomach disappear.

"Buttercup," I began.

"No," she snapped, stepping close, wrapping her arms around me, her body flush to mine, her voice low and intense and sliding over me, sinking in through my skin, settling onto my soul. "You're not going to do this when we've finally figured our shit out. You aren't going to be an asshole and push me away. You are going to fuck me and you're going to give us both enough orgasms to hold me over for a while because you're going to be there, on that fucking team, and you're going to be there a while."

Her mouth pressed to mine, one fierce kiss that sent my heart skittering and my cock hardening. "Then you're going to go back to your place and pack your shit for a good long stay with the Gold because you're fucking incredible and you're going to *be* incredible, and if you're not, if you make me drive my ass down to San Francisco to kick *yours,* then we're going to have a problem."

The coil loosened.

Amusement slid like jelly through my veins, warming me, slowing my pulse, making my movements languid and slow and steady.

"You're going to kick my ass, buttercup?"

A flash of a smile, as though she sensed my panic cooling, my humor growing. "Damn right I am." Her hand slid into my hair. "Even if I have to bring down my shotgun and my saw."

I barked out a laugh.

She kissed me again, long and slow and deep. "You're going to be great," she whispered when she'd pulled back enough to suck in a breath. "So *fucking* great."

"Or you'll saw off my dick?" I said lightly.

"Fuck no, I need that," she quipped.

More laughter bursting out of my throat, that panic disappearing.

This woman.

Leaning down, I swept her up into my arms.

She squeaked. "What are you doing?"

"Orgasms."

Her teeth pressed into her bottom lip; her eyes went hot. But there was no sass, no fire, no arguments.

She just reached between us, wrapped her hand around my aching cock, and said, "Enough to tide us over."

I grinned. "Damn right, buttercup."

Thirty-Two

"You know," I said into the phone. "Tonight was the first time I watched a hockey game from beginning to end."

A soft huff of amusement. "I'm almost scared to ask what you thought."

He sounded tired.

Unsurprising, since he'd worked his ass off. Even as a hockey newbie, I'd been able to see that.

But this was his first game—or well, not the first, but this was the first since...whatever we were, the first since he'd told me about his mom, his implosion, his insecurities.

So, I was going to make fucking certain that he went to bed with a smile on his pretty, albeit somewhat annoying face.

The man had been texting me regularly since he'd left the day before.

Mostly dirty memes and GIFs that were designed to make me smile, but along with the occasional—*At the hotel. At the rink. Back at the hotel.*—they'd made me...miss him.

"What's with that face, buttercup?"

I blinked, returned my focus to the screen and video call that was showing that pretty and slightly annoying man. "What face?"

"The face that says you miss me."

He rolled over, the crisp, white sheet sliding down his bare chest, the chest I'd kissed my way across less than forty-eight hours before. He smirked, tugged it lower still, showing me *all* the goods that had gotten me in trouble with missing him in the first place.

Terrible man.

"I don't miss you," I said, adding when he sniffed, "I just miss your cock."

He snorted, but the man had never missed an opportunity to talk, touch, or bring attention to his penis, so it didn't surprise me when he reached down, wrapped one big hand around his cock and stroked.

I choked, on my own spit, I'd be the first to admit.

But that man stroking his own cock, the taut skin moving over the hard jut of his erection, the tip glistening with precum had need tearing through me, setting fire to my veins. I was wet. I could feel my desire gathering at the tops of my thighs, my nipples beading against the fabric of my sleep shirt.

"Whatcha got under that big ugly shirt, buttercup?"

Ugly? Yes, I was wearing an oversized blue cotton shirt with a huge print of Wish Bear on the front. But she was adorable, and he had no right—*no right!*—to insult the fluffball of adorableness.

"Wish Bear isn't ugly," I snapped.

A sexy grin, that hand still stroking, making it very difficult for me to concentrate on what had gotten my feathers ruffled in the first place. "That shirt is."

"You're an ass."

"I fucking *love* it when you get all growly with me."

More heat. More dampness coating the tops of my thighs. More...need for this man who was nearly four hours away.

"You're sick."

"You like it."

A shake of my head. "No, I don't."

Now his grin was absolutely unrepentant. "Put your fingers between your thighs, buttercup. They come up dry, and I know you're telling the truth."

"You're—"

"An asshole, I know. Tell me again." He stroked faster, his groan rumbling through my phone's speaker. It might as well have been against my skin for how my body reacted.

Burning up.

Trembling.

Fighting the urge to rip off my "ugly" shirt and put my fingers between my thighs, to show him he was right. That I was turned on and wanted him here and—

Fuck it.

He seemed to make it his mission to shock me.

I needed to give him a taste of his own medicine.

So, I propped the phone up next to me, reached for the hem of my shirt, and whipped it over my head.

Showing him what I was wearing under it.

Which was...nothing.

"Fuck," he groaned, his muscles straining as he jerked his cock.

"I want you to stroke yourself," I ordered, rubbing my hands along my chest, squeezing my breasts, brushing my thumbs over my nipples, pretending they were his hands, his fingers.

His hand worked.

Sweat began to glisten on his skin.

"I want you to pretend it's my hand wrapped around your cock, that I'm there with you, that when you come, it's on my breasts."

"*Fuck,*" he hissed, the head of his cock turning an angry red, moisture beading, making slick sounds.

Or maybe that was from me, from my hands, my fingers between my thighs.

"Spread your legs, buttercup," he rasped. "I want to see you, want to see those slick folds." I sat up, rearranging the pillows, shifting the phone so he could see between my legs and spread my thighs. Wide.

Not shy.

Not scared.

I'd learned to own this part of me.

This man had given me nothing but pleasure and confidence. He felt as deeply as I did.

He was...the most dangerous person I had ever met in my life.

And the safest.

Because he made me feel safe.

But he didn't let me sit in that feeling, curl into it, sink into the peaceful oblivion. He pushed me to grab for more, to *take* more.

"Rub your clit," he ordered. "*No*, not like that." A growl. "Rub it like I'm there. Rub it like how I would. Hard, buttercup. No fucking mercy. Rub your clit like I'm demanding you come on my fingers, my tongue."

I shuddered.

Then I rubbed harder.

And—oh God—that was good.

"Don't stop, buttercup. Keep going but push a finger inside. Hard."

I did what I was told, sliding my middle finger inside my pussy, curling it forward, hitting my clit from the inside and out. "It's not enough," I whispered, hips jerking.

"Then give yourself more."

Another finger.

And then another, until I could pretend it was his hands on my clit, his fingers inside me, his lips and teeth and tongue sending me up that mountainside.

"Fuck," I whispered.

"Don't stop."

"*Fuck*," I whispered.

"Don't *fucking* stop, buttercup."

My head flopped back against the headboard, gaze catching on his through the phone, holding scorching blue eyes for a moment before my gaze drifted down his body.

Pecs.

Abs.

Cock.

All glistening.

All begging for my attention.

All driving me closer to that edge.

Pleasure wound itself tight in my belly, the ends of that strong spiral twisting taut until one side sparked, caught, and went alight. Like a lit fuse, it ignited, burning rapidly.

"Axel, baby," I begged.

"Don't fucking stop. Don't—"

"I'm gonna come."

"Do it."

His expression was feral, all the muscles of his arms, his torso, his neck standing out sharply in relief.

"I'm gonna—"

"*Do it.*"

I shattered, my back arching, hips bucking, moan escaping from between my clenched teeth. By some small miracle, I managed to keep my eyes open, and I was rewarded with the glorious sight of Axel falling over the edge too.

Jaw clenching.

Curse words tangling with my name as his hand worked, as... white jets of cum shot out of his cock, coating his belly, making my mouth water and wish I had it on my body, my tongue, my taste buds.

A swell of exhaustion chased the wave of pleasure.

Drawing my lids down as I tried to catch my breath.

"Fuck," he rumbled, recovering a lot quicker than I had— because professional athlete and all that. "I wish I was there."

My mouth tipped up, and I couldn't resist teasing him,

couldn't resist giving him that sass he said he liked. "I'm glad you're not."

A groan, his hand clenching something—oh, a T-shirt—rubbing roughly at his belly. "So fucking mean," he growled. "Is that any way to treat the man who just made you come?"

"Is this the point in the conversation where I remind you that I took matters into my own hands?"

"Is *this* the point where I tell you I really fucking miss you, and not just your body?"

My breath caught. "Axel," I whispered.

"Buttercup," he murmured, and the warmth in that filled my veins with helium, so much until I felt like I could float. He tossed the soiled shirt aside, tugged the sheet up to his waist, and following suit, I used a tissue to clean up then snagged my shirt, pulled it over my head.

"How was the rest of the festival?"

"The kids had a blast," I said. "I'm still not a huge fan of plastic gourds and candy corn, but I did get a slice of delicious chocolate cake today, so it wasn't a total loss. Though I do still have to get through the parade tomorrow and all of the breakdown." My lips twitched. "I *am*, however, a big fan of a certain mystic with a painted-on mustache."

He groaned.

"Is that sound of displeasure because you're sad you don't get to see the parade?"

"No," he muttered. "It's sad for two reasons—one, I'm now officially on the team diet plan, so that means no chocolate cake for me on any day but a Cheat Day, and two, the guys have learned of my moonlighting in the fortune-telling booth."

My lips twitched higher, but I managed to keep my voice neutral when I asked, "Is that a bad thing?"

"Well, considering my nickname is now Balls, yeah, it's not ideal."

I giggled. "How'd they get to Balls from the Fantastic Finnegano?"

"Fortune Teller to Crystal Ball to Ball to Balls." A grunt. "Because apparently Ball doesn't roll off the tongue quite as well as *Balls.*"

I giggled again.

"God, I love it when you laugh."

God, I love *you*.

I almost blurted that out, barely caught it on the edge of my tongue. My heart began pounding—too much, too soon, just...too *much*. But I forced my voice to be light. "Even if it's at your expense?"

A shrug. "There are worse things when it comes to the woman who makes me jerk myself off on FaceTime."

"Well, gold star for me then, huh?"

"When it results in orgasms, fuck yeah." His laughter joined with mine then he yawned, rubbed a hand over his face.

"I should let you get some sleep."

He nodded. "Heading out on a road trip tomorrow."

"I know." Then to his raised brows, "I've now made a study of the Gold's schedule. It's in my calendar, and I've even upgraded my streaming service, so I get the games."

I'd done that even though it would take a little longer to get out of the black, but then today I'd sold Picard to a petting zoo in the next town over for a decent sum. He'd get loved on every day. I'd earned some extra cash.

And maybe even some sandwich money.

"I'll give you some money for that next time I see you."

"Axel," I said firmly. "I don't want your money, so don't offer to give it to me and ruin both our good moods."

"Bailey."

"I miss you more than wanting to argue."

He stilled. "Buttercup."

"Exactly." I curled up on my side, cuddled up under the blankets. "Now take the win, rest up, and focus on hockey."

"No ladders."

"Had to get one last order in, huh?"

"Well, I can't let you be the only one who's good at them." A beat. "Promise?"

My heart squeezed, affection for this man filling every single one of my cells. "Promise," I whispered.

And then, Axel Finnegan, former nuisance and world-class asshole, gave me the gift of a gentle smile and soft words.

The best part?

I knew he'd saved those just for me.

Thirty-Three

Axel

A tap on my shoulder from Calle, one of the offensive coaches, had me glancing up at the former National team player. She'd blown out her knee, taken up coaching, and was killing it.

"Next up," she said, just as the whistle blew to stop the play on the ice.

We were on the penalty kill, down a man because Coop was in the box for a trip, and I wasn't normally on the PK squad.

But I wasn't going to argue.

Not when we were down one goal, another could put the nail in the coffin for this game, and we couldn't afford to just give up two points in a long season where every single point made a difference. More wins meant more points, meant a better playoff position.

Home ice advantage.

Better seeding.

And...I was thinking to the future, about what we could do as a team, instead of worrying about living up to the promise of now.

Bailey would give me that gold star.

Bailey...

I missed her.

Ridiculous right? I'd spent twenty-five years without her, and all of a few days with her, if I wasn't counting the nightly phone calls and regular texts, and I felt like I was missing part of myself.

The ice, the game...that felt right.

Not being in the same town to share it with her?

That blew.

But I knew she was watching. Every game. Every night.

Her commentary was hilarious because of her limited hockey knowledge—hating their third jerseys, calling the puck a ball, asking when halftime was—but...even though she wasn't here, even though I had that missing piece sitting heavy in my chest, I didn't feel alone.

And I wasn't going to stop.

Not now.

No fucking way.

Plus, I'd picked her up a present and was going to give it to her two days from now. We had two days off after the next game, and I was spending them in River's Bend.

With Bailey.

Tonight?

I was going to make her proud.

Determined, I jumped over the boards, lined up, and took the face-off, winning it back to Logan who chipped it up off the glass.

Then it was a race down the ice—first a conservative one (because I didn't want to get caught up and leave my teammates down *two* players), then it became a balls-out one when I realized that I had a very real chance at getting to the puck before the other team's defenseman.

My heart pumped, my lungs burned, my quads were on fucking fire.

But I didn't feel any of that.

Urgency.

That was the chief feeling.

I needed to get to that fucking puck.

The defenseman bumped me, and not expecting the fucker to have caught up enough to make contact after I'd already passed him, I nearly ate shit.

But I recovered quickly, kept skating.

Ten feet from the puck.

Five.

Two.

One.

I got it on the blade of my stick, just barely corralling it as my opponent slammed me hard into the boards.

I'd been expecting *that,* though, so I rolled with the check, exhaling so my breath wasn't lost, so that I could keep the oxygen coming, my body moving. A kick brought the puck in front of me, and I got my stick on it again, freeing up a little bit of space.

Giving me enough time for me to glance up at the clock, to see that the penalty only had three seconds left.

Another crushing hit, slamming me into the boards.

But my mind was already five steps ahead.

I needed to protect the puck.

For three.

Two.

One.

Then a burst of effort, of movement that broke the hold the defenseman had on me, that shoved me past the other one who'd come in to double-team me. I saw a flash of black, another, knew that Blue had followed me into the offensive zone, just like I knew that Coop was streaking in behind him, his penalty having ended and our man disadvantage coming to an end, allowing him to jump back on the ice and join the play.

I gained a foot, knew I had a moment—and only a moment— to look, to get my bearings, to get the puck to my teammate.

A flick of my wrists.

A pass from the corner to the front of the net, floating past Blue, jumping over his stick.

But that was okay...

Because Coop was there.

A shove had the defenseman off my ass. Then I was moving to the net, to the far side, sneaking up behind the goalie.

Coop faked a shot, passed it to Blue.

Who'd seen my cut, my positioning, and passed the puck over.

Five feet, four, three, two—

I wound up.

Swung down.

My shot...hit the goalie in the pads as he read the play and slid over, blocking the puck.

But the goalie was moving too fast, and the rebound didn't make it to safety, didn't fly out into the corner or out of the zone. It dropped...right into the center of the crease, the small cylinder of vulcanized rubber bouncing.

Right *fucking* there.

I lunged forward, jabbed at the puck.

Sticks slashed down around me, hands shoved, mouths formed curse words, but I got my blade on that puck, and I hit it fucking *hard*.

Hard enough that it slid forward, shooting forward, drifting toward the goal line.

Over the goal line.

I saw it in the net.

And then I was shoved forward.

Harder than that puck.

I fell forward, eating ice, tasting blood, dodging the skates suddenly surrounding me as my teammates came to my defense, doling their own pushes and shoving, chirping, and cursing.

But I couldn't give one fuck.

Because...the puck was in the net.

The score was tied.

I was earning my keep, my place.

I was thinking about these men—and Brit—as my teammates.

Progress.

Fucking finally.

———

I was checking my phone in the locker room after the game.

But I didn't get a chance to open the texts that were waiting for me from Bailey before Brit sat down next to me, lips curving at the edges. "I see you flushed the bullshit."

Setting my phone down, I gazed at her innocently. "I don't know what you're talking about."

"Bullshit...*Balls.*"

I grunted.

God, that fucking nickname.

"What do they call you? Smiles?" I asked, considering her biggest sponsorship was for a popular toothpaste brand and her grin was well-known, having graced many a magazine cover and billboard.

"No," she said.

"Grinny Weasley?"

She snorted. "Now, if Mandy got a hold of that one." A nudge of my shoulder to hers. "You're doing good, kid."

Stupid that the sentiment meant so much.

But I didn't have time to process that, not when my phone buzzed. Brit snagged it from beside my hip before I could react—fucking quick ass glove hand—and glanced at the screen.

"Who's Buttercup?"

Fucking *hell.*

I snatched it from her, narrowed my eyes.

"Another problem you solved because of Auntie Brit." She smiled beatifically. "So, when do I get to meet her?"

I scowled. "Never," I muttered.

She was completely unfazed. "You know the crew would accept her."

That I didn't have any doubt of, not now that I'd spent a full week with the team, saw how tight they were, how much like a family they functioned—and not the fucked up one I'd grown up with, but an actual family that loved and cared about each other.

"I know," I said, shoving the phone under my leg—on the far side for good measure and safekeeping from Brit's reach. "But... we're new, and she lives in River's Bend."

Brit winced. "The long-distance thing sucks, but River's Bend isn't that far, you know."

"I know," I said. "I guess the bigger thing is that I only just got her to agree to see me. I don't want to push too much too fast."

"Wow."

I frowned. "What?"

"Just surprised, I guess. A big, tough, alpha hockey player admitting that he needs to take things slow and steady? Color me surprised." A toss of her blond ponytail, a flash of that million-dollar smile. "Apparently, River's Bend makes them insightful and sensitive."

Heaven help me if the guys caught wind of *that*.

"I'm not from River's Bend."

"You did a good job of making a spot for yourself," she said, voice quiet. "And not just as a shit-stirrer."

I grunted again. "A certain goalie helped kick my ass in gear."

Now I got the full Brit smile. "Flatterer."

"Wants this conversation over-er."

She punched me in the arm. "No broody assholes, puh-lease. Especially, since I came over to do you a favor."

That sounded...ominous.

People didn't do favors, not for me, not without strings anyway.

Except...people did.

People on this team. People in River's Bend.

I pushed that realization down, focused on Brit.

"I have an apartment not far from the arena. It doesn't make the commute to the practice facility all that great, but it's close enough and convenient for home games, and best of all it's empty, furnished, and free, since Lucas and Rome"—two rookies who'd been signed right after training camp at the beginning of the season—"moved out."

"I—" My words faltered because I didn't really understand.

She plunked a set of keys into my hand. "Hotel life gets old real quick. The apartment is yours for as long as you need it."

"I haven't signed the contract yet."

"Word is it'll be ready for you when we land in San Francisco."

"I—my agent—" He hadn't said anything to me. In fact, I'd been trying to get in touch with him from the moment I'd been called up and had gotten nothing but radio silence.

One of the reasons I hadn't signed yet.

Not the only one, considering they hadn't asked me to sit down and actually put pen to paper yet.

But...maybe that was because my agent was a fuckup?

Shit.

My temples began to ache, and I resisted the urge to rub them. Another thing to deal with when all I wanted was to get home to Bailey.

"Another word of advice?"

I blinked up at her.

She handed me a card. "Call Prestige, bump your shitty agent, and get Olivia to represent you. She's a BAMF and a total shark and is used to negotiating with the back office. She'll get you the deal you need."

"I—" I fumbled for a few more moments, scrambled to find the right thing to say.

How did this woman know?

Brit stood, clapped me on the shoulder. "And maybe call her tonight."

My brows dragged together.

A shrug from the goalie. "I might have already told her that you were interested in new representation. No offense, but Manny Douglas is shit."

I sucked in a breath.

Shook my head.

The power of Brit.

"Are you related to a woman named Billie Rose?" I asked as she started to walk away.

Consternation on a pretty face. "No, why?"

"I think you'd better do a 23andMe, just to be sure."

A flick of that ponytail, another smile. "Sounds like I'd like her."

"It'd either be love or a battle to the death."

Laughter. Another clap of my shoulder. "I like you, Balls. You're good people."

I started to reach for my cell, stopped when she called, "Oh, Balls?"

Rolling my eyes, I glanced up. "You'll manage the distance," she said softly. "She somehow managed to get through all of your walls, wound her way through the barbed wire around your heart. You'll figure out a couple hour drive." A nod that was nothing if not encouraging. "I know you will."

And then she strode away, leaving me to my text messages.

With a set of keys in my hand.

A business card in the other.

But, most important, with hope that I'd finally sorted out my shit.

Thirty-Four

BAILEY

I was finishing up the touches on my dinner sandwich—this week's selection was salami, cheddar, with a fancy Dijon mustard that made me feel especially bougie. Of course, the bread was the cheapest variety I could find to pay for that fancy mustard.

The farm...was a money pit.

Gramps's old truck had needed new tires.

Another pipe in the "remodeled" section of the house (and, yes, that was air quotes because I had serious doubts about how complete the remodel had been) had a leak. I was thinking it was more like a lipstick-on-a-pig situation rather than actually going in and updating the things that needed updating.

New pipes to replace the eighty-year-old ones? Nah, that would be too smart. They hadn't actually replaced them all. Instead, they'd done a poor patch job, and now that poor patch job was responsible for me having to tear the carpet out of another bedroom. It was ugly, but still.

New wiring because the updates my grandparents installed in the seventies might be a fire danger? Of course not.

But fancy carpet and tile and wallpaper?

Oh, absolutely.

Now a large portion of that wallpaper was in the trash, along with the sheetrock it had been adhered to.

And I'd spent the rest of Picard's money on pipes.

And fancy Dijon mustard was going by the wayside once this bottle was done.

Because wiring.

And circling back to money pit.

Sigh.

For now, I'd turned off the breakers in the remodeled section, had made sure the water was off in that part of the house.

I'd had a few electricians and plumbers out to give bids, and now the fancy Dijon mustard fund was going toward pipes and wiring.

Fun times.

But I'd make it through.

I always did.

Plus, now that I was splurging on fancy streaming services, I had plenty of things to watch while I stuck to my sandwich diet.

Go me.

I took my plate into the family room, still sans carpet and couch, but I'd commandeered Gramps' old recliner from the barn.

It smelled like horse and faintly like Gramps. His cologne, the spice and sandalwood mix that I would never forget. Sitting in it felt like he was giving me a hug, so even though I'd had to toss that old, ugly couch of Gran's and the memories that came with it, I'd found this.

I was reaching for the remote when I heard tires crunching on the gravel outside, saw the flash of headlights across my driveway.

Considering how far outside town I was, I didn't get a lot of casual visitors.

I was catching up with Dessie tomorrow, a promised full report at her place, and I had no doubt that Billie Rose would tag along for the reporting. Frankly, it was a miracle that I'd gotten nearly a ten-day reprieve from the conversation, and I had to chalk that up to Billie Rose wrapping up the Harvest Festival and prepping for the Holiday Parade.

More parades.

More snotty-nosed kids and picture frames and twinkly lights.

I smiled.

Maybe I could convince Axel to take another turn at the Fantastic Finnegano. I found that I had a particular fondness for the fortune teller tent.

I set my plate aside when the headlights flashed through my living room windows, telling me that this wasn't a turnaround, but rather a car parking in my driveway.

"Damn," I muttered, not feeling particularly social, but also knowing that if it was a neighbor who needed assistance, I wouldn't be eating my sammy any time soon.

A push to my feet, a pause to grab my shotgun—because a woman who lived alone in the middle of nowhere couldn't be too careful—and moved to the front door, reaching the hall just as the bell rang.

Keeping my gun at my side, but ready all the same, I opened the door a crack.

And felt my heart go *whoosh*.

Axel was on my porch—fully clothed, sadly. He had a bag over one shoulder, another in his hand, and was wearing a suit that was slightly wrinkled but still hugged his body in all the right places. Powerful thighs. Broad shoulders. Biceps a woman could (and I had) cling to. His eyes warmed when he saw me, danced with mirth when his gaze flicked down.

"Do you have handcuffs?" he asked.

His voice was...a warm blanket wrapping around me.

"What?"

Grinning, he pushed the door open, nudging me back, his bags hitting the floor. My shotgun was plucked out of my hands and settled into the rack I had mounted on the wall.

Then his arms were around me and my face was in his chest and...home.

I was standing in my house, and it felt like I'd finally come home.

"Hi, buttercup," he murmured, running his hand over my hair, wrapping his other arm tightly around me. "Miss me?"

"Just your dick," I returned.

Then felt his chuckle in my soul. "I missed you," he murmured.

"Meh," I said. "I'm the pain in the ass who orders you around and threatened to shoot you."

Another chuckle. "I told you I'm open to anything in the bedroom." A nip to the top of my ear. "Or out of it."

I choked.

He laughed, swept me up into his arms and marched into the living room, steps faltering when he took in the space. "What the fuck, buttercup?"

He knew about the leaks, the carpet, the missing sheetrock.

I'd also told him I was taking care of things. Which I was.

It was just sometimes on a ranch like mine, other things took priority, and then...there was the whole money thing.

Still, all I said was, "I have it under control."

"You *have* no carpet." A beat. "Or furniture."

"Gramps's chair is good enough for the moment. Plus, I'm not going to fix the trimmings until the base is settled." His gaze flicked to mine. "I have bids for plumbing and electrical, since the first leaked again and the second is a fire hazard." I pushed lightly at his shoulders, indicating that he should put me down.

Which he understood, apparently, because he walked over to Gramps's recliner, set me down.

Gently.

Always gently—except in bed, of course.

Then he gave me a little bit of rough. Which I liked.

"I didn't know you were coming up," I said softly, reaching for his hand and trying to tug him down into the chair next to me. He came close but didn't sit. "When do you need to go back?"

"Tomorrow night."

My belly went squiggly. "Yay," I whispered.

His fingers smoothed back my hair and he kissed my forehead. "Sorry, it's not longer."

"You and your dick are here," I said lightly. "That's enough."

Heat creeping into the edges of his eyes, warming that icy blue to a temperate river to heated springs. He started to answer, and I braced myself for whatever filthy thing he'd say that would set my clit buzzing, nipples hardening, but before he replied, he turned, and I saw his gaze hit my plate perched on the crate I was using as a coffee table.

A breath that had his broad shoulders rising and falling, his frustration a palpable presence in the room.

I went for a change in subject.

It seemed most prudent. "So, how are you feeling with every-thing? You're looking good on the ice. That...deke—I think they call it—was on the top ten plays of the week."

"It's 9:30," he said, completely ignoring my attempts at conver-sation change.

"Uh, yeah? Are you tired from the drive? Do you want to go to bed?"

Yes, please.

I'd really prefer *that* topic change.

A muscle in his jaw flexing. He nodded at the plate. "Is that dinner or a bedtime snack?"

I pulled my hand back, tucked it into my lap. "Dinner," I admitted.

A sigh. "Fencing?"

"That had me working late?"

He nodded.

"No." I swallowed. "Um, I—a broken water line."

Another sigh.

Now, I shrugged. "The cows need water."

"So, you did what?" The question was quiet, his face suddenly impenetrable.

"It was only a ten-foot trench I needed to dig and run a new line on." I grinned, not sure why he was all growly when I damned well wasn't going to stop taking care of the ranch, of myself, but not wanting to bicker about it when we had all of a day together. "The mud was the worst part, but I bet you would have loved it. All that muck and wet clothing, the only thing I was missing was someone to wrestle with."

He grunted. "Ten feet," he muttered, eyes sparking.

And I lost a thread of patience. "Look," I said, "you have your job, this is mine. I can handle everything the ranch throws at me, and I have for years. And, a word of warning, I'm not going to tolerate you getting all growly and protective when I'm just trying to do my job." I dropped my hand onto his shoulder. "Most importantly, I'm doing fine. This is all normal maintenance and putting out fires and just day-to-day for me. I promise." A beat. "And how you're acting right now makes me feel like you don't think I can do it. Even though I know I can because the only reason the ranch is here right now and not some tract of homes because the bank foreclosed is because of me."

Fingers on my cheek, stroking gently. "You're right." He tugged at the end of my ponytail. "I'm sorry, buttercup."

"Thank you," I said, and I meant it. I was doing my best to support him, support his job, even though we were new. I needed the same from him...and I needed the apology when he overstepped, I needed him to see me, see what I was doing.

A kiss to my forehead before he plunked the plate in my lap. "Eat."

It was more order and grunt than request, but both made my

heart roll over in the best way possible. Because he was taking care of me, but in a way that wasn't overstepping, or at least didn't insult my ability to take care of the ranch.

Myself on the other hand.

Well...he wouldn't be the first person to point that out. "Did you eat?"

He nodded. "I've got my approved meal plan food in my bag. I'll just put it in the fridge."

"Okay," I said as I picked up the sandwich, but before I took a bite I saw his face, saw the *concern* on his face. "Axel, honey, it's all good."

Half of his mouth tipped up. "Yeah."

Then he moved back out into the hall, asking me what else was up as he headed into the kitchen.

"Not much, I mean, Gramps's truck decided to be a bastard, but I managed to get it up and running before I put my limited plumbing skills to work on the trough. Just call me Jill of All Trades."

He came back in, carrying the bag he'd had in his hand on the porch.

"Of course, considering it came with a side of mud wrestling, it reminded me that I definitely need a professional to take care of the house. Otherwise"—I smiled, took another bite, and spoke around all that yummy Dijon— "it would take me a decade to finish the house."

The vibe I was getting from him was oddly intense, but he didn't comment, just sank down onto the arm of the chair and watched me eat the sandwich.

When I was done, he took the plate, asked, "Still hungry?"

I shook my head.

The plate went to the crate.

But still, he didn't say anything.

And now I was getting a *weird* vibe.

"What is it?" I asked when he didn't say anything, just stared out the windows, hand stroking through my hair.

"I have something for you."

"Okaaay," I murmured when he didn't say anything further.

After a long moment, he added, "It feels big."

I inhaled, let it out slowly. "Do you—I mean—we don't have to do it today if it feels like it's too much."

He shifted off the arm of the chair, big palms resting on my thighs. "I want to fuck you senseless because that feels familiar and safe and something I know how to do." My throat went tight. "But...I want something different with you. I want...*more.*"

"Axel," I whispered.

"So, I want to give you something, but I'm sort of freaking out that it's too much too soon, especially since I haven't even gotten to take you out on a date yet, and we've been...I don't know, a couple, together, my girlfriend, *more*. Fuck"—he shoved a hand through his hair—"now I sound like a goddamned idiot."

"No," I said, sliding forward and wrapping my arms around his shoulders. "You're not an idiot. I...we're not doing this in any way that's normal. But...you know parts of me that no one else does, and that doesn't scare me. *You* don't scare me, Axel Finnegan. Not any longer. Not since I've seen that big heart of yours." I ran my thumb along his jaw, the bristles brushing over my skin.

"Big...heart?" He'd relaxed, expression gentling, but his eyes were filled with that Finnegan mischief.

I rolled my eyes as I sat back and extended a hand. "Pretty puh-lease!"

THIRTY-FIVE

AXEL

Why was I so fucking nervous?

Because she was important.

Because she was more.

Because—

I focused on the task at hand. "Right," I said, reaching into my pocket. "There are actually two presents, and if you don't like them, it's no big deal, I can—"

Her hand came to my free one, squeezed lightly.

"I'm sure I'll love them." Her lips turned up into a crooked smile. "So long as it's not an engagement ring—"

I pulled out the small box I'd shoved in my pocket.

The small *ring-sized* box.

She made a choking sound.

I plunked the box into her hand.

"I—" She visibly recoiled, and suddenly I fought back my laughter. "Axel, I'm sorry, but I don't want to get married again."

Considering what her ex-husband had done, I didn't blame her.

"Open it."

Her throat worked and her hands shook as she tugged open the box. "Oh," she breathed, so much relief in those two letters that I lost my hold on the laughter.

She glared up at me. "Not funny."

I tugged her into my arms, the tension gripping my insides breaking. She didn't want to marry me, and that was cool, that was actually refreshing. We were what we were then, in that moment. We were new and learning and...it was just us. "No marriage, buttercup. Just us, and...all your secrets."

I gave her my best evil villain laughter.

She swatted at my shoulder, but when I pulled out the necklace I'd spotted in the store's window, the one that had made me think of her, that I'd *had* to stop and buy for her, she gasped quietly.

"That's—"

"You gave away your secret when you mentioned Picard."

Her bottom lip trembled as she ran a finger over the charm. It was a silly thing, a cow in a traditional red shirt, something that I was only beginning to know about because I'd begun streaming the show in my downtime.

"You weren't supposed to pick up on that," she said softly.

"Well, I might not have if I hadn't heard you call that horse Data."

She groaned, but her lips were curving. "It's really cute," she whispered.

"I know," I whispered back.

Her hand came to my jaw, and her eyes were wet when she said, "Thank you."

"It was nothing."

"No." Her eyes were wet. "It's not nothing to me."

"Okay, buttercup," I murmured, wrapping my arms around her. "Okay." And then I held her, just held this woman who'd somehow become important to me, who was fierce and brusque and soft and sweet, a fucking juxtaposition that made me want to find out every single secret, everything that made her laugh or smile, everything that made her sad, made her cry. I wanted vengeance on her ex. I wanted to hunt down anyone who had hurt her. I wanted...every single piece of my life tied to hers.

After a few minutes, her sniffing stopped, and she pulled back slightly.

"Just what you wanted, right? A crying woman at ten o'clock at night after driving for four hours?"

Amusement in my belly.

Laughter in the air.

"Should I give you the other present?"

"I don't think I'll be able to handle it. Not unless you want a watering pot in your arms."

"Meh." I leaned back and over, grabbed the box, and plunked it into her lap. "Full disclosure. This wasn't all me."

A frown.

"Brit helped me arrange it. Well, no"—I shook my head—"Brit *arranged* it."

"Brit, goalie Brit?"

I nodded. "She wanted me to formally issue an invite to the Gold family."

"I—"

"She's *my* Billie Rose."

Bailey pushed back her hair. "Oh, Lord."

"Yeah."

She shook the box lightly. "Now I'm scared to open this."

"It's not going to jump out at you."

"You said you didn't arrange it, so how can you be sure?"

I shifted, scooping her up so that she was in my lap and my ass was in the recliner. "Because I know what's inside."

"Oh."

"Yeah." I tugged her ponytail. "*Oh.*"

She tore off the black ribbon (that I hadn't tied on) then the gold paper (that I *had* used to wrap the box).

Then opened the top.

She started, breath sliding out on a hiss. "*Axel.*"

My jersey. Or, well, a game-weight Gold jersey with my name on the back. Slowly, she pulled it out of the box, her touch reverent, almost as much as mine had been the first time I'd ever seen my name on a Gold jersey. It was big and important and...it fucking meant everything.

My name there.

Her getting the weight of it.

She clambered out of my lap and tugged it over her head, and I laughed when I saw how it engulfed her, hanging off her hands, dropping nearly to her knees. "You're kind of small, buttercup."

"Well, not everyone can be a behemoth like you."

"True."

She cocked her head to the side, a jaunty smile on her face. "You're imagining me in this without anything underneath it, aren't you?"

"I'm *always* imagining you naked," I said.

But imagining her naked with the exception of my jersey skating over her thighs, my name on her back, her body wet and aching and ready beneath that material and just for me...yeah that was fucking *good.*

She reached for her waist, and in a flash, her leggings were on the floor.

A glance showed me her underwear was tangled in the black material, but even as I was processing that, her arms were moving inside the jersey, and there was a flash of skin, a flash of mouth-watering curves.

Her shirt landed at my feet.

Then her bra.

Then I caught a glimpse of a peach-shaped ass, wet, glistening folds as she bent, slid off one sock and then the other.

Growling, I jumped to my feet, snatched her to me.

She squeaked, the socks dropping from her hand to the floor.

"Fucking teasing," I said, picking her up and tossing her over my shoulder.

"You like it."

My hand sliding up her thigh, cupping that ass for a moment before I dipped my fingers into her slick pussy. Wet. So fucking *wet*. I brought my fingers to my mouth, sucked them deep, apples and woman on my tongue.

"Axel—" she gasped.

"Too much?" I asked.

"Not enough."

A tart reply that earned her a smack on her gorgeous ass.

"Too much?" I asked again.

"No, baby," she said, turning her head, nipping at my jaw. "I want you to give me everything you've got."

It was a fucking miracle there was any blood left in my legs, enough in my brain to carry her to her bedroom when all I wanted to do was drop her to her feet and fuck her right there on the hallway floor.

But I had enough—just barely—to make it to her bed.

And it turned out that I had enough to give her everything I had.

———

I'd turned off her alarm and stumbled my way through chores, luckily having heard her describe her mornings enough to hold the animals over for at least a few hours.

She needed her rest.

She was on her own too much.

She needed someone to take a little of the pressure off her shoulders. I didn't completely understand where that protective urge came from, especially when I'd spent my life protecting myself and avoiding contact with anyone who might require more than I could give them.

Which was sex, orgasms, nothing more.

But I wasn't that with Bailey.

And I was going to be away a lot. I'd signed a contract, one that converted mine from the Rush into one that would keep me on the Gold.

For three years.

It was entry level. One way. It meant I was going to be on the roster, and I was going to stay there.

So, I couldn't be here all the time.

Which was why I was turning off alarms and making coffee... and studying the contents of her fridge.

And looking at the bills piled on the countertop.

And staring at the bids for new plumbing and electric for the house.

And...hating that I hadn't realized exactly how much she was struggling. I'd brought her a necklace and a jersey, and she'd sold her fucking cow to pay for a streaming service so she could watch me play hockey.

She'd dug a ten-foot trench, wrestled with pipes in the mud.

Hurt her back.

Fallen from a ladder.

By herself.

She didn't ask for help.

Wouldn't. I might not know every single thing about her yet, but I knew that she wouldn't.

So, I was brewing coffee and doing what I could.

And if I took some pictures with my phone of those bills, if I scheduled a grocery delivery because her fridge and pantry were mostly empty (more so than should be for any person, even if it was just for one person in this house) then so be it.

I couldn't be here every day.

I *could* find a way to make sure she was protected even if I wasn't.

"What are you doing?"

I spun around, casually shoving my phone and nodding to the bowl I'd begun prepping on the counter. "Bemoaning my breakfast."

Her hair was a mess, eyes half-mast, lips swollen, throat scuffed from my beard.

She was wearing my jersey.

She was the most beautiful woman I had ever seen.

I poured her a cup of coffee, offered her some of my overnight oats (she refused, sticking with the black brew), and when we went down to the barn (after she'd put on pants and shoes) and her face softened when she saw my clumsy efforts at completing her morning routine, I knew...

She wasn't just my now.

She was my future.

And it was my job to make sure she was protected.

THIRTY-SIX

I frowned at the truck in my driveway.

It wasn't Axel's little sedan and anyway, my hockey player —yup, *my* hockey player was currently on a plane, heading for Seattle.

But the white work truck looked familiar.

So did the man who was coming out of my house.

"Jerry?" I asked, bringing Gramps's truck to a stop and manually (because it didn't have automatic *anything*) rolling down a window. "What are you doing here?"

The man, black hair, beer belly, and a typically genial smile, slid to a halt.

By a pile of pipes.

Um.

What?

I'd gotten a quote from Jerry, but I wasn't going to go with him, not when his bid was the most expensive. He did good work, but, frankly, I wouldn't be able to afford him and also do the electrical.

Hell, truthfully, I couldn't afford either.

But I'd planned on dipping into the savings I'd managed to squirrel away, and I could go back to PB&Js, and I could maybe even pick up some evening shifts at Monroe's.

I'd get to hang with Dessie *and* practice my beer pulling techniques.

All I'd ever wanted.

Yay!

And yes, that was sarcasm talking.

"Um," Jerry said, drawing me back to the conversation at hand. "I'm fixing the pipes."

I blinked.

Then bit back my curse. "Is there a reason you're fixing the pipes when I haven't actually *hired* you to do the job?"

Now it was his turn to blink.

"I got the check, Bailey, and the request to start as soon as possible." He cleared his throat, shoved his hands into his pocket. "I had a cancelation this morning, so I figured I'd get a jump on it while you were out in the field."

My temple was starting to pound. "But was I the one to make the call, Jer?"

That had him freezing.

"It wasn't me, yeah?"

If there was ever an *Oh shit* moment to cross someone's face, Jerry's was the quintessential one. "But I cashed the check already. I used it for the down payment on Jennifer's room and board."

My other temple began to pound.

Jennifer was his daughter who'd gotten into a kickass school after being waitlisted in the fall. I knew, because this was River's Bend, that she was starting in January, and apparently, she was starting because of the proceeds from this job. Proceeds that could have only come from one person.

"Do you want me to stop?" he asked.

"No, Jer. Thanks."

Relief in his eyes before he nodded and hurried back to the pipes and then headed back into the house. I opened my mouth, almost called him back, and then realized it was on me.

River's Bend was safe.

Really safe.

This far out from town with so few visitors?

Even safer.

Thus, I rarely locked my doors—when I wasn't trying to keep naked troublemakers out, that was.

Apparently, I needed to make a habit of that if Axel was going to start doing things like this.

I grumbled as I pulled out my cell, typed a message to Axel, knowing that he was unlikely to get it since he was in the air, but as I turned back to the house, to the pile of pipes and the plumber who was fixing up the ranch house, my heart wasn't annoyed.

It was...touched.

"Oh, Axel," I murmured, "what am I going to do about you?"

Not run. Not avoid.

I was going to live.

I was going to embrace what might be.

I was going to take care of a certain hockey player who had spent years pretending he didn't care about anyone but himself.

Because he deserved it, needed it...and I needed to give it to him.

All of that was true, and my heart might be soft for him.

But I still cursed that certain, troublesome hockey player when I saw another van pull up.

A&E Electric emblazoned on its side.

———

"I ought to flay you alive, Axel Finnegan," I snapped, later that evening.

Much later because Axel had just gotten off the team bus, after he'd gotten off the team plane, after they'd taken on Seattle and won again that evening.

A six-game streak since Axel had been pulled up.

He was looking good.

On the ice, I thought, based on my limited experience. But mostly off it. Granted we hadn't spent loads of time together, but we'd spent enough now for me to read his moods, to understand when he was rattled and nervous.

And he was...settled.

Confident.

Secure.

Part of that was from the contract.

He'd made it, and while I knew that he probably was thinking about Rogers' injury and how it impacted his rise, I wasn't seeing it impact him as much. I could pick up nerves, especially if we talked before the games, but when we talked after each match up, I could see a difference. Day by day, I was watching his confidence grow.

That didn't mean I was going to put up with his bullshit, though.

"Because I'm sexy and you miss my cock?" he asked, and though we were on audio only as he drove back to the hotel room —a room he'd not so subtly left a key for me to use if "I happen to be in town" before he'd left two days before—I knew that he was smirking at me. Unfortunately, he *was* sexy, and I definitely missed his cock, almost as much as I missed the way he wrapped himself around me when we went to sleep.

But that was beside the point.

"I'm not a charity case, Finnegan," I growled.

"I know that, *Donovan.*"

"So, what the hell are you doing paying for repairs on my house?"

"Is this about the carpet?"

I blinked. "What carpet?"

A muttered curse. "Right," he said quickly. "It's about the pipes and wires and shit."

My sigh rattled through the speakers of my phone, echoing in my ear. "Axel, please tell me that you didn't buy me new carpet."

A beat then, "She'll be there tomorrow. You pick out the kind you want and the furniture you need—"

"I don't *need*—"

"And if you don't pick it out or try to cheap out or put her off, then I have given Desiree strict instructions to work with Margaret to pick out what she thinks you'd like and need."

My teeth clicked together. "You've given *Dessie* strict instructions?"

"Yup."

"To work with Margaret Butcher."

The only interior designer in River's Bend, and also the only Margaret I knew.

"Yup."

"For *my* house."

"Yup."

"Okay, I've said it once, you arrogant, pushy bastard, but I'll say it again, I am *not* a charity case!"

Yes, I was yelling.

No, it wasn't my finest moment.

But seriously? What in the fuck-all did this man think he was doing?

"No," he snapped, and the sharp tone made me blink, made me realize exactly how gently he'd been treating me since that day on Main Street, since he'd found me behind the dumpster. "No," he said again, taking a breath and evening out his voice. "You're not a charity case, buttercup. But you are *my* woman, and I can't be on the road or four hours away in San Francisco worrying that your fucking house is going to catch on fire, or the pipes are going to burst and ruin something that's more important to you than ugly-ass carpet." He sighed, and I knew he was shoving a hand through his hair, frustration mussing the strands. "I can't worry about you and play one hundred percent, because you're important to me, because I need to know that you're good." A breath. "I can't focus on work here when my heart is there and doesn't have food in her fridge."

Well, I guess that meant that Billie Rose wasn't the one who'd stocked my fridge.

Which was what I was focusing on because him saying that I was his heart?

Oh, mama.

That meant a lot.

That meant...*everything*.

"Baby," I whispered.

"I know it's too much," he said. "I know you like doing things on your own. But...I need to do this for you, I *want* to do it. So, will you let me?"

My pulse was galloping through my veins, sending my blood zooming through my limbs, making my head spin, my tongue feel swollen, my throat tight. Could I let him?

Every cell in my body was screaming no.

I couldn't trust him.

I *couldn't*.

But...

Couldn't I?

"I'll pay you back," I managed to force out.

"In orgasms," he countered so quickly, so dryly that the tension in my body faded, that amusement took its place.

And I laughed.

I was leaping forward into oblivion, into a dark, unlit abyss that I didn't know how to navigate, creating ties between us, putting myself in his debt, and...

I was laughing.

"In *money*," I countered.

"Sure," he said easily.

Too easily.

"You're never going to cash my checks, are you?"

"Fuck no."

I groaned, plunked my head back onto my pillow. "What the hell am I going to do with you, Axel Finnegan?"

Love him.

I was going to love him.

That was what was at the bottom of the abyss.

And...somehow, I couldn't find my fear, my barbed wire, my concrete to shore up my defenses and keep him at a distance.

"Orgasms. Blow jobs. Your sexy pussy on my face as you ride yourself to an orgasm."

"I'm sensing a theme here," I said dryly.

"Well, that's what happens when my woman is hot as fuck and I can't stop dreaming about making her come."

I bit back a groan as heat blossomed in my body.

Luckily, though, he went on, easing up on the talk that was making me horny and without my man to soothe the ache. "Add in the occasional sandwich and hockey commentary where you talk about halftime and how our jerseys are the prettiest."

"That was *one* time!"

But I didn't miss the fact that he'd said *our jerseys*.

Didn't miss that he was settling in further.

He chuckled then asked softly, "We good, buttercup?"

I sighed. "We're good, baby."

"Good, honey. Now go to bed."

A yawn delayed my reply. "Are you almost back to the hotel?"

"Pulling into the garage."

"Okay," I whispered. "You make sure you sleep soon, too."

"I will."

My finger moved to the end button, pausing when he asked, "Promise me one thing?"

"Yeah?"

"No floral."

And that was how the man made me fall asleep with a laugh on my tongue and a smile on my lips.

Thirty-Seven

Axel

"You don't have much stuff," Brit said, letting me into the apartment.

I had a key, but it had felt weird to let myself in when I knew she was inside, doing a last-minute check of the place.

Her eyes hit the backpack I'd brought with me upon leaving my hotel room, and I wasn't imagining the hint of disapproval in those hazel depths.

"I have to make one more trip," I admitted. Truthfully, I'd left most of my shit back in the hotel. Partly because I was hesitant to move into the apartment, to be in debt to Brit, to accept something so big from a woman I was just starting to know, but just as I'd come to terms with the fact that I *was* going to accept something this big from a woman I was just starting to know, housekeeping had begun knocking on my door. Normally, they'd just come back when I was out, but the woman today was determined to come in and get started, and had all but barged her way in.

New to the job, I supposed.

But who was I to stop her from finishing her work, especially when I was leaving anyway?

Still, her coming in to clean meant I'd ended up rushing around, dodging her as I tried to shove enough in a bag to make it seem like I wasn't taking Brit's favor for granted while she worked.

Eventually, though, I'd had enough to fill my backpack and had slipped out into the hall, leaving her to it.

Or probably, more accurately, getting out of her way.

Though, she'd pretty much been done by then, leaving the cart in my open doorway as she'd fussed with something on the cart outside the door.

Oh well, all I could do was make sure to leave a good tip for them when I checked out. For now, I was dealing with Brit's slightly disappointed expression as her gaze went from the bag hanging over my shoulder and slid back up to my face.

"Did you think it would be full of tampons and unicorn pillows?" she asked archly.

"I'll have you know unicorns are my favorite animal." A shrug as I set my backpack on the counter. "Plus, tampons are excellent for nose bleeds."

"So, what? You weren't sure if it was going to be a shithole, Balls?"

"No, Brit," I said, guilt slicing through me. "That's not—"

A punch to my shoulder. "Breathe, Axel. I'm fucking with you. I get it," she said. "It's hard to shed all the bullshit and natural to be cautious. Especially because we're like fantasyland with the way we stick together. I'm just glad you're here, one bag or ten." She passed me a clicker and her voice went no nonsense. "Now, this is for the garage. There are two parking spots"—a grin—"so your girl can come visit."

"And so you can get your gossip fodder?"

That grin went unrepentant. "Damned right."

"She's busy and works a lot."

"Good."

I frowned.

"That means she won't be hung up on fancy Axel Finnegan and his fancy hockey skills." A finger to her bottom lip, tapping once, twice. "Maybe Fancy would be a better name for you. God knows that you showed off those *fancy* hands last night."

"Concrete hands, you mean."

She giggled.

"Also, Concrete isn't a good nickname either."

"Better than Balls," she pointed out.

There was that.

"Well," she said, hopping up onto a plain gray barstool and resting her hands on the white marble countertop, "I should probably leave you to take that trip back to your hotel room, let you have a chance to move in."

"Why do I sense a *but* coming?"

Her million-dollar smile. "Because there is one."

And right on cue, there was a knock at the door.

"Apartment tradition," she said, hopping down and moving to pull open the wooden panel. "You get to host the first Cheat Day."

As I processed that, the door was tugged wide, and the guys began pouring in, bags of food and beer and the odd cheerfully-wrapped box in hand.

Less Cheat Day.

More housewarming.

In a borrowed apartment, with the utilities set up and rent that was minimal (because I'd refused to accept free, and Brit and I had come to a compromise) and—

I was one of them.

I *belonged*.

Because I contributed and worked hard and—the truth settled deep inside me—because I'd done it.

On my own merits, but not alone.

Brit had helped and Billie Rose and Bailey and—

I wasn't in a vacuum.

I couldn't do it solely by myself.

But I could *earn* my way.

I could make the most of this chance, this life, this—

I accepted a beer that Coop shoved in my hand, laughed at a joke Brit told.

I could make the most of this team who could become my family.

THIRTY-EIGHT

BAILEY

"This is crazy," I whispered as I navigated the winding San Franciscan roads. "Really fucking crazy, Bailey."

It was late.

Middle of the night late, like it was closer to morning than night late. But I'd been *kept* late because Desiree was fucking *into* home decorating and she and Margaret hadn't let me leave until I'd looked through every fucking stitch of fabric and carpet and flooring option.

Three days of that.

Three days of decorating discussions in between taking care of the ranch and dodging the workers in my house and—

I'd been ready to scream.

Luckily, Billie Rose, with all her first-rate gossip skills and her nose for knowing when a River's Bend resident needed help, had come in that evening and sprung me.

She was going to be on ranch duty for the next twenty-four hours.

Which meant...I was going to my first hockey game.

Ever.

Well, I hoped I was.

The Gold were playing tomorrow night, and I was hoping that I could buy a ticket, or maybe my hockey playing man had the hookup and could secure me one, or—

However it happened, I was going to get into the Gold Mine and watch Axel play.

Eek.

But first, I was going to use that key he'd left for me.

I was going to surprise him.

I was going to give him copious orgasms and then we were going to sleep together, and I wouldn't have to get up early to feed the animals and—

"There," I whispered, spotting the hotel and shifting over a lane.

Of course, since this was San Francisco and none of the streets made sense and traffic was ridiculous, even in the middle of the night, I ended up circling the block twice before I managed to maneuver Gramps's old truck into the parking garage and cram it into a stall.

But I'd made it.

And now...nerves.

I had never done anything like this. *Never.*

Not once in my life had I dropped everything to come and surprise a man in his hotel.

Not once since Colt had I even been open to putting myself out there to a man.

For a man.

And yet, here I was.

The churning in my gut was so intense that I nearly backed my way out of that stall, turned away, and made the drive home.

But...I couldn't.

I was done letting my past rule my present.

"Exactly," I muttered, grabbing my backpack and slinging it over my shoulder. A breath. Shoring up my spine.

Then opening my door.

Was it with shaking hands? Yeah.

Was I doing it anyway? Damn right I was.

I locked up, moved to the lobby, and headed straight for the elevators.

Up.

Stopping on Axel's floor.

Searching the signs, finding the right direction to turn, and then...I was there. Outside his door.

To knock or not to knock.

To breathe or hyperventilate.

To run screaming away through this hallway or to...run screaming through this hallway.

To...use the key on the lock and push open the door.

The lights were mostly off—but then again, it was late. So, I carefully set my backpack down, moved quietly down the hall, and headed for the bed.

Five feet.

Four. Three.

Two—

The light flicked on.

I blinked.

Blinked again.

Because what the fuck?

The covers flew back, and I spun away, thinking for a minute that I was in the wrong hotel room, horrified that I'd broken in and seen—

That.

A woman.

A woman I *recognized.*

What the fuck?

What. The. Fuck?

It was the girl who'd spilled beer on me, who'd complained that Axel never went out anymore and...she was naked.

And skinny and pretty and *naked*.

And pissed.

"What the fuck?" she snapped, snatching the comforter off the bed, and holding it to her body—a body that was much nicer than mine, it had to be noted.

"Shit," I said. Wrong room. I had the wrong room. "I-I'm so s-sorry," I stuttered, slamming my eyes closed for a moment before I realized I needed to get the fuck out. I turned and...I saw Axel's jacket hanging over the back of the chair.

Axel's bag on the floor.

Axel's shoes in the corner of the room.

Axel's cologne on the dresser near the TV.

Stabbing.

He was stabbing me. He wasn't even there, and he was sinking the knife into my flesh.

"Where is he?" I asked.

"He needed...nourishment," said the woman.

Nourishment?

Like...he needed to regain his strength after a long night of activity?

No. He wouldn't do that. He wouldn't. There had to be an explanation for this. Like she was crazy and had broken into his room. But the door hadn't looked like it had been tampered with, or at least it wasn't kicked in, the lock not working. I'd needed to use the key.

So...maybe this wasn't Axel's room and she'd stolen...almost everything he'd brought down from River's Bend?

Or—

I turned back, opened my mouth to say...something.

She beat me to it. "I think my favorite part of Axel"—a laugh —"besides his cock, of course"—another laugh and it pierced right through me—"is that tattoo. *Whew.*" She fanned herself. "The way it wraps around his ribs, how it dips down and nearly touches that scar just above his hip...*fucking* chef's kiss."

That was...very specific.

That was...making it very difficult for me to think that she wasn't in Axel's room because she'd gone full psycho ninja, but rather because he'd invited her.

"Tell me," she said. "Have you ever tried to take him deep, but he was so big that you choked?"

I had.

Because he was.

But I'd been working up to it, had all but been making it my fucking life's work to be able to take that big cock deep.

"Why are you here?" I asked.

"He *brought* me here."

"No," I whispered. "He wouldn't do that."

"Because he's with you?" she asked and there was that laugh again—piercing, knife-like, *painful*. "Oh, honey, Axel doesn't do monogamy. Hell, he rarely does one woman at a time." A smirk. "Unless, that woman is enough for him."

Thunk.

That wasn't right.

Yet...I was here.

This wasn't happening.

This wasn't—

I needed to go, to get the fuck out of this room. I needed to get away from this woman who was adding to the stab wounds, who was slowly, incrementally bleeding me dry so that I could breathe and think and reason this out—

I needed to *go.*

A breath.

I whipped away from the woman, from the scene that was fucking with my head, that was cutting me deeper by the second.

"Where are you going?" she trilled. "Stick around and maybe both of us can play."

I was going to be sick.

In that room, with that condescending woman looking on and talking about threesomes with the man that I had been in love with.

Swallowing hard, trying to keep the bile down even as it burned up the back of my throat, even as my stomach churned and roiled anew. Sweaty palms, shaking legs, but I managed to move to my backpack, to wrap my fingers around one of the straps.

I started to pick it up, but I was too off my game, too shaky and barely holding on and—

My fingers spasmed and my bag dropped to the floor, the contents scattering.

I fell to my knees, started grabbing my shit, shoving it back in, even as she laughed at me, as she kept talking.

But all I could hear at this point was buzzing, her words no longer distinguishable. My pulse was pounding in my ears, the steady thrumming making it impossible for me to process anything.

Especially while I was scrabbling for my lip balm and my phone charger and my tiny bottles of travel shampoo and body wash and conditioner.

Nails biting into my shoulder. "Look, bitch, I'm talking to—"

I had to go.

I *needed* to go.

One more stretch had me snatching the last of my things, had me breaking free of her grip, and then I was on my feet, shoving her back. Spinning for the door, yanking at the handle.

I pushed into the hall, ran for the elevator.

No.

Stairs.

I couldn't wait for the fucking elevator.

So, I shoved through the metal door, rushed into the stairwell, pounded down the stairs until I reached the parking garage. Tears were burning in my eyes, were *escaping*, dripping down my face, but I knew, *knew*, I had to first get to Gramps's truck.

Out of the parking lot.

Away from that room, from this hotel.

I needed to get someplace safe.

Thirty-Nine

A siren blared outside my windows, startling me.

Totally unused to the sounds of the city after having spent so much time in River's Bend.

Groaning, I stretched, snagged my cell, and glanced at the time. Too fucking early.

Too fucking early even to call Bailey.

We'd only exchanged a few texts in the previous days, mostly her cursing me for putting her through HGTV Bootcamp and me snarking about an orgasm count that kept growing.

But I had the day off and was planning to drive up to River's Bend to see the progress, see if I could coax a favor out of Billie Rose to watch the ranch the next time I had two days off in a row.

I wanted to bring Bailey down to the city, wanted her to see the apartment, and depending on how long Billie Rose was willing to grant, to bring her to the rink...and—heaven help me—introduce her to the team.

Brit was going to be thrilled.

I was fucking terrified...and ready.

That too.

The conflicting emotions meant that it was unlikely I was going to go back to sleep.

Last night had gone on later than I'd planned, the guys busting out board games—and look, *I* was competitive about all things, but the Gold squad took *Ticket to Ride* to a whole new level.

There were set matchups and brackets and playoffs and—

Everyone had stayed late to watch Coop, Blue, Logan, and Rome battle it out for first place.

Which had, surprisingly, gone to Rome.

Apparently, that meant he had to host the next board game throwdown.

Fine by me.

I'd gotten my ass handed to me in the game. I needed to study up, to practice, to come back ready to take those fuckers—cough, I mean my *teammates*—down.

The siren went again.

Sighing, I pushed out of bed. I needed to get my city ears back if I wanted to sleep in. But since I was awake, I might as well get the rest of my shit from the hotel before heading up to River's Bend. Check out, drop my shit, sneak up for a taste of my woman that would need to tide me over for another week.

A quick shower—and a quick thanks for Brit, whose nosy ass had invaded my apartment and brought me fresh linens.

Then I was heading out of the apartment building, getting in my car, driving across town.

I parked in the underground lot of the hotel, frowning when I thought I saw Bailey's truck, but she'd specifically told me yesterday that Margaret was bringing her to the flooring store to make her final selections.

So, another old truck.

But the sight of it made me smile, made me miss her.

Maybe I could call her on the way back out, she'd be up by then, could yell at me about the home décor choices, and I could hear the way her voice went soft when I told her I was coming up to see her.

Sliding my card on the reader, I moved into the lobby, waited for the elevator to open, and got on.

Thirty seconds later, I was stepping into the hall, swiping my keycard for a second time, this time on the door for my room.

I pushed in—

And then didn't process what in the fuck-all I was seeing.

What. I. Was. *Seeing*.

Lights on.

The bed a mess.

A phone in the hall. I stopped at that, actually backed up into the hall, making sure that I had the right room, because, well, it was fucking early, and it was easily possible that I wasn't operating on all cylinders.

But the placard to the left of the door told me I was in the right place.

So, I moved back inside, and the first thing I did was stoop down and pick up the phone. It wasn't mine, obviously, and when I saw the case, my gut clenched. But it wasn't until I hit the button on the side, saw the picture of Picard on the screen, that my nape went ice cold.

Bailey's.

It was *Bailey's*.

I should be excited—the truck, the phone, the evidence that Bailey was here in San Francisco. But...something about the lights being on, the lack of a greeting, the way my belongings were spread around, as though someone had gone through them.

Bailey wouldn't have gone through my stuff.

She wouldn't be asleep with the lights on, her phone on the floor, the room a mess.

She—

"Hi, baby."

Not her voice.

Not Bailey's.

I looked up and saw a naked woman, and that naked woman wasn't Bailey.

But I *had* seen her before.

She was...the housekeeper. The one who'd all but demanded her way into my room.

Yes, she was that woman.

But also...

I saw the tattoo above her breast, the glint of glitter on her skin, and another memory floated up in my mind. She wasn't just a housekeeper. She was from River's Bend. I hadn't recognized her yesterday because she'd changed her hair, because I didn't spend a lot of time looking at her face, not when she spent the majority of her time with her tits nearly hanging out. But naked, she was familiar enough, and I remembered her love of the sparkling stuff, remembered that it was in some sort of lotion that she wore, and the glitter always clung to the guys' skin after they fucked her. And most of the guys had fucked her.

Though I hadn't.

Yeah, I'd fucked pretty much everyone willing to have me over the years I'd been in town, but I'd never fucked *her*.

There was something desperate about...Candice? Cassidy? No, *Candi*. With the traditional "i" and a fucking creepy-ass expression on her face.

But I'd fucked her friend, and I'd done it at Joel's place.

On his couch while Joel had taken Candi to his bedroom.

And when I'd finished, when I was getting dressed to leave— because that was what I did then, fuck, come, go—she had been standing in the doorway. Naked.

Watching us.

Watching *me*.

Like she'd been ready to join in.

I'd been drunk enough to brush it off, and hell, I'd been with enough people over the years to not give a fuck that someone might have seen me having sex.

"What the fuck are you doing?" I asked, shoving her back when she came close.

She stumbled, lips parting on a gasp, tears immediately forming in her eyes.

Fucking tears.

Dammit.

I didn't have time for this.

"I'm here for you," she said, those tears slipping over, immediately turning her mascara into raccoon eyes.

I stepped close, didn't miss the way her eyes lit up. But all I did was stick my face in hers and demand, "What did you do to her?"

Candi's tears dried in an instant—because they were on command. "To whom?"

"To Bailey, you fucking bitch."

Her lips pressed flat.

I resisted the urge to throttle her. "Did you hurt her? Did you hurt, Bailey?"

Candi's chin lifted. "I just told her the truth."

Don't touch her. Don't touch the bitch because then I might kill her. "What truth?"

"That you're not happy with her." Her hand came out, and I stepped back. "That you'll only ever be with me."

"You've lost your fucking mind."

I reached in my pocket for my cell.

Should I call security? The police? Who would sort out the shit-show in my room sooner? I was backing toward the door, considering just that, when her face screwed up, something scary sliding across it.

Fuck the call.

Fuck retrieving my shit.

I'd buy new stuff.

If she'd put this poison into Bailey's mind, I needed to find her as quickly as I could, stop her before she ran off and did something stupid.

I reached for the handle, yanked the door open.

"I love you, Axel. Don't go—"

Her voice was close enough to make me spin back around, and I barely had time to brace before Candi launched herself at me.

"Oof," I grunted, pushed Candi back when she tried to latch her mouth to mine.

A moan when our lips brushed, a groan when I shoved her, not so gently away. "Get dressed," I snapped, and when Candi didn't move, I wrestled open the door, thrust her into the hall.

Then slammed it shut.

Took two minutes to grab Candi's shit.

The look on her face as I chucked it out into the hall told me that my first call was going to be to the police.

The woman had lost her fucking mind.

But first, Bailey.

I needed to get to her, make sure she knew that nothing had happened. Even if that meant navigating the crazy in the hall.

Except, the moment I reached for the door, Bailey's phone began ringing.

Billie Rose.

Fuck.

I swiped, answered the call. "Hey, Billie Rose. I need your help—"

"Axel," she said, cutting me off completely. "We have a problem."

FORTY

I t took until I was nearly home for my tears to dry, my breathing to calm, for me to carefully consider all the thoughts spiraling through my head.

We hadn't made any promises.

We hadn't exchanged any vows.

We'd barely spent any time together.

I was...expecting too much. We hadn't agreed to be monogamous, and it wasn't like he'd asked me there and then I'd caught him with his dick in another woman.

I'd gone down to surprise him.

But I'd been the one who'd ended up surprised, wounded, hurt, broken, no...*shattered*.

He was finally getting to live out his dream.

I was just...old, beaten down baggage.

Holding him back.

Each thought had me shrinking into myself, the big, open world I'd begun tiptoeing into closing down, walls slamming into me, making it difficult for me to breathe, to think, to *drive*.

I pulled over, rested my head on the steering wheel.

And then I screamed.

So fucking loud that I nearly jumped out of my own skin, and *I* was the one making the godawful noise.

"No!" I yelled. "Just fucking *no!*"

This wasn't right.

This wasn't *him,* wasn't what Axel and I had.

It just...wasn't.

"So what?" I whispered, catching my own reflection in the rearview. "What are you going to do about it?"

Call him.

That was the first step.

But when I reached into my backpack and tried to grab my cell, it wasn't inside. "What?" I yanked the zipper fully open, dumped everything onto my seat. Lip balm, underwear, a change of clothes, my tiny shampoo and conditioner bottles. My phone charger. My hairbrush.

His jersey.

That one hurt.

I breathed through it, kept searching.

But no cell phone.

"Fuck," I whispered. "Fucking hell." I looked around, like the rolling hills outside River's Bend would give me my answers.

And they did, I supposed.

I was less than thirty minutes from home.

I'd start there, track down Billie Rose, and then I'd call Axel.

I'd figure out what was going on.

I wouldn't panic and run and shut him out. Not without talking to him first.

"Right," I whispered, taking another breath, trying to calm myself as I shoved my shit back into my bag, as I calmly checked over my shoulder and then pulled onto the road. "One step at a time."

I could do this.

I could be calm and sure and logical with my actions.

So, I drove through the winding roads until I reached the turnoff for the ranch. Then I bumped my way down the gravel driveway, relief pulsing through me when I saw Billie's little SUV was in the driveway.

I'd use her phone.

I'd call Axel.

It would be okay.

No matter what happened, I would be okay.

Blond curls entered my periphery as I pulled to a stop, just barely visible over the top of Billie's car. They moved my way quickly, but I didn't suspect anything was amiss.

Billie Rose did *everything* quickly.

I snagged my backpack, forced myself to be calm as I hopped out of Gramps's truck. "Billie, hey, I need to—"

In a millisecond, she was in my face. "Get in your truck," she whispered. "Get in your truck and get out of here."

"What?"

She began shoving me back, reaching for the door handle.

"Get in and drive to my place—"

"My baby!"

The voice was nails on a chalkboard.

The voice was...my mother's.

Gasping, I looked around Billie Rose and saw my mother, looking tan and thin and clad in designer hippie clothes. Looking the same as the last time I'd seen her when she'd dumped the problem of the ranch in my lap.

She extended her arms. "Come and give your mommy a big hug. I've missed you so much, baby!"

That was a blatant lie.

It always was.

But my gaze had drifted beyond her.

To my father.

He nodded in my direction but didn't pretend he'd missed me.

There wasn't any love lost between us, hadn't ever been. Mostly because our relationship was transactional, and one-sided, and he'd never had time for me except when I could do something for him.

"Shit," I muttered.

Billie Rose gave me another shove. "Honey, I need you to go. Right now. Straight to my house and—"

My dad shifted, and I saw there was a third person with them.

That third person made me understand why Billie Rose was so determined to get me back into the truck.

That third person was a man.

One I'd thought I known.

One I'd thought I'd loved.

My heart dropped to my feet and panic gripped every single cell in my body when Colt stepped out from behind my parents.

———

Thank you for reading! I hope you loved meeting Axel and Bailey! The next book in the Rush Hockey trilogy is FILTHY PUCKBOY. **I never expected to fall for a puckboy...but now I can't let him go...**

CLICK HERE TO GET FILTHY PUCKBOY NOW>

And if you enjoyed BIG PUCK ENERGY, you'll love the sexy, sweet, and close-knit Breakers Hockey crew. The first book in the series, BROKEN, is now live!

It is sexy, hot, adorable and such a fun read. You will not be able to put this down!" —Amazon Reviewer

———

I so appreciate your help in spreading the word about my books, including sharing with friends! Please leave a review on your favorite book site!

You can also join my Facebook group, the Fabinators, for exclusive giveaways and sneak peeks of future books.

SIGN UP FOR ELISE FABER'S NEWSLETTER HERE: https://www.elisefaber.com/newsletter

————

Want an exclusive story featuring more yummy hockey players?
Then click below to join Elise's newsletter!
http://eepurl.com/bdnmEj

————

And join Elise's fan group, the Fabinators (https://www.facebook.
com/groups/fabinators) for insider information, sneak peaks at
new releases, and fun freebies! Hope to see you there!

————

Rush Hockey

Big Puck Energy
Filthy Puckboy
So Pucking Over It

ALSO BY ELISE FABER

Breakout

Checked

Coasting

Centered

Charging

Caged

Crashed

A Gold Christmas

Cycled

Caught

Cap

Covered

Breakers Hockey (all stand alone)

Broken

Boldly

Breathless

Ballsy

Rush Hockey Trilogy

Big Puck Energy

Filthy Puckboy

So Pucking Over It

Love, Action, Camera (all stand alone)

Dotted Line

Action Shot

Close-Up

End Scene

Meet Cute

Love After Midnight (all stand alone)

Rum And Notes

Virgin Daiquiri

On The Rocks

Sex On The Seats

Life Sucks Series (all stand alone)

Train Wreck

Hot Mess

Dumpster Fire

Clusterf*@k

FUBAR

Roosevelt Ranch Series (all stand alone, series complete)

Disaster at Roosevelt Ranch

Heartbreak at Roosevelt Ranch

Collision at Roosevelt Ranch

Regret at Roosevelt Ranch

Desire at Roosevelt Ranch

Phoenix Series (read in order)

Phoenix Rising

Dark Phoenix

Phoenix Freed

Phoenix: Lex Tal Chronicles (rereleasing soon, stand alone, Phoenix

world)

From Ashes

In Flames

To Smoke

KTS Series (all stand alone, series complete)

Riding The Edge

Crossing The Line

Leveling The Field

Scorching The Earth

Cocky Heroes World

Tattooed Troublemaker

About the Author

USA Today bestselling author, Elise Faber, loves chocolate, Star Wars, Harry Potter, and hockey (the order depending on the day and how well her team -- the Sharks! -- are playing). She and her husband also play as much hockey as they can squeeze into their schedules, so much so that their typical date night is spent on the ice. Elise is the mom to two exuberant boys and lives in Northern California. Connect with her in her Facebook group, the Fabinators or find more information about her books at www.elise-faber.com.

f facebook.com/elisefaberauthor

a amazon.com/author/elisefaber

BB bookbub.com/profile/elise-faber

O instagram.com/elisefaber

d tiktok.com/@elisefaberauthor

g goodreads.com/elisefaber